CREATION OF MADNESS

Linda B. Myers

ABOUT THIS BOOK

Creation of Madness is a work of fiction. Nations, characters, places and happenings are from the author's imagination. Any resemblance to actual persons - living or dead - events or locales is entirely coincidental.

No part of the book may be used without written permission, except in the case of brief quotations in critical articles and reviews. Email inquiries to myerslindab@gmail.com.

Originally published as *Lessons of Evil*.
2019 edited and published as *Creation of Madness* by Mycomm One
©2014 by Linda B. Myers
ISBN: 978-0-9986747-8-0

Cover design by www.introstudio.me
Interior design by Heidi Hansen

For updates and chatter:
www.lindabmyers.com
Facebook.com/lindabmyers.author
myerslindab@gmail.com

DEDICATION

For my sister, Donna Whichello

This story would not exist if not for her story.

CHAPTER ONE

Nutcrackers think they know everything, but they're clueless. Abishua learned that years ago from the psychobabble at Oregon State Penitentiary. He was paroled early because of all the 'progress' he displayed. The assholes had no one but themselves to blame for the bloody mess he made of a girl the first night of his freedom. Back in 1970. He'd avoided prison ever since, nearly twenty years.

At the moment he was clipping his fingernails over the office waste can, thinking about the newest mind fucker. *She'll fail, too. They all do.* She'd never have proof of a damn thing. Not when each of his creations had a spy embedded deep inside, a spy who reported back to him and nobody else in his Seekers of the Absolute Pathway.

Abishua looked at his fingertips, satisfied with his handiwork. "Cadman," he said to his oldest son who was, as always, nearby. "Keep an eye on Laura Covington. Be sure she doesn't push too far."

He turned his attention to the child sitting motionless at his feet. "It's time," he said.

Tick, tick, tick.

CHAPTER TWO

Dr. Laura Covington sat in her hellhole of an office, the knees of her long legs bumped up against the wall. She wished she could open a window except she didn't have one. "That's what I get for climbing *down* the corporate ladder," she muttered.

After years as a corporate psychologist in Portland, Oregon, she'd kissed her slick environs and high-paying job good-bye. The far grittier world of Community Mental Health had called to her. This was where she'd find the people most in need of her counseling skills. 1989 would be her year to reach out to the troubled souls clinging to society's lowest rungs. So she leapt at the job opening for an experienced psychologist in Rapid River, a small town in the Oregon desert.

She craved the mental challenge, and boy oh boy, did she ever get it. Almost nobody was as challenging as, say, Woodrow in his aluminum cone hat warding off the aliens. Or Vlad who bit into himself if he couldn't corner a rodent. Clinical vampirism wasn't one of those things she'd encountered in the corporate sector.

Be careful what you wish for. Her mother's warnings often came to her. There were so many of them to choose from.

Laura's thoughts wandered to her predecessor, Sarah Fletcher. When she'd gone through Sarah's files in her first weeks on the job, Laura had been impressed with the senior counselor.

"Where did she go?" Laura asked her new boss, Tom McClaren.

"Somewhere in Seattle," he answered. "I'm not exactly sure where. Private practice, I think."

"She took good notes. Left me a lot to go on with the clients."

"Maybe, but don't believe everything you read."

"What do you mean?" Laura was surprised by what sounded like criticism.

"Oh nothing. Except Sarah sometimes got a little too...imaginative. We want your take on things. You have better credentials, and that's what we're paying for."

Maybe Sarah Fletcher didn't leave by choice. Laura wondered if Tom was referring to the woman's work with Multiple Personality Disorder. Not all counselors believed it existed. Maybe they doubted the diagnosis because they'd never worked with such a dysfunctional population as that at Community Mental Health. But Laura was open to all sorts of trauma-based syndromes.

Just because you haven't seen it, doesn't mean it isn't real.

She was particularly eager to meet her next client.

***

"Who are you?" asked the wide-eyed young man hovering at Laura's office door. He looked as ready to run as a feral cat.

Laura stood. When he started to back away, she sat down again. "I'm Dr. Laura Covington," she said. "I'm your new psychologist. Please come in."

"Where's Sarah?" David Hollingshead slowly closed the door then crept as far as her only client chair. He was in his mid-twenties, with golden brown eyes that looked older than his years to Laura. Older or tired. And definitely frightened. His clothes were faded, timeworn at stress points, and his shoulder-length auburn hair had some kind of white flecks clinging to it. But he was at least clean enough to have no body odor. *An improvement over a lot of my new clientele.*

Laura thought David would be handsome if the scar on his cheek had been stitched together by more talented hands. He was gaunt, but in decent physical shape as far as she could tell, and he had no telltale signs of drug or alcohol addiction. *He must be doing something to take care of himself.*

"Sarah Fletcher left the department several weeks ago," Laura said as he perched on the chair, looking ready to take flight if necessary. "Didn't she tell you?"

"Maybe she told the others. But they didn't tell me."

It was her first inkling that David and she were not alone in her tiny office. According to his file, he originally came to Community Mental Health in 1987 from the psych ward at the Rapid River hospital, diagnosed with Multiple Personality Disorder. Sarah Fletcher had left a brief note that she concurred with this diagnosis. But his file was surprisingly short on details considering the full reports she left on other clients.

"I'll miss Sarah." He seemed dejected by this turn of events.

"Yes, I'm sure you will. Transitioning to a new counselor is never easy." Several of her clients felt abandoned by her predecessor. After all, they had been. It wasn't all that easy for the new counselor either, taking over a group of people who'd rather she wasn't there.

"Talking upsets some of us. And we don't all like change."

"I understand. I wasn't sure if you'd come today since you missed your first appointment." Laura kept her voice low to begin asserting her authority in a tranquil manner.

"I missed an appointment?" David looked befuddled. "I'm sorry."

"I'm glad you're here now. I've read your file, so I know a little about you. But I'd like to ask you a few questions just for background, okay?"

"We'll see how it goes," he said, with the hint of a smile, and he settled back into the chair. He could meet her gaze, unlike many of her clients. In fact, his eyes seemed fastened on her, the way a prey animal might view a predator.

"Did Sarah discuss your diagnosis with you?"

He was clutching the edge of her desk, and she

could see the tension in his slender hands. He lifted one and pointed to his own head. "Yes. She said I'm not alone in here. I didn't believe it. But then I worked it out, and she was right."

"I know you don't trust me yet, David. That will take time. But if you listen to me, I will do the same for you. And we'll continue working on it together."

He shifted, hooking his feet around the chair's front legs.

"I thought you could tell me a little about your job," Laura said, choosing the easiest place for many people to start talking about themselves.

David never took his eyes off her. She began to feel like the target of a dissection, skin peeled back and organs exposed. It was difficult for her not to glance down to check whether her buttons were behaving.

Finally he said, "We don't like it in here. It's too tight."

"Yes, the room is very small. Would you like to move your chair closer to the door? I could open it, but I don't want you to worry that we'll be overheard."

"Being shut in," he said, voice almost a whisper. "It scares the Little Ones."

She felt a tingle of excitement. *The Little Ones?*

She needed to solve this simple issue of space if he was to believe she could help with harder problems. "Would a room with windows help?"

He nodded. Laura called Lovella the receptionist to book the downstairs conference room. "Let's move there, David. We'll meet there until the, ah, Little Ones, know they can trust me."

They sat down together, the only two people in a conference room that could seat sixteen. A glass wall separated them from the sounds and goings on at the front reception desk. Vertical blinds screened the windows that faced the street corner, but strong sun filtered through. It was usually sunny here in Oregon's high desert country, not as gray as Portland where Laura had lived before.

"This is better," David said.

Laura read the relaxation in his body language. *The Little Ones must be happier.* "Good. Then we'll meet here until my office is comfortable for you. Now, can you tell me about your job?"

"I'm a pretty fair woodworker, cabinet maker, any kind of finish carpentry," he said. "That's what I did when I was on the road a lot." *Ah! That explains the white flecks in his hair. It's sawdust!*

As the session progressed, David lost the wariness that had accompanied him into her office. When their time ended, Laura felt they had made a good start. Maybe he'd come to accept her in place of Sarah Fletcher.

CHAPTER THREE

"He said he'd diaper babies or old people if need be, but not me," Diaper Man howled.

Dr. Laura kept a straight face as her client described his break up with the guy he called his main man, his hunka hunka, his love torch.

Diaper Man was a middle-aged schizophrenic. He also enjoyed wearing a diaper. This in itself would not have been issue enough for him to receive free counseling, since it wasn't exactly a threat to society. But it's what he most liked to talk about.

Laura listened to his story then reminded him about the dangers of hanging around public restrooms to find another soul mate. She saw to it that he got his anti-psychotic meds from the psychiatrist and made it clear that he mattered to her as well as to all the other people at Community Mental Health. That was really what he needed most. To matter.

As the only PhD in Rapid River's Community Mental Health Department, Laura spent part of her days conducting psychological testing for all the other counselors. Her own caseload was enormous, as well. Some clients like Diaper Man could hold a job, but most were so disoriented or disabled that employment was out of the question. They lived in hole-in-the-wall apartments or missions or alleys. She was their last line of defense, and she vowed to do everything for them that her education, experience and emotions prepared her to do.

Nonetheless, she had her favorites. Like David Hollingshead. The idea of a multiple was so new to her, so fascinating. After their first appointment, David always appeared on schedule. Laura went to the lobby to meet him each time and escort him into the conference room.

As she came down the stairs, she could often hear him chatting with the ancient receptionist. Lovella had a face as wrinkled as a shar-pei and skin the color of a dark chocolate mocha. Her salt and pepper hair was pulled back with dagger-length clips, and heaven help the strand that tried to escape. Her most startling feature was her bosom, encased today in a white blouse so starched it looked rigid. Nothing about the receptionist was soft, except she appeared to dote on David. Today, her face was cracked open in what could only be called a smile. But after Laura collected David for his session, the receptionist returned to her dour self.

"You!" Lovella snapped at the frail-looking fellow sitting on a straight-backed waiting room chair. "Don't tear pages out of that magazine. I'm not telling you again."

Laura closed the conference room door, enjoying the sunny room as much as David did. It was time for him to confront issues over his failed marriage, so she got to it as soon as they were seated. "In your file, I see that you and your wife have separated."

David appeared flustered. "That's not easy to talk about, Dr. Laura."

"You're right. Most of our work together will be hard." *Come on, David, don't balk.*

"Well...if it's important. Cathy cleared out. Has her own place now."

"Did she know about your diagnosis?"

"She beat feet before the hospital shrink gave it a name."

"He said in your record that you were losing time, that intervals would pass and you wouldn't know what happened. Did Cathy know about that?"

He brushed a forelock of auburn hair back from his eyes. "She just thought I was spacey. 'Earth to David,' she'd say. She complained that I never listened to her, that I'd lose my head if it wasn't screwed on. But mostly, I don't know, I guess we were just apart a lot."

David began to swivel the conference room chair back and forth. Laura read it for nervous tension. He'd said it wasn't easy to talk about, and his body was agreeing.

Could a wife really not know her husband was losing time? Or is David just very good at hiding it? "Tell me why you were apart so much."

He stopped to light a cigarette. None of her clients was fazed by the new anti-smoking craze. They all still puffed away. Assessing his slender frame, she thought he should be spending his money on food instead.

"Cathy worked late a lot. She wanted the overtime. I was building houses as far away as Medford. Our crew stayed in crappy motels all week. Everybody got tanked at nights just 'cause we were bored. I thought I passed out a lot. Turns out, it wasn't from booze. Sarah helped me see that I was losing time. But I didn't know it back then.

"I sometimes woke up with aches and wounds I couldn't explain." He cocked his head and rubbed a finger down the red scar on his cheek. "No idea what happened here. Anyway, our crew only got back to Rapid River on weekends. I saw Cathy then, if she wasn't working all the time."

"When did things start to change for you two?"

David stared out toward the reception area, but Laura doubted he was actually seeing anything as he reminisced. *A mild kind of dissociation common for us all.*

"My boss bolted a while back, leaving a lot of unpaid bills. Work isn't easy to come by anymore. Sometimes my church hires me to build furniture they can sell. It's not a lot, but I thought at least I wouldn't have to travel so much. I could be with my wife more." His eyes misted with tears. "It wasn't long after I stopped travelling that Cathy left me."

Laura gave him time to regain his composure then asked, "Did she say why?"

"She started to gripe about money, and we fought about it. Then one day, she said I scared her, even slapped her. But I can't believe that. I don't remember any of it. I love her. I'd never hurt her."

His golden brown eyes were as imploring as an animal shelter poster. He seemed innocent enough, but for the first time, Laura felt a prickle of apprehension. *Should I be alone with this man?* From where she sat, she could see through the glass wall to Lovella and the activity around the reception desk. It calmed her. She felt safe enough to continue. "Why would Cathy say you hurt her if you didn't?"

He stopped swiveling the chair and leaned toward her. "I've thought a lot about that. I think she wanted to punish me for losing my job."

"What finally made her leave?"

"I didn't get it. She accused me of having another woman. I said it wasn't true. And it wasn't. But, then she said she'd actually seen me with some bimbo, at a bar one night when she stopped with her friends after work. Then she thought I was more than a cheat. A liar, too. And she walked out."

He took a deep ragged breath and leaned back. "The thing is, I really didn't have another woman. At least not one I remember. I went ballistic."

"I'm not surprised. That kind of event is called a stressor."

"I'll say. I was angry, felt lost. Without a job, without my wife, not knowing what to believe, well, I fell apart. The shrink used a word -"

"Decompensation."

"Yeah, that's it. Cops picked me up where I passed out in an alley. I was liquored up, been cut pretty bad. They took me to the emergency room. Once the docs patched up my gut, they wheeled me down to the psych ward. They kept me ten days, booted me out, and told me to come here."

When she'd had her corporate job, people came to Laura between meetings with sales and marketing, not after a life-threatening fight in an alley. Her clients here at Community Mental Health lived close to the edge. She still wasn't used to the violence.

"Let's talk more about losing time," she said.

But David was done talking for the day. "I think it's time you meet the others," he said, rising to leave. "I'll bring them next session. Some of them want a word with you."

***

Later that afternoon, Laura was reviewing her notes when she heard a knock on the frame of her open door.

"Laura, could I speak with you a moment?" said Tom McClaren, her boss. His carrot top clashed with his florid complexion, but his comical Howdy Doody freckles didn't fool her. She knew he had the street smarts to be of enormous value to the department, especially when it came to negotiating federal, state, and county codes and funding.

She turned off her tape recorder, shut her notebook, and invited him into her office with a smile. "It's nothing much, but *mi casa es su casa*."

"This isn't exactly a social call. I hear that you've been using the conference room to see one of your clients." Howdy Doody frowned.

"Yes. David Hollingshead has issues in a small room with no windows." She indicated her office with a hand gesture worthy of Vanna White.

"Why's that?"

"He says the Little Ones get scared."

"Oh, for heaven's sake. Not that again." Tom rolled his eyes. "By now he should be comfortable with you."

Laura stiffened, not liking her competence to be questioned. "He is comfortable with me. Just not with the office. I see nothing wrong with using the conference room as long as it's available."

"Well, the department does. It just doesn't look good. It's for government or hospital conferences, not individual counseling."

"But I still don't -"

"So please conduct your sessions in your office from now on. And keep in mind, these people are very cunning. They can fool you. With your corporate background, you might be a little, oh, shall we say naïve about them. You need to control them, not the other way around." He smiled, turned and left.

Must be hard to walk with a stick so far up your butt. A hot blush of anger crept up her chest and neck. She'd hoped to leave officialdom behind in the corporate world, but the red tape was pretty binding here, too.

The next week, Lovella called her from reception when David arrived. "Oh, and you should know there's a meeting in the conference room."

"But I booked it for this morning," Laura protested. She'd ignored Tom's request.

"You been trumped by the Man."

"I'll be right down." She grabbed her coat, purse, notebook, and galloped down the stairs. David was standing at the reception desk, talking with Lovella. Laura shot an angry look at the group in the conference room and saw Tom's eyes meet hers. She controlled herself enough not to flip him a bird, then said to David, "How about we go for a walk today? I'll buy you a Coke, and we'll talk."

"That's okay, Dr. Laura. The Little Ones say they'll be all right in your office now that they know who you are."

Barriers were coming down with her client if not with her boss. Tom would think he'd won, but she reminded herself that this was about David, not about her. So back up the stairs she went. David took a seat in her office while she put her purse in her desk drawer and hung her coat on the back of the door. Then she looked at him, indicating the door with her hand, "Okay?"

He nodded, and Laura shut it. She took her seat, turned toward him and began, "I'm sorry about the conference room. We don't always see eye to eye, but Mr. McC..."

"Fucker don't know his head from his dick." David's face was a mask of anger.

Startled, Laura said, "Well, you needn't worry about him, David. I can..."

"Who you calling David? What a pussy that one is."

Laura's heart beat a little faster. She'd heard lectures about it, read about it, but…"Then who are you?"

"Name's Weasel. I speak for the Defenders. The others don't do shit without my say so." Weasel's voice crackled with tension. He seemed to take more space than David, squaring his shoulders like that.

The hair on the back of Laura's neck stiffened. "Where is David?" *Other than sitting right here in front of me. Holy shit!*

"He's taking a little time out." Weasel's face was far more animated than David's. He leaned back and sprawled his legs out in front of him. A challenging posture. Sure of himself. Macho.

"Is he being punished?"

"He should have slapped that fucking boss of yours from here to Toledo." Weasel bared his teeth, an expression totally alien on David's mild countenance.

Laura fought the instinct to leave. "No! There will be no threats to any member of this staff." *Including me. Especially me.*

"Yeah. That last nutcracker was a pussy, too," Weasel said.

"Do you mean Sarah?" Laura asked, trying to keep pace while her head was saying wait, just a minute, give me time to catch up.

"That's the one. She was cowed by that prick, too." Weasel/David removed a toothpick from his shirt pocket and began to chew on it. "Some of the Forum liked her, though."

"The Forum?"

For the next half hour, Weasel the Defender spun a tale bizarre enough for *The Twilight Zone*. Almost none of it had been in Sarah's notes. It was electrifying for Laura, watching one person play different roles. *Dr. Jekyll, meet Mr. Hyde. Eve, here are your three faces.*

Laura learned that David and Sarah had

developed the Forum together. It was a senate inside David with three representatives of different personality types called the White Hats, the Little Ones, and the Defenders. Together, through bickering, wheedling, and bullying, they held sway over David, the host who most often faced the public. Any of the others could take over, make him feel pain, or keep him from it.

"That last mind fucker said we have to keep the weakling safe or we're all in danger."

"That last mind fucker was right." Laura heard nothing but Weasel. Not the clock, not people in the hall, not the floor fan oscillating through its slow pattern. Nothing existed for her but David and, well, whoever.

"Now that Sarah left us, I could kill him for all she cares." Weasel spat the toothpick into Laura's wastebasket.

"That's not true. You all still need to take care of David. There's only one body. Kill him, and you all die." *Kill? Die? What am I saying?*

"Who has to take care of me?" David asked, his body gathering into a less pugnacious posture. His shoulders slumped, and his facial features returning to benign. "Which one are you talking to?"

"David?" Laura asked, her voice the least bit unsteady.

"Of course it's me." David smiled. "You better be careful, Dr. Laura, or people will think you're as crazy as I am."

***

After David left, Laura reveled in her amazement. One client had entered and exited her office, but two had been in there with her. She had decisions to make about what the hell she really believed. She was frightened of being foolish, exhilarated by the unknown, intrigued to know more. In her corporate role, she had dealt with rage management, alcoholism, family issues as they impacted the breadwinner. But nothing at all like this. She needed to do research and do it fast, but she doubted the Rapid River Bookstore was equipped to handle Weasel.

I just hope to hell I am.

CHAPTER FOUR

By five-thirty Laura was often stressed out, but that's when her real job began. It was time to pick up Wade at Lil Pals Day Care. A kid had not been her idea. Neither had living with her seventy-year-old barracuda of a mother, Eudora, who tripped over her trench coat belt while disembarking a city bus. Now the old lady had a trick knee and was a little too shaky to live alone. Eudora moved in with Laura just in time to relocate with her from Portland to Rapid River.

God help me.

Almost the day of her mother's move-in, Laura inherited a five-year-old boy, Wade Sanford. A former corporate client named Laura the boy's guardian in her will, then proceeded to drink herself into a fatal high speed accident. At forty, and starting a new career, the last thing Laura wanted was motherhood. But the boy had nobody else, and Laura knew what could happen to a troubled child enmeshed in a flawed system. Like it or not, she simply couldn't let that happen. *What the hell am I getting myself into?*

"You're not my mommy," Wade declared with a trembling voice when they first met in a lawyer's chilly office.

"No, Wade, no I'm not," Laura said, wishing she'd

paid more attention in child psychology classes. "But I liked her a lot. And I bet I will like you, too."

"You probably will. People do," he agreed solemnly.

"I do already," she said, smiling at him.

"Are you my Gram? The other kids have some of those. And you're old."

"Well, I guess I'm old enough to be your grandmother." *Are guys just born knowing how to hurt your feelings? Is forty really that old?*

"Okay, then. You can be Gram. I've always wanted one. They take kids to zoos and buy them stuff."

And so, the deal was struck. Laura would be Gram, and Wade would be hers. After a couple months of haggling with courts, trustees, state and county agencies, Wade came to stay. Laura found herself at the helm of a precarious little family, whose issues were still nine-tenths under water.

Most days, Laura felt better prepared to be a cosmonaut than a mother. And this kid was an especially big mystery. Wade came with nothing more than records of inoculations and a small insurance policy that his mother had left for his upkeep. With no known father and a deceased mother, Laura recognized the boy had been handed powerful fodder for abandonment issues.

Fortunately, Laura's mother Eudora and Wade took to each other right from the start. "You Dora?" the boy had misunderstood when they met. From then on, she was Dora to him.

Eudora was the first to notice that Wade seemed

entirely too docile, too obliging. Laura liked the calm, but it concerned her mother. "Part of the time he should be nasty as a cornered badger. You know, pushing the envelope, throwing a hissy."

"Don't you think he's simply scared of rocking the boat? He must be worried about doing the wrong thing."

"Maybe. But count on that dam to burst any time now."

"I'll get some child psychology books."

"Well okay, but I don't think he's old enough to read them."

***

Sure enough, the dam did break. Maybe Wade had gotten comfortable enough to test her, like any kid would. Or maybe with his sad background he needed to see whether she would abandon him, too. Whatever the reason, the battle commenced that very afternoon. Laura picked Wade up at Lil Pals and took him to a late appointment with the pediatrician.

"I don't want to go," Wade pouted.

Laura was patient. "You need a physical to be in day care. It's a good idea. I've heard Dr. Latimer is a very nice man."

The pediatrician's waiting room was cheery to a fault, with a jumbo fish tank, a Lego metropolis, rocking horses, and a rainbow mural on the wall. Laura thought the canned music was probably called something like *Gladness & Glee*.

Apparently, Wade wasn't fooled by any of it,

knowing that you got poked with needles in places like this. "No shots, Gram," he announced, scowling up at her and pulling back so she had to drag him across the room to the chairs.

"If Dr. Latimer says you need..." Laura began as she seated herself.

"No shots," he repeated, standing in front of her and stamping a foot.

"... to have a shot, then I expect you to be a big boy and..."

"NO SHOTS," Wade power-shrieked, then kicked the chair leg, narrowly missing Laura's ankle.

"Wade, stop this!" She was so surprised by the outburst that she figured her mouth must be as round as a donut hole.

"No shots, no shots, no shots," he wailed.

The receptionist stared at Wade, then at Laura. The other mommies stared. The other children stared. A nurse peeked out from the inner sanctum and stared. Laura felt her composure drain away along with any semblance of parenting skills. She blushed so hot she wondered if this was the first attack of menopause. She stared wide-eyed at her child, marveling at his transformation into Devil Boy. And then she caved.

"All right, Wade. No shots."

Instantly, Wade brightened and began playing with the waiting room toys, engaging with the other children, in general being a model citizen. Still basking in the glow of victory, he handled the visit with Dr. Latimer like a champ. The doc listened to his heart, looked into his ears and eyes, told him to take deep breaths. He pronounced Wade a healthy specimen of five-year-old boyhood if ever he'd seen one. And nothing about shots was mentioned.

The child beamed, but Laura left the office as wilted as the last rose of summer. She was pleased Wade was healthy, but she wanted to kill him. She'd suffered a humiliating defeat at the hands of a child who had no PhD in psychology at all. Eudora had been right once again. The dam had burst and a cornered badger had emerged.

That night, Wade crawled onto Laura's lap holding his teddy bear, and they went through *Goodnight Moon* once again. Based on how often he requested it, it was the best gift she'd given him so far.

"I'm mad at my Mommy," he finally admitted quietly.

"Tell me," Laura said.

"She yelled at me. A lot."

"Why did she do that?" It would be cathartic for him to talk. It was good for her, too, since she had no idea what had happened to the child in his first five years.

"I made her head hurt."

A five-year-old would be rough on an alcoholic's mornings after.

"She locked me in. I was scared." His little voice was as full of heartbreak as a scream. "I told her, 'I hate you, Mommy.' So she went away. But I didn't mean it."

Laura hugged him tight as he cried. "Now you listen to me, Wade. Nothing you did made your mommy go away. She cared for you right up until it was my turn. You don't have to feel bad or worry about that, not ever."

She hoped it sounded convincing to him. And she hoped she could eventually convince herself. She still wasn't sure the decision to keep him would be the best for her. He needed her, but the reverse simply wasn't true. She wanted to love him as openly and fully as Eudora did from the very first day, but for her it was a new direction and she had no map.

CHAPTER FIVE

The Prophet Abishua chose his name because it meant 'deliverance.' It helped him convince a deluded band of followers that he was their pipeline to salvation. He called them Seekers of the Absolute Pathway, and he thrived on their consuming need to find a purpose to their little lives.

"Children are the bricks and mortar of our enterprise," Abishua would preach to his flock, and when alone with his son Cadman, he would instruct, "You must use them accurately to create the sturdiest foundation."

In the early days, raw material was difficult to come by. The cult was too small to produce enough of its own children, so others had to be procured. But that was no problem. Like all psychopaths, Abishua was without a conscience. He was also charming and compelling enough to manipulate gullible people anyway he wished. He taught his cult women how to steal little ones, telling them it was for the children's own good. "Raised by their parents, they're in danger of society's basest behavior. Raised by me, they will achieve salvation." He instructed the women to find poorly supervised playgrounds in nearby cities like Portland or Eugene or even Seattle. One would use a puppy to lure a child close enough to the street for the others to snatch the kid up and drive away forever.

The method worked but was too dangerous to use often. Abishua was gratified that the cult had now grown to the point that it had enough fertile men and women to keep the babies coming. They could adequately provide children for the kiddy porn that he sold internationally.

Like any wise entrepreneur, Abishua maintained a secondary source of supply to keep his business healthy. He placed a mole in the town's leading day care center. "Get to know each child," he told the mole. "Discover what makes them unique, what they love, how they're most vulnerable."

The day care was an incubator for Abishua's own precious creations. Some children were more likely candidates than others, effortless to break. He told the mole, "Keep your eyes open for a particularly imaginative child, one for whom storybook characters easily come alive. A child who can spend time alone, intrigued with his own thoughts and fantasies. A child who's already been abused or abandoned."

This child was a real find, precious raw material worth the time and risk it took to create a masterpiece all his own. The call he'd just received from the mole alerted him that such a child was at the day care now. The boy was the son of the meddlesome Dr. Laura Covington.

Abishua had no sense of humor. But he'd observed how it worked in others. He was aware that if he could feel any emotion whatsoever, this would have been the funniest joke he'd ever heard.

CHAPTER SIX

Why isn't there anything in Sarah's notes about the Forum? Laura thought about it until she developed a theory. As Sarah worked with the Forum to create a place where David could safely function in society, he would no longer be a danger to himself or others. That would be the end of the county's obligation to him. Maybe Sarah stopped keeping notes in order to avoid coming to the end of the counseling sessions. *If she was intellectually hooked, how far toward fusing the personality system into one entity did she hope to go?*

Or maybe there had been notes. Maybe Tom did away with them because he didn't buy the diagnosis.

At noon, Laura grabbed her colorful clutch from a desk drawer and left her office for lunch. As she came down the graceful old staircase, she looked around at all the eye candy of the landmark building that housed the Rapid River Community Mental Health Department. It had been a hotel when it was built in the early 1900s. Laura imagined that, back then, loggers from the surrounding hills came there for nights that were a damn sight wilder than a good night's sleep.

The building was rehabbed extensively and brought up to city codes. Delightful hints of the hotel's heyday were carefully retained by some unnamed rehabber who'd actually given a damn. The flooring was replaced with industrial strength tile that caused her wedges to clop, but the ceiling was the original tin. It was painted dove gray now, and the embossed square pattern was still an eye stopper. Cornices were intact as well, creating a border of leafy swirls all around the ceiling. In order to maintain the look of the hotel, the lobby was wallpapered with a geometric pattern that would have been just the ticket in 1910.

What had been the hotel's front desk was now Lovella's realm. The wide staircase with its beautiful old banister once led to the guest rooms above. They'd now been cut down to pigeonholes that served as offices for the counselors, nurses and visiting physicians.

Laura imagined herself, tall and elegant, sweeping down the staircase in ankle length cotton batiste and lace, with her curly chestnut hair pulled up into a pompadour. Men would all have suspenders, bow ties and handlebar mustaches. In her imagination, a piano player in the lobby tickled the ivories with *My Gal Sal* and *Barney Google*.

When she exited the building, her fantasy popped away, and she went back to mulling over Sarah's notes as she walked down the street to meet Helen Waring. Laura and Helen had been friends for years, ever since their days as college roommates. That had been one of the big draws for changing locations. Helen helped Laura choose a house and make the move from Portland.

Black Walnut was a fern bar that served

homemade soups and massive sandwiches, along with its own ales and seasonal beers. Laura saw her friend at a table in the crowded room and was surprised she was not alone.

Helen was the editor of the *Rapid City Review*. "It's the beer. That's why these guys are here," Helen said as Laura took the only empty chair. "They helped themselves to my table. You know newsmen drink by the bucketful."

"An ugly stereotype," the one with the killer smile said. He extended a hand to Laura. "I'm Rob Cooper, and this is the Mule."

"That's Harvey Mueller, ma'am. Pleased to meet you."

Laura knew Helen had a volatile but long standing thing with the Mule and was glad to finally meet him. "He's stubborn as one," Helen had told her. "I suppose that's why I can't push him around, so it's not all bad." *Something had to explain the attraction*, Laura thought while assessing the slouch and Adam's apple that made the Mule a homely Abe Lincoln.

Helen was short and round, the opposite of the Mule. Her idea of business casual was sweat shirts and jeans. Helen had no interest in rinsing the grey from her hair, or adding a touch of foundation to soften her complexion, or using a pencil to define brows and lashes that were too blonde to be seen on their own. Her smile lines made her look like a kind woman, one that might say, "There, there," and bake you cookies when you were feeling blue. But she had a sharp wit that made her editorials terse and opinionated. Laura knew that Helen enjoyed making an adversary as much as a friend. Laura was sincerely glad to be the latter.

"Laura Covington is the new kid in town," Helen explained. "A college pal of mine, now a counselor at the county loony bin, so you two better watch your steps."

"Actually, loony bin is out of favor these days," Laura said. "We professionals prefer nut house. I'm the new nutcracker."

"Ouch," said the Mule.

"Have a seat, Laura." Helen invited. "How's it going?"

"Well, I'm working with my first Multiple," Laura enthused as she took the last empty chair.

"Multiple?" asked Helen.

"You mean like Sybil?" the Mule joined in.

"Isn't that stuff just woo-woo?" Rob added.

"Easy, easy!" Laura held up her hands. "Back off. No wonder people don't hang with packs of journalists."

Rob and the Mule were reporter and photographer, she knew from the by-lines and photo credits in the *Review*. They were both tall and slender, but while the Mule slouched at the table, Rob sat straight and alert. The reporter was dark-haired and craggy-faced, handsome in a leathery, outdoorsy sort of way. He seemed a little too mature to be a reporter at a small town paper. *Mid forties, maybe?* She wondered if he was an avid skier, hiker or mountain climber. That could keep a journalist here instead of attracted to a bigger city's bigger stories.

"We see all types of dissociation," Laura said, defending her corner. "MPD is a perfectly acceptable diagnosis in the DSM-3."

"MPD in the DSM-3? Is that a new language?" Rob asked.

"Multiple Personality Disorder in the *Diagnostic and Statistical Manual*. The third edition is the one used by us up-to-date nutcrackers," she said, smiling at Rob.

"But some shrinks say it's hooey, right?" Helen probed. "Wonder if there's a story in this for the *Review*."

Laura shot her visual arrows. "Not from me. But you can always contact the head administrator, Tom McClaren. I'm sure he'd love the publicity."

"Okay, cool your jets. I'll drop it. For now."

The Mule said, "Anyone wants me to help with their fries, go ahead and order them."

A mooch as well as butt-ugly? Laura ordered a turkey on rye with fries, with no intention of sharing. Helen was going to have to enlighten her about the Mule.

But this Rob guy? Well, to steal a phrase from Diaper Man, he could surely be a person's main man hunka hunka love torch.

CHAPTER SEVEN

Life with Eudora could be just as volatile as Laura's workdays. Laura recalled a morning when they were still living in Portland, before she'd agreed to take in Wade.

"Well?" Eudora had demanded from her position at the stove. The little woman loved to cook and firmly believed her daughter couldn't. Laura had been mostly kicked out of her own kitchen other than to eat at the dinette. She took it fairly gracefully, recognizing that her mother needed a job to feel useful. *And also, what a deal.*

"Well, what?"

"Well, when are you picking him up?" Eudora waggled the pancake flipper at her daughter like a flexible sword.

"Eudora, I'm afraid he'd be better off with someone who has time for him."

"I have time. What else?"

"I don't know a damn thing about kids. And this one will have a boatload of problems."

"I know kids. Was one. Raised two. What else?"

Sigh. "You have to have time, know-how and staying power. You're, um, *getting on* a little, don't you think?"

"And maybe you're a little too dimwitted. You go

around wanting to help your fellow man, then along comes one little child, and you run like a jack rabbit." As Laura recalled, by the end of that breakfast, the only woman still speaking was Jane Pauley delivering the news.

This Friday evening, Eudora and she were sitting in the living room of Laura's new house. Old house, really, having been built in the 1910s. Her Portland condo was sleek, with industrial chic décor. The Ice Palace, her mother called it. But this house had been remodeled to suit the taste of the 80s, and she'd decorated it to be warm and cozy, in order to cut the ties with her former digs. In the loft overhead, Wade was playing with his farm set of plastic animals, making moos and clucks and whinnies.

Laura kicked off her shoes, wiggled her toes, and silently thanked Princess Di for making lower heels popular again. She started to tell her mother about a problem she was having with her boss, Tom. "I'm really in the trenches, working with brain injuries, mood disorders, appalling trauma. I love the challenge. But Tom is a roadblock."

Books on Multiplicity were not a popular expenditure with Tom, so Laura ordered everyone she could find and paid for it herself. "Hundreds of bucks to do my job better," she complained, fondling the five-pound volume that had arrived that day.

Eudora looked up from her *Cosmopolitan*. "Really? Well maybe you ought to spend another fifty on more child psychology," She rolled her eyes upward toward the boy farmer above them.

"What do you mean? Is something wrong?" Laura asked, suddenly concerned.

"Oh no, not physically. Nothing's wrong that a few minutes of real emotion from you wouldn't cure."

"What are you talking about?" Laura bristled. "I spend time with him, take him places, buy him things."

"Honey, you have to spend heart with the child as well as time. Put away your books. Tell him jokes, laugh at his. Give him hugs out of context. Share a Twinkie or a box of Nerds. It's not about the number of minutes, but the number of memories. You'll find he's very easy to love."

Always a pleasure, these little chats, old woman. Laura shut her book, then stared blindly at its cover. Eudora was right, of course, damn it all anyway. *But why? Why am I more invested in my clients than in Wade? What's holding me back?*

She decided what she'd do to buy time while she worked on that puzzle. She'd give him something with immediate emotional impact. Something of his very own to love.

God help me.

***

Wade was having a terrific day. Gram had promised to get him a cat, and today was the day.

"It's Cat Day!" he piped into her ear, shaking her awake at seven Saturday morning.

"Mrphhh," she croaked. "Cat-astrophy day." She squinted at the clock and whined, "They won't be open for hours, Wade."

"But we need to be first to get the best one." He pulled the covers off her bed and began to bounce up and down on the mattress next to her.

Sitting up and stretching, she muttered, "That's more action than this mattress has seen in months."

"What?" Wade asked, still bouncing.

"Nothing," she said, then staggered off to the shower. Wade watched the second hand on the clock, giving her four whole circles around the dial before he began pounding on the bathroom door.

"Can't you hurry?" Wade thought Gram was such a slowpoke with all those face creams and eye goop and hair stuff. He just threw on his clothes and he was ready. *What's wrong with girls, anyway? And Gram was so bossy!*

"We're going nowhere until you clean up your room," he heard her yell out from the bathroom.

"Gra-aaa-am." He made three syllables out of the word.

"Don't make me say it again."

"Shit," Wade muttered.

"What did you say?" She threw open the bathroom door, with the dryer still blowing her hair around like a tornado.

"Nothing," he yelped then galloped into his room to pick up yesterday's clothes, his coloring book, and three Tonka trucks. He buried everything under his Smurf bedspread then pulled it up to his pillow. There, she'd never guess.

"Go wake up Dora," Gram said once she was dressed. "Try that jumping up and down stuff. It ought to work."

When they all were ready, Gram drove to the animal shelter but the sign on the door said they didn't open until ten.

"Told you so," said Dora.

"Did not," said Wade.

"Did, too."

"I'll tell you *both* what. Let's go to the pet store first," said Gram. Wade noticed she was clutching the steering wheel pretty hard. "We'll still get back in plenty of time."

Luckily, the pet store opened at nine. Gram took a cart and went off to buy cat food, litter, a litter pan, and a cat carrier, which was all pretty boring stuff. Wade took Dora by the hand to the cat toy aisle where he was allowed to pick out any two playthings. He looked and looked.

"What's the hold up, Wade?" Dora asked.

"I can't decide."

"Well, if I were a cat, I'd want these feathers on the stick," she said, batting a hand at the colorful little tuft.

"Gram says no sticks in the house."

"She can be an old poop, can't she? I think just this once it will be okay. And I'm her mom so that makes me boss. But don't tell her I said that."

They loaded their purchases into the Camry and headed back to the animal shelter. After a fifteen-minute wait, it opened.

"We're the first ones here. You're the best, Gram!" Wade rejoiced.

She reached down and gave him a hug. "No,

Wade, *you're* the best." Then Dora looked at Gram and gave her a smile.

Wade wondered what that was about but just for a second. He was too excited over the cat to think about much else.

The animal shelter man was old, rotund and cheery. He was Harold, and his badge called him a volunteer at the shelter. Harold took them to a room where the cats were caged.

"How will I choose, Gram?" Wade asked, believing she could answer anything ever since Dora called her a Know It All.

"I think you'll just know, Wade. They say pets choose you."

They began to walk the rows of cages, and Wade peered into one after another. One had two kittens curled up together.

"I want two," he said.

"Wade, we discussed this. Only one."

"But why?"

"One kitty will be plenty for you to take care of. Maybe we can get another someday, but we should start with just one for now."

Harold nodded and agreed. "Very wise, very wise."

Grown-ups always stick together. Wade continued looking in all the cages, even crouching down to the bottom row. Suddenly, a chocolate brown paw shot out and tapped him on the nose. Startled, he straightened up, then squatted cautiously once more. Again the paw stretched out but this time found

Wade's cheek and patted it gently a couple times. Wade stood up and said to the shelter man, "This one wants me. And I want him."

"This little brown cat?" Harold asked, bending down. Wade thought he was so fat he might tip over as his bulk shifted, but he seemed to settle okay. "Why, I think you have very good taste, young man," he said as he opened the cage and scooped up the cat. "I believe there must be a touch of Abyssinian in here, based on the size of these ears. Now put out your arms."

Harold lowered the cat into Wade's waiting grasp. Wade stared at it, and it studied him back. He broke into a smile saying, "Look, Gram, his ears are so pointy. Like that Spock guy you talk about."

"What a good name for him," Gram smiled, looking happy for the first time that morning.

The little cat began to purr and cuddled against Wade's chest. The decision to take Spock home was made by all parties, right then and there.

"I chose you, like Gram chose me," Wade explained to the cat on the drive home.

***

Spock took immediate possession of the house. Laura had naively assumed it would stay in Wade's room, but Spock refused to read the house rules. He was always in Wade's shadow or he dogged Eudora. Laura was his third choice but any old lap in the storm. She hated the way he laced around her legs while she transferred laundry from washer to dryer, and he knew it, which was all the more reason to do it.

Sunday afternoon Laura was sitting at her desk tucked in the open loft space, looking at a tri-fold brochure. Spock had knocked over the little ceramic bowl of paper clips next to her Compaq computer, and she was distractedly picking them up while she read. Occasionally, she took a clandestine peak at Wade who was sprawled on his tummy, tongue circled over his upper lip, drawing pictures and coloring them in. The cat was curled up asleep in the small of his back, after a boisterous game of slapping around his color markers. *What more can you ask of nine pounds of attitude than friendship?*

As she watched Wade draw, she reflected that he was a child good at passing time in quiet concentration. He could go off in a world of his own. Sometimes when she called him to dinner or to do a chore, she had to call more than once. At first she thought he was being willful. But if what she had recently read about children post trauma was true, he was likely taking expeditions around the inside of his own head, working out all the changes in his young life. He was a little too focused, maybe, but if it helped him manage stress, it had to be okay.

Right?

She turned back to the brochure, and began filling out the form on the last page. It was for a counselors' conference in Portland in a month's time. The subject was dissociative disorders like MPD.

Her boss had refused to pay for the trip, saying,

"We have far more pressing needs for our limited educational budget." So she would book a flight to Portland for the Friday evening before the conference, and pay for it herself. It was a damn good thing she'd worked long enough in the corporate sector to afford to work at Community Mental Health. She would be home Sunday night, and miss no work. *The day may come when he'll be sorry he didn't pay more attention to dissociative clients. Or to me.*

CHAPTER EIGHT

"Oh no," Laura groaned when the alarm bleated her out of bed on Monday. "Bowling." She tried burying herself under the covers, but the snooze alarm showed no mercy.

Monday mornings were always frantic, what with weekend crisis catch-up. But this Monday was also Mental Health Outing Day. Tom explained it to her this way. "We consider socialization to be good for many clients, to improve their interpersonal skills by mixing and mingling. All the counselors take turns as chaperones for these events."

"What about you, Tom?" she had asked.

"Well, no, I am an administrator, not a caseworker. This takes the finesse of you people." He pronounced *you people* as though he were referring to large maggots.

Jenny, Diego and Laura headed up the party on this Monday morning. As usual, Jenny reminded Laura of an aging flower child with her loose fitting smock and long gray tendrils caught up in a macramé band. Diego was a Guatemalan who specialized with Hispanic clients.

"Tom said this takes finesse," Laura muttered to Jenny after buckling seat belts around the hips of several clients in the Mental Health Department van.

"The only finesse I need is how to buckle a seat belt without touching anyone inappropriately."

"Especially when so many *want* to be touched inappropriately. Diego says he'll drive if you and I bowl."

"I can't just get a latte and watch? Surely my PhD is worth some damn perk."

"Absolutely not, Dr. Covington," Jenny laughed. "We all interact so every client receives an enriching experience. It's part of our Equalize and Socialize Philosophy."

Diego said in a whisper, "And they like it if we let them win."

"That ought to be no problem," Laura answered, having not entered a bowling alley since her undergrad days.

Once the counselors shepherded everyone into Rapid River Lanes, their clients congregated around the shoe rental, each requesting a pair in a size that might or might not be accurate. Eventually, Jenny, Diego and Laura worked their way through broken laces, double half hitch knots, and flattened insoles until everyone was more or less properly shod.

Some clients were as likely to drop balls on the lanes as roll them. Some helped each other; some took advantage of each other. But they all appeared to have a pretty good time. At one point Laura observed Veronica, a deaf schizophrenic, signing frantically to the voices in her head. Maybe she was explaining the rules or telling them to shut up so she could concentrate. Woodrow's aluminum cone hat helped him communicate with other worlds, but it was of no help with his bowling score. Diaper Man seemed thrilled when he actually knocked over all the pins with one throw, but everyone was soundly beaten by a sufferer of Asperger Syndrome who high-fived no one and acknowledged no congratulations. *So much for socialization.*

By the time the shoes were returned, the counselors cleaned up the spilled popcorn and Coke, and the group was loaded back into the van to return to Community Mental Health, Laura was drained. Her eyes burned from the alley's cigarette smoke, her head hurt from the noise, and she had a blister on her heel from the left bowling shoe.

It wasn't quite noon.

Right after a desk lunch of yogurt and a PB Max from the vending machine – *where the hell is my will power these days?* – Laura met with her client, Colleen Garrison.

Colleen was pretty in the way of waifs, with eyes to rival Bambi's and skin as pale as milk. She was in her early twenties but could easily pass for much younger. Colleen wore fluid garments that might have been appropriate for a Renaissance fair. Today she had even braided velvet green ribbons into her coal black hair. It all added to her air of fragility. *It's the posture and look of submission that make her appear so defeated.*

"You look nice, Colleen," Laura said, "I like how you've done your hair."

"Really? Or are you just saying that?"

"Really. I will always tell you the truth." Laura

knew that paranoia was Colleen's way of relating to the world. She came to Community Mental Health regularly for her lithium. Laura's job was to be sure she was taking care of herself, and that the bipolar mood swings were under control. After their session, Laura would send her on to the visiting physician for a refill of her meds.

But just lately, Laura had begun to wonder. Did Colleen react to lithium as she should? She was capable of anger, but her mood swings weren't really severe. Instead, she seemed constantly depressed. Was she actually taking the lithium? Nor was she as self-absorbed as Laura would expect from a bipolar candidate.

Could the diagnosis be wrong?

"Last week, we talked about the importance of a support system. Do you remember?" Laura looked up from the notes she had made.

"People I can count on. To keep me from going bonkers."

"Well, I might not put it quite that way, but yes. You said it was okay for me to talk to your boss. About going bonkers at work." Community Mental Health tried to keep clients working if possible, so Laura often called on employers.

"Yes?" Colleen said in a suspicious little voice, narrowing her eyes.

"Mr. Harrison said everyone at the library likes you, even if you get overemotional sometimes."

"Sometimes I just get so mad," Colleen twisted a bangle around and around her wrist. In so doing, she brought attention to the scars that the bangles were no doubt supposed to hide.

"That's when you count on your support system. Like your roommate, Emma. When you get upset with someone at work, don't say a cross word to them. Instead, call Emma."

"What if she's not home?"

"Then call me."

"What if I can't reach you?"

"By then your feelings of anger will have passed, and you can go back to work all calm again."

Colleen now played with her braid, twisting it around a finger. Emotions galloped across her face. "Well, okay. It might work. Maybe."

Laura considered this a success of sorts, even though Colleen would likely lose ground before her next appointment. Progress was, at best, stagnant. After the girl left, Laura taped session notes for transcription, ending with a reminder to think more about Colleen's diagnosis.

She took a break and checked her watch, realizing David was late for his appointment. When Lovella finally called to say he was on his way up, Laura could hear the concern in the receptionist's voice. "He looks like crap. You find out who did this to him, you hear?"

Yes, ma'am.

When he limped into her office Laura gasped at the swelling below his eye. "David, what happened?" She winced at his obvious pain as he slowly sank into her visitor chair. His body must be a battleground of bruises.

"Don't know. Guess I must have slept on the wrong side of the bed," he said with the ghost of a smile.

"Like sleeping caused *that* shiner. Did you get into a fight?" She looked at his hands, but the skin on his knuckles was neither broken nor swollen.

"The pussy never landed a punch. Just let the fuckers kick the shit out of him."

"Weasel?" Laura asked, thinking the change in personality must be the one who represented the Defenders.

"Yo."

"I thought you were supposed to take care of the body? Not let David get into fights." Laura was surprised she was irritated with him. *I'm actually angry at him, and he doesn't exist. Well, sort of doesn't. Weird.*

"We're very sorry, Dr. Covington. We try to make the Defenders keep David out of fights, just like you said. But they can be so pigheaded." This was a different voice, one with a gentler tone and better diction.

As Laura watched, Weasel's macho legs-spread and balls-out posture morphed into a new presentation. He crossed his legs, ankle on knee in a less aggressive pose. His face relaxed and he smiled at her. Laura felt her own skin chemistry react as if another, far more attractive man had entered the room.

"Hello. Who are you?"

"I'm Nathan, a White Hat. I work with the Defenders and the Little Ones to keep David from getting hurt. But this weekend we all failed."

"What happened?"

"David saw his ex, Cathy, with another man," Nathan said, sadly shaking his head. "David was so upset that he hit a low life bar and started to drink. None of us could make him stop. Then, Weasel got disgusted with him and thought it would do him good to man up. He took over and picked a fight. Two big guys slapped David around, but we didn't let him hit back. So they gave up, and we took him home. To get him someplace safe."

"Then you did protect him, Nathan. The Forum did its job," Laura said. *Way to go, Sarah.*

The White Hat smiled, looking pleased to be told he had done well. "Maybe, but it irritated Weasel."

"Why doesn't David ignore the Defenders when they get aggressive?"

"It's confusing. Weasel gets him in trouble sometimes, but out of it, too. He's a lot stronger than David or me, so we need him. Frankly, I think some of those Defenders are hard for even Weasel to control. The rest of us try to hold things together. Sarah Fletcher helped us see that, before she left us." He stopped for a moment, looking so sad that Laura thought he would weep. "And Dr. Covington, we're afraid."

Suddenly, he was a child, grabbing the sides of the chair and kicking the end of her desk repeatedly with one foot. He hunched forward, and looked around as though expecting someone behind him. "Some of us are really, really scared."

Good God. "What part of the system are you?"

"I'm Rose."

"So you're a girl?" Laura asked. Unable to stop herself, Laura used a softer voice, as though speaking to a worried child.

"Yes, Dr. Laura. I watch over the Little Ones. And we're all frightened."

"Are they little girls, too?" *If I pander to him as though he were a child, does that mean I am buying into all this? Is that making it worse?*

"No, they're all boys."

"Then why do you suppose you're a girl, Rose?"

"You know, Dr. Laura. It's a girl's job to take care of the boys. We raise the boys until the men take them."

Laura couldn't help a sharp intake of breath. "Did the men take David?" She knew David must have suffered abuse in the past. Only severe trauma could cause this degree of identity dissociation.

"When he was very small, men came for him again and again." David/Rose crossed his ankles and tucked his feet under the chair. "I can't talk for long. I'm not strong enough if the others tell me to stop."

"I understand. We'll stop when they do." *Yeah, sure I understand.*

"That's when our Little Ones first appeared. Some are for hitting, and some are for doing bad things, and some are for having their bottoms hurt."

"But David doesn't know they've suffered?"

"It's my job to be sure the Little Ones never tell so he'll never know. Know. No. No!" Rose cried and was gone.

"Never do that!" growled Weasel, frightening

Laura with his intensity. "She can't say, she can't tell."

"But, but why?" Adrenalin rushed into her system.

"Keep pushing and David will die. We'll all die." For the first time the Defender himself looked fearful. "There's more than you see, there's more than you know." Then he was gone.

Slowly David returned. "Wow," he said hazily, then felt dampness on his cheek. "Was I crying?"

Laura felt like she'd been tripping. "I met the Little Ones," she said calming herself now that Weasel was gone. "Do you know Rose?"

"I know about her. Is that who was crying? Is she okay?" He seemed as concerned as he would be for a real child. Of course, Rose *was* a real child to him.

"I don't know, David," Laura admitted. "We'll be working on it together. But we can't keep her okay unless we keep you okay. So you need to tell me about the fight you had. One of the others told me you were beaten in a bar. Do you remember where you were?"

Laura needed him to confront this issue, but if she pushed too hard, he would simply disappear into another personality. She didn't know whether he could take another switch for now. She was pretty sure she couldn't.

"I don't know. I was at church and the next thing I know, I'm back in my bed with a headache and sore all over."

"So it happened early in the day?"

"No. In the evening. Church is in the evening."

"Which church is it?"

"I can't say. But I was there. I … I have to leave

now." David stood quickly and smoothly as if ignoring the body pain he'd exposed at the beginning of the session. He careened from the office so fast he knocked the floor fan against her waste basket, overturning both.

When Laura called after him, he turned with a look of dread. Someone within him mouthed, "Please help us." Then David rushed down the stairs and was gone.

CHAPTER NINE

Cadman was a steadfast worker but an unimaginative one. While some parents might have hoped for more, the Prophet Abishua knew it was for the best. His son was too limited to have delusions of running the cult himself. He would never be a threat. In fact he lived to please his father. Abishua could assign him the grunt work, leaving himself free for less menial matters. And once assigned, Cadman would carry out his duty with the dedication of a working dog.

So training the boys to shoot became Cadman's job. "It is important to the welfare and perpetuation of the cult that all boys be proficient with guns," Abishua had instructed. "You must improve their performance on the shooting range." And then he told Cadman how.

"Always have losers as well as winners. Reward the satisfactory children, but punish the failures. Require the older boys to oversee the younger. By increasing their responsibility you will increase their motivation to please. And the younger ones will want to perform well for their role models."

"Yes, Father," Cadman said, apparently never realizing that Abishua was manipulating him as well. "Teach the older ones to congratulate the younger who excel each month. Then teach them then to punish the low scorers with loud, angry taunts. They should jeer all the more at the ones who cry."

Abishua then told Cadman what to do with the loser. The child with the very lowest score each month must play a game of paintball. He had to stand naked before a firing squad, wearing only a helmet with a face mask. The older boys would shoot him in the groin, chest, back, buttocks, whatever he turned toward them to ward off the hail of stings. His parents should be forced to watch.

"Even the most resolute child will always beg them to stop eventually. When it is over, he is to be shunned by the other children until his bruises disappear." Abishua stopped and smiled at his son. "You'll soon find there's no teacher like humiliation."

Cadman beamed with his new responsibilities. "The boys will improve their scores and thank you for the opportunity."

Abishua never doubted that they would.

CHAPTER TEN

"Know anything about night churches?" Laura asked Helen that evening after antipasto, pasta aioli and garlic bread. Helen was a kitchen disaster, so she was always ready for an invitation to Eudora's home cooking.

"Night church. You mean like Sunday evening socials or youth groups?" Helen asked, leaning back into the overstuffed chair to make a little more room for her overstuffed belly.

Wade and Spock were in bed. Eudora had toddled off to her room with one of the tabloids that tickled her so. Before leaving, she'd said, "I have to find out about this Nancy Reagan / Kissinger Love Tryst. Helen, you really need this caliber of journalism in the *Review*."

The two friends were settling in Laura's living room for an evening chin wag, as Helen called it.

"No, night as in an actual church service." Laura set a plate of fruit on the coffee table and served herself a coffee spiked with Bailey's. Helen claimed to be too full for another thing. Laura looked around the cozy living room, her gaze ending at the low burning, crackling fireplace. She felt relaxed and warm in this cocoon. At home. *No more Ice Palace*.

"Don't know of one," Helen said. "Why?"

"One of my clients mentioned it. He said it was last

night but was pretty vague about where."

"Was he too drunk on the communion wine to recall?"

"No. Too dissociative."

"Dissociative. Your Multiple, huh?" Helen snorted. "You're just as out there as your mother's taste in journalism."

"There're all kinds of dissociation, Helen," Laura sighed. "Most of us have it now and again."

"Give me a break."

"No, but I'll give you an example. Have you ever driven home from work and been so involved in your own thoughts that you end up in your driveway with no clear memory of getting there?"

"Yeah, I guess. That's dissociation?"

Laura nodded. "They call it highway hypnosis. Or, have you been so engrossed in editing one of the *Review's* stories that you didn't hear the people around you talking?"

"Yeah sure, but that's a long way from *sometimes you feel like a nut*." Helen sang the jingle.

"Maybe, but it's only a matter of degree." Laura added another touch of the sweet Irish crème to her coffee, then nudged the fruit plate across the coffee table toward Helen. "There are physical problems like schizophrenia that are controlled with medication and counseling. More or less." She waved her hand back and forth. "Then there are disorders that are emotional in cause. A multiple personality might be mistaken for schizophrenia, but it can't be controlled with the same meds. It's caused by trauma to a very young child."

"Example please." Helen melted even deeper into the chair, having selected a pear slice after all.

"Say a little girl is raped by her father or finger fucked by big brother."

Helen winced. "That's disgusting. Gross me out!"

"No shit, Sherlock. But it's 1989. Didn't you know that children are for adult entertainment these days?" Like most counselors, Laura was repulsed by the malignant deeds people could do. "Anyway, say this little girl is a creative sort, maybe one who already has an imaginary friend."

"I had one. She was the best friend I ever had."

Laura flipped a bird her way then continued. "This little girl develops another imaginary friend that feels all that pain so the girl doesn't have to any more. It's a protective device for a child to make it through all the shit people throw at her. Makes it possible for her to continue living and even loving them.

"But this friend doesn't go away as the child grows up. She's there forever, as a shield through her life. Or maybe it's even a he, if daddy was a back door man. Or maybe there's more than one if the child's needs are very great and the abuse went on for a prolonged period."

"I guess it's easy to laugh at things you don't understand. But this MPD stuff isn't so funny after all," Helen sounded chastened.

"Well, it *can* be, I suppose. In my client's file there's a birthday card to Sarah, the counselor before me. It's just from him, but signed by four different people."

"You're kidding."

"No, ma'am." Laura resumed her lecture after stretching her stockinged feet toward the fireplace. "These personalities are all made up by a frightened child so each is single-dimensional, filling a specific need. They often have childish names like Angel or Darth." *Or White Hats or Little Ones.*

"Darth? I thought these were good guys."

"Some are dangerous and might even hurt the body. Slit the wrists or inflict burns."

"Why the hell do that?"

"Some Multiples have a personality that punishes perceived sins, or another that fills the host with guilt. 'If daddy raped me, I must have asked for it.' That kind of thing."

"I think I get it, Laura. But circle back around to this night church. How does it relate?"

"Well, I don't know. But this client, he functions pretty well. He saw or did or heard something that spooked him, maybe at a church service. He might have been beaten there. And his trauma started sometime when he was a little kid. I'm worried that the menace that hurt him as a child may still exist. A parent, an uncle, maybe a secret society."

"In that case, you be careful, Laura. Sounds potentially dangerous. Also sounds like there might be a story we should pursue."

If Helen's ears could perk up like a hunting dog's, Laura figured they would have. "I really can't go on record with this, Helen. Client confidentiality. So not another word from me."

"Oh? Then I don't reveal my source and tell you who asked for your phone number."

***

Laura didn't have to wait long to find out. Rob Cooper, the *Review* reporter, phoned her the next day. "I'm going over to Three Fingered Jack tomorrow to interview a llama rancher who won some big prize for her herd. Mule's coming to take snaps, and Helen's joining, too, if you'll come. Afterwards we can grab a burger and hear a local blues rock band that is really pretty awful."

Laura hadn't dated since moving to Rapid River. *Who has the time?* But this Rob did have a killer smile. His long eyelashes and those pumped up forearms weren't bad either.

"Like, how could I resist some really awful music?" she asked.

"I thought you'd be impressed. I'm a smooth talking guy. We'll pick you up at your place after work. Helen says she knows where it is. Um, you might want to wear some turd whacker boots."

"Turd whacker?"

"You know, like shit kicker? Sod buster? Hell, you been standing on cement all your life, lady?"

"I'll see if I can trade in my high heeled sneakers at the farm co-op."

After the call, Laura felt a pleasant glow. It was nice to know your original equipment was attractive even after the big four-o. *Might be even nicer to find out if it still works.* She had never looked for a long term relationship after her marriage broke up. But she wouldn't run from one. In the meantime, she was happy with occasional mattress aerobics and required no more commitment than that.

The next afternoon, she picked up Wade at day care then rushed home, tossing aside the khaki pants and Izod top she'd worn in the office. She changed into an extra large sweater that cinched with a wide belt and flattered her small waist. Over silky little nothings, she pulled on acid washed jeans that made Eudora comment, "How the hell did you get into those ... and who else is gonna?" Eudora didn't always talk like other mothers.

Finally, Laura pulled her hair back with a banana clip. Then she removed it, refluffed and moussed until she had hair almost as big as the *Flashdance* cast. She struck a pose in front of her full length mirror and was pleased with the results, right down to her pointed-toe ankle boots. They were as close as she could come to turd whacking attire.

Rob seemed delighted. "For a doctor, you're one hot cowgirl."

That may be, but Laura had never been around large farm animals so she was nervous, especially when the Llama Lady gave her a llama on a lead. She gave one to Helen, too. "All my babies have to learn how to walk on leads to be good pack animals."

Llama Lady, whom they quickly dubbed LL, was an appealing rancher who'd worked the Oregon range about as long as there'd been sagebrush and tumbleweeds. The sun and wind had taken its toll; her skin was as tough as a rawhide bone.

"This is Jezebel, and that's Delilah," she said, handing leads to Laura and Helen. "You go walk these beauties while the boys and I talk."

"Don't they spit?" Helen asked.

"The boys?"

"No, the llamas."

"Oh. Not much. Besides their aim ain't all that great. They can kick, though, so stay at the front end. Take a hike down the lane, then come back and see if you can get them to step across that hose over there."

"A hose? They have trouble stepping that high?" Laura asked.

"Nope. They think it's a snake, and they hate snakes. But they got to learn not to shy."

Helen and Laura watched the others disappear into the barn, Mule taking photos as LL talked to Rob. Laura was intrigued by the view of Rob's backside, not that she would ever admit it.

"Have I mentioned I hate snakes, too?" Helen said. "And did she really call them beauties? Look like tall ugly sheep to me."

"Or short cute camels."

Once they started down the lane, the llamas followed so docilely it was possible to forget they were there. Laura enjoyed the evening stroll in beautiful high country with her old friend. An evensong of chickadees and song sparrows accompanied the cattle and horses grazing in a checkerboard of pastures, alfalfa fields, and sod farms. The young crops smelled sweet, hiding almost all the aroma of cow pies.

"So tell me about Rob," Laura asked.

"You're on your own there, kid. I've known him for years and like what I know, but those are some still waters. Used to work in Chicago after Nam, then came back here, where he's from to begin with. He was already at the *Review* when I started. Damn good reporter. Too good for Hicksville, to tell you the truth. But he seems determined to stay. I've always figured something spooked him into coming back home, but he keeps it to himself."

"I don't want to get attached if he's a jerk."

"Funny. He said the same thing about you."

When the newsmen and LL came out of the barn, Helen and Laura were on one side of the hose with Jezebel and Delilah on the other.

"We've failed, I'm afraid," Laura apologized.

"Hose 2, llamas 0. Oh, and about spitting?" Helen said, wiping at a wet spot on her arm with a wad of Kleenex. "Their aim isn't all that bad."

Before leaving the ranch, Laura asked the Llama Lady if she could bring her five-year-old grandson Wade out for a visit one day. She knew he'd like to explore a real working ranch.

"No problem at all. I like the company," LL said. "I even have a gentle old mare he could ride around a paddock. If he helps me clean out a stall."

"It's a deal," Laura smiled, noticing Rob look at her quizzically.

"Here's to a couple of top ranch hands," the Mule toasted Helen and Laura later in the bar. The burgers were scrumptious, made from grilled bison. Laura never had the mild, low-fat meat before, and enjoyed it immensely. Along with the thick, hand cut steak fries.

When the music began, it was too loud for them to hear each other, and it was every bit as bad as Rob promised. He grabbed her hand and headed for the floor. Helen and the Mule started dancing, too. The top of Helen's head just about reached his shirt pocket. Rob was a naturally smooth dancer, but Laura could see she surprised him by being the real performer. She had style that was almost catlike, and no inhibition about giving him a run for his money.

"That's the second time you've surprised me," he yelled over an appalling version of a ZZ Top favorite.

"When was the first?" she hollered back, tossing her chestnut curls out of her eyes.

"I sure don't know any other grandmothers that look like you."

She laughed a rich sound far more melodic than the band. The bar was hot, the dance floor crowded, and she was feeling just fine, from her big hair to pointed-toe ankle boots.

That night, Rob dropped Helen and the Mule off at the *Review* office to find their own ways home, then drove Laura to hers. On the way, she told him more about Wade and Eudora, and how they found themselves living in Rapid River. "New beginnings for each of us," she said.

She turned to face him as much as the seat belt would allow. "How about you? How did Ace Reporter

Rob Cooper wind up in Rapid River?"

"Actually, I started out here. Raised just up the road in the ski area. Worked summers on fire crews until I earned enough to make it through J school at U-Dub in Seattle. I worked for the city desk at the paper there until I went to Nam. Met the Mule over there. When I got back, the *Chicago Tribune* was hiring investigative reporters. I thought it was time to give a big city a shot, so I moved there. Spent a few years chasing after the mob, Mayor Daley, the best pizzas and worst baseball teams in the world."

"How'd you end up back here?"

He said nothing for a while then smiled. "Let's just say it was the weather. If you're going to get six feet of snow at a time, I want to be where I can ski on it."

The evening ended with a promise of phone calls and a slow, sweet kiss.

I like what I know so far. But he's a puzzle. Wonder why he really came back to Rapid River?

***

The high desert night was always cool, with air clean of anything except a whiff of sage and pinon pine. The moon lit a landscape as littered with eerie rock formations as its own lonely surface. Rob drove toward home with his window open so the chill kept him alert.

He'd had no shortage of sexual liaisons. He knew he was okay on the eyes, but he wasn't vain. *Hell, I'm no Tom Selleck.* It was more that he was a man in his forties who was single, employed and had all his teeth. He'd never married, although he'd had a couple of live-ins, one of them even a serious commitment for a bunch of years. Not wanting to become a daddy had put paid to that one.

I'm not on the look-out, but I'm not not on the look-out either. He was open to a relationship or arrangement or whatever the hell you called it these days. But he carried his own sad baggage that he didn't feel like dumping on anyone he loved.

Then along came Dr. Laura Covington. She'd just appeared in the Black Walnut and strutted right into his heart. He was fascinated by a woman of her accomplishments, a woman who was committed to making life better for a handful of the neediest people in the Pacific Northwest. And, okay, he was fascinated by those breasts, too. Would tits that full feel firm or as squishy as Nerf balls?

She'd been a damn good sport about the llamas and the wretched music tonight. *But is she too city for me?* He had a hard time picturing her camping in the wild. But would she at least enjoy a quiet evening in front of a fire? Maybe nude, so he could stroke that golden skin and find out if it felt more like silk or velvet. Would her moves be urgent as she wrapped those long legs around him and drew him closer, deeper?

She had owned that floor tonight like she was the inventor of dancing. As the bar – and he – got hotter, he'd been able to inhale even more of that exotic spicy scent that seemed to emanate from her chestnut hair.

At this point, Rob was only sure about one thing. If he didn't quit thinking about it, he was going to have to spend a few minutes beside the road before he continued on toward home.

A coyote howling in the lonely night sounded pretty much like he felt.

***

The psychologist in Laura loved to dig around in someone's head. Maybe she was simply nosy. Whatever, she was intrigued by Rob and his secretive past. She eagerly awaited developments. *Maybe he won't call, maybe we'll be friends, maybe lovers.*

Lovers it turned out to be, as they demonstrated the next week at a house party given by friends of Rob. A pile of lightweight coats on the bed, soft cashmeres and leather jackets, proved too inviting to ignore. Laura stretched out on the yielding depths of her own down vest, as Rob stroked her skin until she tingled with desire.

"You suppose there's a condom in any of these pockets?" Laura muttered, and Rob proved he still lived by the Boy Scout motto. They were as well-suited as former lovers who found each other after a long separation. Afterwards, they cuddled in silent bliss until a party guest came in search of his jacket. Laura buried her face under a car coat, feeling like an ostrich with its head in the sand.

"Excuse me," the guest said, apparently to Rob's naked backside. "Could you hand me that Pendleton wool there ... thanks so much. Sorry to be a bother."

"No problem, dude," Rob managed.

"'Night, Cooper. 'Night, Dr. Covington." The third wheel left.

"Who the hell was that?" Laura whispered.

"No idea. But he recognized my ass or your tits."

"Not that your ass isn't spectacular, but I think it's more likely he saw us come in here."

"Now that we've gone public, I guess I'll be writing a column about this tomorrow."

"Well, then let me give you something to write about. Come back here."

***

"Is that you, Laura?" Eudora called when Laura got home that night.

It's like I'm a teenager sneaking home. Laura walked back to her mother's bedroom.

"Did you have fun?" Eudora asked. She looked up from her romance novel, whose cover portrayed an embrace that would take two experienced contortionists. "What did you do?"

That, Laura thought, still pleasantly sore from the memory. "We went to a party. It was nice. How did you and Wade get along?"

"He had a rough evening. He put on his pjs, then wanted to watch TV until you came home, and I said no. He informed me I sucked and threw the pop corn bowl. Then he stormed up to his room and raised the roof. I mean a major league tantrum. I went up when it got quiet to be sure all was well. He'd fallen asleep, so I left him, and came to bed myself."

"Sorry, Eudora. You shouldn't have to tackle those stairs. I'll speak to him about it in the morning."

"Oh, no, don't. It's best ignored. He needed to blow off some steam. I'm sure it had everything to do with you being gone for an evening."

"So who's the psychologist now?" Laura smiled at her mother and was rewarded with a smile back.

"You like this Rob person?"

"Yeah, I think I do. He's different. Not a lot of game playing, at least I don't think."

"Helen likes him?"

"Yes. She introduced us."

"Good."

"Good?"

"Left on your own, you'd choose another nincompoop."

Life with Eudora meant tolerance for unyielding opinions. She'd never forgiven Laura's ex for finding another woman. "Thanks for the vote of confidence," Laura said. "See you in the morning."

She thought about Wade as she got ready for bed. She knew he was continuing to test how far he could push, if he could really trust them to stick around. He'd be doing it with his own mother. She knew that. But it still didn't change how lousy she felt when she didn't make him happy.

CHAPTER ELEVEN

Monday morning Laura asked Lovella to call local churches and find out which ones had evening services.

"You plan on repenting your wicked ways?" the receptionist asked, wrinkles above her eyebrows raised to punctuate the question. It was common knowledge among the counselors that she had to like you before doing a task for you. Fortunately, Laura had passed whatever litmus test Lovella used.

"David went to a church service the night he was beaten. I'd like to know more about it."

"You think the congregation went too far with the laying on of hands?"

"Not that, necessarily. But some of them might have gone along to the bar afterwards. David doesn't know what happened, but maybe they do."

"I'll get back to you." Lovella's fondness for David no doubt helped get her in gear.

Between clients, Laura thought briefly about Wade. *I'll spend more time with him soon. Really I will.* But then, a breakthrough session with Colleen claimed her attention.

"Somebody should just off me," Colleen said, as depressed as Laura had ever seen her. Observing the thin white scars on Colleen's wrists, Laura knew the girl had already tried it a time or two. Was there a personality disorder at work here? One that was emotional in nature so it wouldn't respond to lithium? Suddenly, Laura was sure her client was not bipolar.

She's a trauma survivor.

The signs were there. Laura's gut told her the girl had suffered physical or sexual abuse, and it might still be happening. Colleen had all the related feelings of unworthiness and paranoia. She couldn't maintain a long-term relationship with a friend much less her husband. Laura knew from the file that Colleen had allowed him to take their little girl when he left her. She wouldn't have done that if her husband were the abuser, would she? Something else was at work here. Did she give up her child because she felt undeserving, even contemptible?

Colleen should be drug-free, at least until the trauma could be explored. Laura was excited with her discovery, until Tom McClaren tapped on the door frame later that day.

"I'm getting to know that knock, Tom. Like an opening volley of gunfire."

"Volley, Laura? Gunfire? That sounds rather hostile."

"Forgive me," Laura relented. He might be an irritant, but he was her boss. "You're right. Have a seat."

Tom perched on the edge of the client chair. "I did want to talk about Colleen Garrison. I know she was here again today."

"Yes, we're breaking some new ground," Laura

said with enthusiasm.

"New ground," he said, pausing to nod. "New ground. You know, she has been a client here for quite some time, always with the same problems."

"Yes, but I think one of those problems might be an incorrect diagnosis."

Tom looked appalled. "You're questioning the other caseworkers and the doctors as well?"

Stay calm. Take a deep breath. "It is very hard to tell the difference between bipolar disorder and many identity disorders. It can take a lot of time and effort. Please believe it's not meant as a criticism. In fact, reviewing cases is one of the very reasons you wanted a PhD on staff, isn't that right?"

"Well, yes, that's one reason, of course. But providing for Colleen Garrison is taking far more time than it used to, and at a higher resource level. I also want you to devote your energies to the testing that only you can do."

She knew the department received extra government compensation for testing, and that it took a PhD to administer the IQ tests and personality evaluations. But she did not allow herself to be sidetracked. "Tom, Colleen is not bipolar. I think she has been abused, and may still be under attack. It will take time to dig back to the truth."

"But Laura, digging to the truth is not always our mission."

"It isn't?" Laura was actually dumbfounded. *Digging* was Psychology 101. *Digging* was what she loved the most.

He took on a tone he might use to explain patty cake to a child. "In private practice, getting to core issues would be a goal. Followed by years of therapy. But here, a community mental health worker has to help clients get to the point they can function adequately, and no longer pose a threat to themselves or to society. The end."

"You're saying I should not do a complete job?"

"If she is still in actual danger, then of course we have to discover it and get it stopped. Otherwise, what's done is done. There is neither the time nor the money to go back to ancient history as long as she is getting by in a reasonably stable fashion."

From the way his jaw line stiffened, she knew he was probably counting to ten with her as she was with him. They stared at each other.

Finally, he rose to leave. "Give what I said some thought. I'm sure we can find common ground that will be comfortable for us both."

Common ground, my ass. You'd fire me today if it wasn't for my PhD.

Laura thought for a while, drumming a syncopated beat on her coffee cup with a pencil. Then she called the visiting physician. He was one of two psychiatrists who provided the department with a day of care each week. After Laura explained her concern about Colleen, the doctor agreed that she had a point. The bipolar diagnosis predated him, too, so he had no ownership of it or reason to refuse trying something else. He consented to weaning Colleen off lithium.

The shrink always had the final word on such

things, so Laura had the support she needed to back Tom down if it ever came up again. She was humming her college fight song when Jenny poked her head into Laura's office.

"Having a good day?" the counselor asked.

"I'm enjoying just how petty I can be!" Laura grinned as she placed a call to Colleen. She told the girl to start reducing the amount of her medication, that they had established a schedule for withdrawal.

"I think you'll like the feeling of being off the lithium," she concluded.

"Yeah, it shits bricks, you know? Makes me feel dopey all the time."

"Yes, it does, ah, shit bricks." In corporate America, Laura had rarely used such colorful language. But what the hell.

You go shit bricks, too, Tom.

***

After Laura picked Wade up from Lil Pals, they sat next door at the Jumping Beans coffee stand. A burst of warmth had snuck up and shocked the daffodils into a wild spurt of growth. Sun melted away Laura's stress, leaving bright thoughts about Wade and Rob and the blessings of life in general.

Wade broke off a chunk of oatmeal cookie and dunked it in his chocolate drink for just the right amount of time before plopping the soggy mess in his mouth. He had the intense concentration of a construction engineer.

Eudora once said that all young people are beautiful. *What rot*, Laura thought. Looking at Wade, she was more than aware his eyes might be a little too close together and his hair too cowlicky to ever be anything but unruly. His front teeth spoke of the orthodontia to come. But she finally saw the wisdom of Eudora's remark. Just the bursting promise of all that youth made him spectacularly beautiful.

What was his genetic code? Who had his daddy been? The dark hair color was his mother's, but that golden skin ... was he maybe half Latino or Italian? Would alcoholism hound him? Could his father sing or write a poem? Was he an engineer?

"What's wrong, Gram?" Wade's question brought her back to the sunny little patio and its aroma of roasted coffee beans. She had been staring at him.

"Just daydreaming I guess."

He frowned. "Are daydreams scary like night dreams?"

"Nope. It was a dandy one about you." *Is he having nightmares? Should I be ...*

But Wade galloped on to the next thing. "We sang songs today, and Jerry called Emily a poo-poo head so Miss Judy gave him a time out. And I drew Trooper Snoop again. Look!"

He rummaged in his pocket for a piece of crumpled paper, then spread it as flat on the table as he could. In the wild splashes of finger paints, Laura could make out a stick figure man with enormous hands, wearing a bright blue outfit. He had dark framed glasses over eyes too big for his head, and a brown line across his middle.

"Very nice, Wade." Looking at the blue suit, she asked, "Is Trooper Snoop a policeman?"

"Yeah, see? That's his club for bashing heads," Wade said, pointing at the brown line.

"It's called a night stick. And does he wear glasses?"

"Gram," he said with disgust. "Those are his binoculars."

"Oh. Of course they are. Silly of me."

"Can I put this on the fridge?"

"You most certainly *may*. It's an awesome drawing."

They finished their drinks, Wade making annoying slurpy sounds through his straw when his glass was empty. On their way to the car, he hopped through the gravel in the lot to make it crunch.

Laura was still thinking about cartoons. Since he'd entered her life, she'd had a crash course in characters, but Trooper Snoop was new to her. She'd like it if Wade felt comfortable going to a cop if he was ever lost or afraid. *Good going, Miss Judy.*

"And guess what else? Guess what else?" Wade exploded while he clambered into his car seat. "Miss Judy says I can bring Spock to school."

"Oh, Wade are you sure?" Laura asked, turning to look at him in the back seat.

"Here's a note," Wade said, extracting another piece of crumpled paper before he fastened his safety belt. This time, Laura flattened the note on the steering wheel and read:

Dear Dr. Covington:

This is to request that Wade bring his new kitty to day care next Friday. Other children have been invited to bring their pets, too, on other days. They all seem to enjoy it. It encourages them to share and show each other how to care about animals. It is also an opportunity to make a new member of our group, like Wade, feel special. We'll be very careful with the cat, and return him to you safe and sound.

Cordially, Judith Loomis

"Well, I guess it will be okay, honey," Laura said to Wade doubtfully. *Twelve kids and a cat, too? Is the woman certifiable?*

"Yay! Let's go. I can't wait to tell Spock."

CHAPTER TWELVE

The next morning, Lovella was on the phone when Laura arrived, but shook a message at her like a little white surrender flag. Laura took it and read it while she climbed the stairs to her office:

Re: Church Services:
No regular evening services, just things like Christmas Eve or summer revivals. But I asked around. There's a flaky bunch out in the desert that meets at night on some schedule. Not weekly ... maybe lunar? Hee hee. Anyway, it's all I found. Call themselves Seekers of the Absolute Pathway. Pathway to where, I have no idea. Probably the mother ship. And you're welcome for my valuable assistance. Lovella

***

By his next appointment, David's eye was no longer swollen and the bruises had faded to a putrid chartreuse. "My muscles aren't so stiff. I don't move like a zombie now." He put his arms out forward and mimicked the walk of the undead as he approached the client chair then plopped down.

"You're in a good mood," Laura said, pleased

when any of her troubled clients found something to smile about.

"Right you are. I got work with a good crew. Installing cabinets in those new houses on Cedar Knob. If it works out, they may keep me on all summer. Maybe I can get Cathy back." The radiance in his gold brown eyes outshone the bruises around them.

"Congratulations, David, that's great."

"No thanks to me. Nathan handled the interview. He's good at stuff like that. That's why he's a White Hat, I guess. He knows the right things to say. Not shy like me. Well, except, of course, he *is* me. Duh."

"Can you call on any member of the Forum whenever you want?" Laura asked.

"Not exactly. Some are good about it but others, they only come around when they want." He chuckled. "I guess some parts of me play hard to get."

"Is there anything in particular you would like to cover today?" Laura liked to give her clients the opportunity to set the agenda before she directed the session.

Nope. The stage is yours, Dr. Laura."

Then I'd like to ask you about the church you attended the night you got into the fight."

"What about it?" The radiance died out. David uncrossed his legs and put both feet on the floor.

"When you were here last time, you couldn't remember going. I've tried to find a church with an evening service, but I haven't succeeded."

"You've been checking up on me?" He didn't sound exactly hostile to Laura, but definitely guarded.

He crossed his arms in a defensive move, and Laura could see his knuckles turning white.

"Well, yes, inasmuch as it is my job to help you stay safe."

"But I can't ... I'm not supposed to talk about it."

"All right then, David. I just wonder if another of the Forum members is actually the churchgoer instead of you."

Pause.

"What the fuck, doc? You think one of us would waste time with wafers and wine?"

"Weasel?"

"Well, it ain't Bo Peep." Weasel slouched back, stretched his legs out forward. He uncrossed his arms, and hooked one over the back of his chair.

"I don't think you'd waste your time, no. But this church isn't a traditional one, is it?" Laura took a tougher tone with Weasel than with David.

"Traditional like *this is the church, this is the steeple*, no. Traditional like *do as I say or else*, yes." He sounded irritated. "Think you're pretty clever, don't you, nutcracker? Think you're so smart?"

"Weasel, I understand that you feel responsible for David. I'm not accusing you or judging you. But I need to know what David is doing if I'm to help him. Help you all."

Weasel lowered his voice to a gruff whisper. "The Seekers called him there, but he didn't go. Another went. That's why he doesn't remember."

The Seekers. They must be the Seekers of the Absolute Pathway, that group that Lovella mentioned.

Weasel sounded petulant. "We can't tell everything. We're forbidden. I told you that before."

"All right. But what other went instead of David?"

"Usually Nathan. This time, I don't know. There's something moving in the back, somewhere behind me. I hear it slither and smell its breath."

In the tiny closed room, Laura could now smell the Defender's nervous sweat. Or maybe her own. "Weasel, can you lead me to whatever it is?" She needed to follow this personality system into its depths if she was to help David find any kind of peace.

"It isn't safe, not for David, not for the rest of us. Maybe not even you."

"I'm in danger?" Laura felt her nerves jangle. *Nervous sweat. Definitely nervous sweat.*

"No more questions. Ask that little bitch. That Colleen."

"Colleen?" Laura drew up in surprise. "Do you mean a client of mine?"

"Ask her what he did to her. What they made David do. In that fucking church in the name of the Absolute. Ask her. Expose *her* wounds."

"Weasel, are you talk ..."

"Sorry, Dr. Laura, so sorry," David said, shaking himself back to consciousness. "Was that the Defender? A shadow rushed away. I'm not sure. It was Weasel, wasn't it?" He stared at her. "Dr. Laura, you look so pale. What did he say? Did he scare you?"

"Do you know a girl named Colleen?"

"Colleen. No, I don't think so."

"Are you sure?"

"No. Only my little sister."
"Your *sister*? Does your sister visit this department, too?" *Bloody hell.*
"She sure does."
"But ... but your last names are different."
"Of course. She was married, you know. She really missed Sarah Fletcher until you showed up. Now she prefers you. Just like I do."
David turned the full wattage of his sweet smile directly on her.

***

"Colleen, we've lowered your lithium for, let's see, ten days now. How do you feel?" Laura was eager to get to the subject of David, but she didn't want to move so fast that she upset his little sister. *Curiosity is my craziness, not hers. Take a chill pill.*

"Well, my mouth isn't so dry, and I don't have such trouble," Colleen lowered her voice, "with the trots."

"Very good. I notice that your hands are trembling less, too. A tremble is one of the side effects of Lithium."

"Yes!" The young woman held up her hands and looked at them. "It's easier for me to work with the library systems now. I really like that."

"Are you sleeping less? Sometimes lithium makes users feel tired."

"Um, no. In fact, maybe I'm dozing off more."

"Well, we need to give it a little more time. It takes the body a while to sort things out. But you're doing a great job," Laura smiled and Colleen beamed with the compliment.

"If you have nothing on your mind to discuss, I have a question for you, Colleen."

"What, Dr. Laura?"

"I wondered if you belong to a church?"

"I used to, but not anymore." The girl looked suddenly sad.

"But you used to go with your brother?"

The change was swift and shocking. Colleen grimaced. Her eyes narrowed until she looked like a different woman, one straining to control severe pain. Laura saw beads of sweat appear on her forehead, and her voice throbbed with sorrow. "Who told you? Who told? Did David? Did her father?"

"Who told me what, Colleen? Are you all right?" Laura was ready to call the department nurse in case this was some sort of seizure.

"Sarah found out, didn't she?" The voice was filled with anguish.

This wasn't a seizure. It was the emergence of a new entity. Colleen was gone. The adrenalin rushing through Laura's system made it hard to stay calm, to think straight. *It's happening again!* "Sarah only wanted the best for you. So do I. What has scared you so? Tell me so I can help."

No answer.

"Please tell me who is speaking."

"I'm Dolores. The one who carries the pain." The voice was so quiet it sounded more like wind moaning through trees. Laura had to strain to hear.

Dolor. An ancient word for pain. "Can you tell me more?"

"I rarely speak. I keep secrets from Colleen so she won't have to know everything they did. I'll let her tell you about the church. But no more than that. No more. Not yet."

There was no magician's flash powder or Ta Dah! Dolores was gone in an instant, and Colleen was back, continuing as though never interrupted. "My church was the Absolute Pathway. I left it, you know. It hurt, but I left. Allen took me away."

"Allen was your husband?" *And you're Colleen, right?*

"Yes. He's gone away now."

"How, Colleen? How did it hurt you to leave the church?"

"I was there all my life. I didn't know anything but the Pathway. People I loved told me it was a good place, and I believed it. But I was deceived. I know that now. Allen helped me see that. They lied. We left, and now they hate me. Now they shun me. I'm all alone except for my brother. It's part of my punishment." Colleen began to weep.

"Colleen, do you know Dolores?"

"Who?" She looked at a genuine loss. "Does she work at the library?"

She doesn't know about herself what her brother knows about himself. Is it possible that a brother and a sister could both be Multiples? What the hell were the parents like? What had they done, and where were they now? These thoughts whirled around in Laura's brain until another one topped all the rest.

What happens when Colleen meets Dolores? Is she better off not knowing? Should I have left her alone with the bipolar diagnosis? Or does the truth really set you free?

Oh shit.

***

"What does she know?" the Prophet Abishua demanded. "What has she guessed?"

"She knows I'm more than one," replied his supplicant creation.

"Of course. Go on."

"She suspects about you."

"What is her suspicion?"

"That there are church services at night."

"What else have you told her?"

"Nothing, Prophet. Nothing."

Abishua's smile was like a crack in the ice. He muttered to Cadman, "The mind fucker isn't much of a threat. She's just a minor irritant."

"Yes, father, but we'll keep watch."

The Prophet turned back to his creation. "You've done well. You will be given your reward."

The Rage was famished and the prize was fresh meat. This one was not as young as the last, but still smooth with downy soft body hair and developing genitalia and a desire to please. The Rage touched and petted, then fingered and sucked again and again, the prize a willing victim regardless of humiliation or anguish. Both the seeker and the sought knew that total compliance was the only way to survive.

The Prophet and his son watched as though it were feeding time at the zoo.

CHAPTER THIRTEEN

Friday morning Laura helped Wade put Spock in the cat carrier. The Abyssinian mix had his own ideas about the dastardly act, yowling as though his heart were broken. Wade's excitement faded fast.

"Is he okay, Gram? Spock, are you okay?"

"He's fine, honey. He's just piss, ah, angry that he has to be in a cage."

"Then he doesn't have to do it."

"He'll be fine once we get to Lil Pals, and he can come out to play. The other kids will really like to meet him. He'll have fun."

"I don't know..." Wade stuck out a belligerent chin.

"I'll tell you what. I'll come pick him up at noon, and I'll bring him home to Eudora. He won't have to stay at day care real long that way."

Wade's face lit up, and Laura's heart fluttered just a little. *I'm getting better at this mother stuff.*

Of course, the office was a genuine mad house that morning. Even before she sat down at her desk, Laura took a call from a cop who said Woodrow was in custody. She talked Diego into springing him.

When the caseworker returned, there was a twinkle in his large brown eyes. "Woodrow was nailing aluminum foil to telephone poles all over town."

"Why on earth?"

"So the aliens will know where to land."

"You mean he wants them to come?"

"Apparently."

"I thought he wanted to keep them away."

"He's had a change of heart. If I see any, maybe I'll just let them take him."

In addition to the threat of alien invasion, the outreach counselors had done a morning sweep. "It's like cops gathering up hookers," Jenny had told Laura her first time through it. Periodically, the outreach group extracted their wayward clients from alleys and parks, luring them to the department with free cigarettes. It was imperative to know alcohol or street drugs weren't blocking their meds.

Once they were rounded up, Laura performed standard tests for complicating issues like brain injuries. She evaluated whether clients were too dangerous to send to the Y or Salvation Army, and Jenny tried to find alternative temporary housing. It was depressing work, even dangerous.

Suddenly, Laura leaped up, yelping, "Jesus! Spock! I'm late." She galloped down the stairs, stopping at reception long enough to tell Lovella she was on a mission of cat salvation.

"You've already saved two loons and several squirrels today," Lovella said, not looking up from the Miss Manners column in the *Review*. "Have at it."

Laura parked in the Jumping Beans lot, waved at the barista, and hustled next door to Lil Pals. All the kids were lying on blankets, napping. All except Wade who sat on a chair near the door. The thundercloud over his head was almost visible. He scowled at Laura, stood and picked up Spock's carrier, startling the ball of fur curled up inside.

"You're late!" Wade accused loudly, attracting Miss Judy's attention.

Laura felt awful. *I'm lower than dirt. I'm a terrible mother.*

"Oh, hi, Dr. Covington," said Miss Judy. "Wade said you were coming. Thanks ever so much for letting us all share Spock. The children loved him."

"It's our pleasure, isn't it Wade?" Laura tried to smile at the cheery woman.

"I want to go home," Wade insisted, his voice escalating as he stood and stamped a foot.

"Wade, I'm very sorry I am late. People at work needed my help."

"I do, too," he whined, trying to hold back tears and stabbing Laura in the heart with a stiletto of guilt.

"I'm afraid he's a wee bit upset," Miss Judy said, then lowered her voice to a confidential whisper. "I think he got overexcited. And maybe jealous when the other kids petted his kitty."

"Do you want to lie down and rest for a while, Wade? Those blankets look really comfy," Laura asked.

"No. I want to go home." He grabbed her hand and began to pull toward the door.

"I have to get back to work ..."

"I WANT TO GO HOME!" A full blown squall was

on the horizon.

"Okay, okay, we'll go home. I'll see if Eudora can watch you this afternoon."

Miss Judy squatted in front of Wade and buttoned him into his sweater. He tried to pull away but she held on until the job was finished. "Thank you for bringing us Spock. Now we know he's your kitty, and we'll always recognize him. We will always be able to find him. In case he runs away. Remember what Trooper Snoop says." She made binoculars out of her fingers and peered through them. "'We'll keep an eye on you.' Now you go home and have a nice rest." She released the sweater, and he shot for the door.

Laura took Spock's cage in one hand and held the door open with her other. Wade hustled out ahead of her, ran next door to Jumping Beans, got in the car, and slammed the door as hard as he could.

"Get in your car seat, Wade." Laura said as she settled the cat carrier on the back seat beside him, then got into the car herself. She rummaged in her purse until she remembered the car key was in her jacket pocket. She started the ignition, but when she looked back, Wade hadn't budged.

"I said to get in your car seat."

"Don't want to." His lower lip stuck out like the spout on a pitcher.

Give me patience. "Please do, and then we can leave."

"No."

"Well then we have to sit here forever and ever."

"You suck."

"So do you." *Thank God for that PhD.*

Their argument caused Spock to commence yowling, and Laura had an inspiration. "Wade, Spock wants to get home so he can get out of the cage. He can't do that without your help. As soon as you get into the car seat we can get him home. He needs your help."

She held her breath. Time passed.

Finally, slowly and deliberately, Wade crawled into his car seat, buckled himself in, and whimpered, "I'll save you, Spock."

Laura drove home, wanting to high-five everyone she passed.

I did it! I outfoxed a five year old.

***

Saturday, Rob came by in his Ford F-150 pickup to take Laura and Wade to the Llama Lady's ranch. LL had been so pleased with Rob's article that she renewed her invitation for them to come for another visit, bringing the boy along.

Laura heard the doorbell but her mother beat her to it. Eudora had not yet met Rob so she waited in the hall to be the one to open the door. As Laura came down the stairs from the loft, she saw Eudora give him a good long look before belting out, "Yo, Laura! This one's a real hunk!" To Rob she added, "Got any buddies for me?"

"None of 'em good enough, Ma'am," he answered.

"I am an extremely fine catch, that's true."

"The good ol' boys I know, hell. You'd just stop

their hearts dead."

"God, it's getting deep in here," Laura said, joining them at the door. Wade was tucked behind her, shy of strangers as always, but too curious not to peek around her knees.

"Eudora, this is Rob Cooper. Wade, come out here. This is Mr. Rob."

Rob winked at Eudora, then held out his hand to the child. "Put 'er there, Wade. That's how real cowpokes talk."

Without getting far from Laura, Wade stretched out his hand for a man-to-man shake. Then, with his left hand, Rob revealed the wide-brimmed hat he'd hidden behind his back. "A guy's gotta have a hat if he's gonna ride a horse."

He set it on the Wade's head, canted at a jaunty angle. It was a white straw model, with a snake-look headband and a couple of colorful feathers. Wade peered at himself in the hall mirror then flashed an enormous grin. "Wow! Gram, look! Like a real cowboy!"

"Um, I was thinking more along the lines of a motorcycle helmet," Laura muttered to Rob.

"Nope. That's for sissies, right, Wade? Don't you worry your pretty little head, ma'am." Rob reached over and planted a smacker on Laura's cheek.

"Cut the cowpoke crap, um, I mean chatter, buckaroo."

"Yes, ma'am." Rob tipped his own hat. "Soon as I say, let's saddle up and ride."

Laura did a slow roll of her eyes.

Wade clambered into the middle of the pickup's bench seat, between the two adults. He cocked his head to look up at this Mr. Rob guy. "You talk funny, like Duke Wayne. Dora likes him in those movies."

"Darn tootin', podner."

"Rob, you said you'd stop." But Laura smiled. *He's a good guy to do all this.*

"You kissed Gram," Wade said. It was flat, somewhere between an observation and an accusation.

Suddenly, Laura wasn't grinning. She looked at Wade whose head was turned toward Rob. *Is he upset?* "Yes, Wade, he did. On the cheek. People do that when they like each other."

"But you're both old." He looked to her with a lower lip ready to pout.

"That's not very nice, Wade. Besides, *old* people kiss."

Wade swung back toward Rob. "Don't you take Gram away."

So that's it! He's worried about losing me. Of course. She didn't want him to worry, of course, but ... *he cares!* Laura's heart fluttered like bird wings.

With a side look to her, Rob said, "Ain't gonna happen, Wade. Your Gram and you are sidekicks. Sidekicks stick together through thick and thin."

"Okay then." Wade pulled the hat down.

"Maybe you'd let me be a sidekick, too."

"We'll see."

Laura brushed imaginary dust from the crown of the hat. "You look pretty cool with it pulled down like that. Maybe Mr. Rob will give you a good cowboy name. Like Dead-Eye. Or Pecos Pete."

"I need cowboy boots, too, Gram."

Laura laughed. "I believe, young Wade, you have already learned how to manipulate women."

"Not a bad skill, son. Not bad at all," Rob said as they drove into the llama ranch drive.

After greetings all around, Laura and Rob watched LL saddle a docile roan, set Wade on top, and show him a few basics about riding. She walked the mare around the paddock, then finally allowed the child to take control. The old horse knew the routine so she continued her slow shuffle around the fence. Eventually, LL clucked her into a trot, bouncing the child until his apprehension gave way to giggles. For Laura, apprehension remained apprehension.

Rob rested his arms on the top fence rail while Laura took photo after photo of Wade. As she snapped, Rob said, "I never had the benefit of riding lessons. The first horse I ever rode threw me so far I nearly took orbit. I just kept falling off until I finally learned how to stay on."

"Sounds like some kind of metaphor for life."

The llamas were an even bigger hit with Wade than the ride. LL introduced him to a newborn. "A baby llama is called a *cria*," she said. "You could name her if you like." The *cria* seemed as curious about the pint-sized human as he was about her.

"Well, she's got black spots like a soccer ball," he said after considerable concentration.

"Then Soccer she shall be," said LL. She showed Wade how to shake out hay and fill water buckets and mix mineral supplements in with grain. "They'd get these minerals naturally in the Andes where they're from, but we have to add them here in the desert," LL explained. After wrinkling his nose, Wade even gave a pitchfork a try and helped clean the stall.

"The boy's a natural ranch hand," LL smiled at Laura. "You can bring him by anytime. I mean it. Fun to have a kid around again."

"That was awesome," Wade beamed on the way home. "I love Soccer."

"Hmmm. Spock might get jealous."

"Soccer's an *outdoor* animal. Spock's an *indoor* animal."

"Women just don't get it, do they, Wade?" Rob said.

Wade puckered his brow. "I don't know, Mr. Rob. Gram is pretty smart most of the time."

This time, Laura thought her heart, poor abused organ, might melt into a puddle of mush.

***

"Seekers of the Absolute Pathway," Rob said at dinner two nights before Laura left for her conference in Portland. The steak house was warm and dark. They were cradled in a big tufted booth, the candle on the table providing just enough light to tell the rib-eyes were perfectly seared.

Laura had her mind on other things just at the moment. Like how Rob's thick hair felt when she ran her fingers through it.

"Helen said you'd asked about them, and she wanted me to pass some info on to you," Rob continued.

Laura loved to see him smile, if only to watch how the skin around his eyes crinkled. Laugh lines, right. Male wrinkles were just flat out sexier than female wrinkles. *I'll bet he doesn't spend fortunes on age defying ointments.*

"It's a fanatical church, or maybe a cult, depending on your point of view. The membership lives outside of town on a ranch. They have fellowship meetings at night instead of during the day. What's your interest?"

My interest is in running my tongue across your chest. She told him about the church her client had mentioned, without revealing David's name. "I wasn't able to find an actual church with night services, but Lovella located this group that sort of sounded like one. You've lived here a long time. What have you heard about them?" She bit into a crusty piece of Italian bread.

Rob ground more pepper on the last bites of his baked potato. "Not a lot, but they've been around for years. I checked the *Review's* morgue for details. They bought the ranch west of town nearly twenty years back, and moved some mobile homes out there. Not a big membership, maybe four or five dozen. Raise a lot of their own stuff, veggies, eggs, milk. I've seen them selling produce along the side of the road. They're in town sometimes, buying supplies or selling woodwork. Some of them with town jobs live here. It would be too far for a daily commute."

"Know anything about their beliefs?" Laura was picking at her meal while the waiter took Rob's empty plate.

"Nope. Just that they call themselves Seekers. Or Absolutists. Rumors come up once in a while, like they do with any group that takes the road less travelled. Nothing other than innuendo, far as I know. They stick to themselves, probably don't even want attention."

"Considering the spiritualists and Satanists and free love freaks out there in the desert, they could be into almost anything."

"Yep. If you want a wacko group, Oregon's the place to find it."

"I know that because I read the *Rapid River Review*."

His eyes actually seemed to sparkle when he smiled this time. "A fine source of news."

"I know the editor personally."

"You know the star reporter pretty personally, too."

"Hard to be much more personal."

"You going to finish that steak?" Rob eyed it with almost as much lust as he eyed her.

"Why do you ask?"

"Sharing your food is a sign of affection."

"Finding out more about the Absolute Pathway is an even greater sign of affection."

"I'll see what I can do."

"Okay, then. Would you like the rest of my steak?"

Over Tia Maria and coffee at the end of the meal, the conversation turned to Laura's family. She tried to explain her relationship with Wade. "Since I never had a kid, I'm struggling with motherhood. I'm reading all the how-to's, of course, but reading and doing are two different things. You have kids?"

"I was never married. And if there are any mini-Coopers out there running around, I don't know it."

"If the mother had to put up with too many jokes like that one, she wouldn't have tried very hard to find you."

"That's why I tell them." He led the conversation back to Laura. "Did you want kids of your own?"

"Not at all. In fact it irks me when people look at me with pity, assuming something is wrong with my plumbing." She sipped her liqueur. "Maybe there is. Maybe I'm missing some vital chromosome that makes me a third sex or something. But I've never been a baby person. And I've analyzed myself six ways from Sunday. I really am pretty sure I'm happy with the decision to have no fruit of the womb."

"Trust me, Laura, you are missing nothing vital." He raised an eyebrow in what could only be called a leer.

More on that later. "I'm not sure I ever even *was* a kid. Maybe because I started reading so young and never stopped. I always felt adult, a natural born worrier, responsible for everything. I guess I started calling my mother Eudora instead of mom because I saw myself as an equal. She had one dependable kid so she could expend exorbitant amounts of energy trying to corral my brother."

"Where's he?"

"God knows. He crews sail boats for a living. Hired by one rich owner after another to follow the wind around the world. He calls now and then when he hits a U.S. port, but there's no sign he'll ever settle down. Eudora's besotted with Wade partly because he's the only grandkid she's ever likely to have."

"He's lucky to have you both, Laura." Rob reached across the table and took her hand. "You're a special person to take him in."

She smiled wistfully. "More like a guilty one, I think. I really did feel I owed his mother something. And the little guy is certainly growing on me. Tantrums and dirty socks and cat hair aside, I guess I'd fight pretty hard to keep him."

She stopped to consider a new thought, cocking her head. "Maybe I was meant to be a little less buttoned-up. I've always been inclined to make plans and follow them. Now, I'm beginning to see it's okay to make plans and deviate from them. All I know for sure is that Wade's an important part of this new life I'm creating."

"I'd like to be, too. Part of your new life," Rob said, staring her in the eyes with a look that seared her heart.

She leaned back in the booth and placed her dinner napkin on the table. "Then it's your turn, Mr. Investigative Reporter. Tell me more about you."

"Mmmm, I'd rather prove to myself that I'm right about all those vital parts."

And because Laura was more than willing to accommodate, they left the restaurant as quickly as teenagers in heat.

The next evening, while Laura packed a carry-on bag for the weekend conference, she thought how much she liked Rob. She had broken her share of hearts, but most of the guys had all been of a type, candidates climbing one corporate ladder or another. She wedged her plastic Caboodles case into the bag, remembering to add her new blue eye shadow and hoop earrings. Rob was a freer spirit, admittedly quirky and less predictable. Maybe a new kind of man was required for her new kind of lifestyle. *The kind of guy who chooses a llama ranch and bad music for a first date.* She laughed as she folded a blouse and tucked it in her bag. If nothing else, she was having fun with him.

And sex had never been better. She loved the easy grace of his sinews and muscles, a flowing physicality from outdoor activity more than indoor gyms. Sex wasn't burdened with performance reviews or oaths of undying love. It was pure pleasure.

Her mind wandered back to Frank, her ex. Choosing a three-piece-suit kind of guy hadn't exactly worked out all that well. They'd started as a team, but drifted apart as their careers overwhelmed them both. He left her nearly a decade ago, and it was a testament to their marital disregard that it had been three days before she was aware he was gone for good. She had just thought he was out of town again.

Maybe Frank had been bored to tears with hearing about her clients. God knows she was bored with his. Or maybe it was those twelve pounds she had gained over the years of her marriage. Maybe her feet were too cold at night or he'd finally had it up to here with her recipe for ham loaf. She'd never know for sure because he hadn't bothered to tell her.

"I don't know what went wrong. It isn't you. Blame it on me. But it's over. I've found someone else." Frank said all those things, and Laura was sure it didn't sound quite so much like a bad country western song when he said it. He was an eloquent asshole after all, capable of getting juries to eat out of his hand, but it all amounted to the same thing. He didn't love her anymore.

Her friend Helen had been there for her then, too. Her reaction on the phone was swift and sure. "What a bung-hole Frank is. The only thing less likable than a journalist is a lawyer."

"Well, if it's any comfort, he always spoke highly of you, too."

"Yeah, I bet. What excuse did the cretin give?"

Laura could almost feel the heat of Helen's anger burning up the phone line. *Too bad husbands aren't as loyal as friends.* She said, "Nothing more than what I've told you."

"So there's no excuse," Helen harrumphed.

"I'd like to think there was some really outstanding circumstance. Like his new bimbo is a ringer for Farrah Fawcett. Hell, who could blame him for that? I'd feel better if it were something special. Instead, it's just all so ordinary."

"He's a dickhead. I hope his scrotum gets caught in the office shredder. There now. I feel better."

Laura actually felt quite a bit better, too.

But why am I thinking about all this tonight? She

brought herself back to the present, and folded a silky robe into the little suitcase. There had been a time that she could count on Frank. Having a partner to really talk with had been comforting, and she missed it. She liked getting to know Rob, and revealing confidences about herself. She wondered if he'd stay interested, or get all worried about commitment.

Even more than that, she wondered why it was so hard for him to talk about himself. Secrets were in there, buried pretty deep. A loss or guilt or something he was holding close to the vest. Discovering another person's confidences was her greatest passion.

If I were a priest, I'd gladly listen to confessions all day.

CHAPTER FOURTEEN

Holly Herkimer accepted that women were chattel to the men in the cult. Some treated them well, as a farmer might protect prized heifers. But most were not so kind.

Holly adored the gentler ones, those who didn't frighten her. She worked hard to please them and to learn all the rules of the Pathway from them. She could ask them the questions she was too intimidated to ask the Prophet Abishua. *He's too important to waste time on me. How could such a great man be the father of a creep like Cadman?* She avoided that one whenever she could manage it.

The kinder men made her feel worthy while painting the picture of a beautiful life ahead for them all. That was the thing about the cult. It raised her up, made her part of something important, bolstered her self-esteem. Even the other women liked her. They taught her to garden and serve, cook and sew. They didn't push her to read or study like her mother had done. They believed a woman could get a little too clever and ask a few too many questions. As long as Holly didn't stumble off the Pathway, she had status within this circle of concern.

Holly knew how easy it was to falter. She had once left the cult and returned to her parent's home. She was pregnant then, and she wanted her mother to be with her through the delivery. Her parents accepted her back home, but they made it clear that they thought she'd been stupid to join the cult in the first place.

"How could you have been so foolish?" her mother asked. "You were tricked by a bunch of hustlers into believing the preposterous."

"Why isn't one of the so called Seekers claiming some kind of responsibility for the baby?" her father asked. "What kind of man is he?"

When her parents questioned the cult, it frightened Holly because she didn't have the answers. She became confused. Her old friends, instead of welcoming her back, made fun of her. Worse than that, members of the cult that she saw in town turned their backs on her. They shunned her because she'd gone over to the side of the lost. They believed it was a danger to themselves to cast their eyes on her.

Holly had never felt so alone. As soon as she was well enough, she bundled up her baby and slipped away from Mom and Dad.

The cult took Holly back, after a period of punishment and penance. She cleaned toilets and floors, worked the hottest hours in the fields, and was taken by any of the men who wanted her. Cadman took his turn first, forcing her roughly from behind. Holly gasped with the humiliation as much as the pain.

In time, she lay face down on the meeting hall floor, prostrate before the Council and begging the forgiveness of the Prophet Abishua. He could have so easily refused her, but he was nothing less than the charismatic leader that she had come to trust and love. He gave her two conditions. She must never deviate from the Pathway again. And her baby would be raised as he alone saw fit. When she agreed with almost no hesitation at all, the congregation rushed forward, lifted her up and welcomed her back with the happiest of embraces. She was among friends once again.

What she failed to consider was the price her child would pay.

CHAPTER FIFTEEN

Laura still owned the Ice Palace so she had a place to stay in Portland during the conference. She'd wanted to keep the condo until she was sure the move to Eastern Oregon would be permanent.

"Looks like Rapid River wins," she told Helen on the phone before catching her flight. "I'll put the condo on the market now."

"It's destiny. I'm used to having you around again."

"Same back at you. I'll spend Saturday at the conference then clean out Sunday morning. There's not much left there to get rid of."

All that remained in the condo were a few pieces of the ultra-modern furniture that had not made the move, including her industrial track lighting, tractor seat stools at the kitchen bar, and a sofa sleeper in geometric neutrals. It seemed cold to her now, even the vertical slats that replaced traditional curtains on her windows.

There was a minimum of essential bathroom supplies, like soap and toilet paper plus the cool gray towels that no longer fit her color scheme in Rapid River. The kitchen had an old coffee maker but no coffee and a clock with a dead battery. The toaster burned one side of a slice while ignoring the other, but it didn't matter because there was no bread anyway. Laura moved around the spartan premises, noticing how the rooms echoed as she walked.

Echoes. Now there's a clichéd symbol of a lifestyle gone by. She missed the corporate office, the swollen paycheck, the allure of a city. Of course. But it didn't hold a candle to the rewards she got from her work now. The job stretched her horizons, and she loved it. *Who wouldn't love Diaper Man or Weasel or Vlad?*

She also miss the freedom to do whatever whenever, no questions asked. She'd worried that her mother would be a judgmental presence, and as it turned out, she was. But at least they'd learned not to speak to each other in the morning before the coffee was ready. Laura was getting better at accepting an observation as just that, not always a judgment.

As for Wade, well, she could no longer put on her make-up nude from the shower, having been captured in the buff once by a little boy barging in, desperate for the toilet. She had no truly personal space anymore and had disposed of anything she'd rather not have to answer for. She replayed a scene in her mind:

"What's this, Gram?" Wade asked, holding up the vibrator she thought was hidden inside the Kleenex box inside her nightstand, a gag gift from Helen when her ex had split.

Crayons covered the living room, and the kid left muddy footprints even if they did live in the desert, and the cat litter always needed to changed. She had to call if she was running late or made a plan that didn't involve them. There was no such thing as time to read

a mystery any more. Sometimes the merger of the little family felt more like a hostile takeover than a planned
...

A knock at the door startled her from her reverie. The building supervisor must be checking why someone was in the apartment. *No privacy even here anymore.*

"Hi, Gunth..." She stopped and stepped back because her visitor was not the plump German janitor. Her visitor was Rob.

"Are you alone?" he asked, already moving into her foyer.

"Yes, but what are you doing here?" she said in complete surprise.

"This," he said, pushing her against a wall and leaning in to her, kissing her with unabashed passion. His hands moved from the wall to her back, drawing her in. She offered no resistance, bending toward him supple as a willow branch. Eventually, he slipped his hands under her shirt, unclasped her bra, then turned her around to cup her breasts with the rough skin of his palms, gently rubbing her nipples with his thumbs.

"Please come in," she gasped. She shut the door then had no time or inclination to say more. But she knew she would have carpet burns on her butt for days.

As they lay on the floor recovering their breath, she said, "Answer my question."

"Please don't think I never listen, but I don't remember your question," Rob said lazily stroking her hair where it fanned across his chest.

She laughed. "What are you doing here?"

"Oh. I called your house, and Eudora gave me the address. She invited me around to give me the key to the front door."

"She didn't," Laura said leaning up on an elbow to stare at Rob, skeptical that her mother would do such a thing.

"She did. And she made me coffee and told me stories about you as a little girl. Showed me pictures, too. I didn't know there actually was such a thing as a bear skin rug. I'd say she's trying to win me over."

"She thinks I need a man."

"You do."

"Not right at the moment." Laura groaned. "I'm sore in places I didn't know I had."
"Who's Gunth?"

"Gunth?"

"Yes. You distinctly said Gunth."

"Oh. Gunther."

"Yes. Who is he?"

"The maintenance guy. Complete with maintenance guy butt crack."

"I don't want you looking at other men's butt cracks."

"I need to get off this floor," Laura said, starting to stand before flopping back down onto Rob's chest. "No wonder old people have joint problems."

"I'm having no problems with my joint."

"What are you and your joint doing here. Really?"

"In addition to thinking you'd like the company, I have research to do tomorrow at the newspaper. Some pushy broad gave me an assignment involving Seekers of the Absolute Pathway. The *Oregonian* has more files, an even bigger library than the *Rapid River Review,* if you can believe such a thing. I have a friend on staff who will let me do some digging while you're studying mixed nuts at your conference."

"Mixed nuts? Hey, do I make fun of your occupation?"

"Well, yes, yes you do. Anyway, if I am allowed to stay here, I will pay for my keep by making breakfast in the morning and taking you out to dinner tomorrow evening and being your love slave. What do you say?"

"Unless you brought coffee, you'll be taking me out for breakfast, too."

***

The Portland Conference on Dissociative Disorders began with a general session for all attendees, which included counselors, caseworkers, psychologists, and personnel from the handful of psychiatric hospital wards in the state. It was followed by a continental breakfast and time for networking before the specialized break-out sessions began. Laura, standing by herself trying to balance a cup of coffee, her purse and her notebook, looked around hopefully. She didn't know a soul. This was a different group of counselors than frequented the corporate functions she used to attend. If nothing else, their wardrobes were nowhere near as slick. The scruffy crowd seemed to be gathering in circles around people who, she assumed, were the day's speakers.

She edged her way to the panel board that listed the break-out sessions. Laura could choose four of the workshops to attend. As she read through the list she came to one entitled *Dissociation and Cult Behavioral Control*. Then she noticed the name of the speaker and her interest level skyrocketed. The speaker was Sarah Fletcher, the woman who had left Rapid River Mental Health just before she arrived. On the panel board, she was listed as an independent counselor, working in Port Townsend, Washington. Hoping to get some time with Sarah after the session, in order to talk about her department and especially her client David, Laura eagerly signed up for it.

The first two sessions, *Trauma Based Personality Belief Systems* and *Techniques for Speaking To and Through the MPD System*, were only somewhat informative. Neither speaker was particularly good, nor offered much that Laura didn't already know from the extensive research she had done. *In fact, I could have done the second one better myself*, she thought as she moved to the third session room.

The Cult Behavioral session was the last before the lunch break. Belief in multiplicity was one thing but in a cult connection was quite another, so Laura didn't expect a huge turnout. Besides, the crowd might thin if the other attendees had the same backache she was getting from the metal folding chairs. *Well, okay, maybe from the sleeper sofa.*

She was surprised to find an even bigger audience than the first two workshops, with a definite air of anticipation. Laura wanted to sit up front so she could get a good look at Sarah and be able to flag her down after the session. She took a seat next to another woman on the aisle in the first row.

"Are you interested in cult behavior, too?" Laura asked the woman just to start a conversation. She looked to be in her late fifties with a self-inflicted hair cut and the kind of sturdy gray suit that had no doubt participated in many such conferences. Large tortoise shell glasses did nothing to hide piercing dark eyes.

"Why yes, yes I am." The woman seemed startled, as though she had been in deep thought.

"I guess that's a no brainer since you're sitting here."

"Yes. Nobody would just sit here to relax on these comfy chairs." The woman smiled back. As they talked, other attendees filled in around them.

"I'm not sure how dissociation and cults are connected." Laura said, then whispered, "I hope the speaker is better than the last two."

"Oh, I hope I am, too." The woman held out her hand. "I'm Sarah Fletcher."

"I'm Laura Covington, and I feel like an idiot." Laura blushed, taking the woman's hand.

"Laura Covington. Why do I know your name?"

"I followed you at the Rapid River Department of Mental Health."

"Oh, yes! Lovella has mentioned you. She likes you, and that's rare."

"If you two still talk, she must like you, too."

"Not particularly. She just likes to gossip, and so do I."

Laura extracted a promise that they could meet over lunch. Sarah then got up and walked to the lectern. The crowd quieted, and she began.

"When we hear the word *cult*, many of us imagine a sacrificial virgin in a flowing gown, on an altar with people in goat-like masks and black robes chanting around her." Sarah smiled briefly while the full house snickered politely. "And, in fact, there are such satanic groups. But the word cult has much broader application. There are hundreds, maybe even thousands of them, active right now in 1989."

Sarah defined cults as groups that mainline society considers unorthodox. "Some are satanic or pagan, some are from Eastern cultures, some promise a better life on another planet. But by far the most have their roots in fundamentalist Christianity.

"Whoever or whatever they are, cults share three similarities. First, their leaders are charismatic individuals, highly sure of themselves, convincing, easy to believe and to adore. To be generous, let's say many buy their own press, believing they are entitled to say and do whatever they wish.

"Second, cults demand that emotional ties to the outside world be broken. Some have existed for generations, passing down their doctrines through closed communities. Some move to out-of-the-way locations. This creates an 'us vs. them' mentality, a groupthink if you will, from which the leadership can build its strength.

"Third, the leader is always a *he*. At least, I've never heard of a woman as the host. Playing God is primarily a male ambition."

Laura heard a few low murmurs in the crowd. She took a look around and saw several people who were making sounds of disagreement.

Sarah must have been aware of it, too. She left the lectern and walked to the front of the stage where she looked around. "Much of what I say today will be controversial. Starting with this. I want to give all you counselors a warning. If you have clients with cult backgrounds, be sure their involvement has ended, that it is only in the past. If they are still involved, you could be upsetting a very dangerous cult leader. Be aware of your own safety as well as your client's. You could be in jeopardy, and I will tell you why if you hear me out."

That stopped the audience rumbling at least momentarily. Sarah went back to the lectern and continued on. "A cult leader may really believe he is a conduit for a greater power, be it God or Satan or an Alien. He convinces his group that following him is the only way an individual can petition this Power. Cult members believe it unconditionally. But, and here is the problem. This cult leader may actually be a psychopath. He has neither conscience nor empathy, taking what he wants to increase personal power. He manipulates and intimidates. He will not take kindly to a nutcracker working against him with his congregation."

Laura thought the glance from Sarah stayed on her a beat longer than necessary.

"As I said, memberships believe in their leaders

wholeheartedly. Remember the 913 souls in Guyana who killed themselves because they were told they were above this evil world. How is such a trusting membership developed? How can anyone be so drawn in? Well, think of yourself as far younger or needier than you are today. While it is true that some people are more receptive to suggestions than others, in everyone's life there is a time of insecurity, searching for answers, vulnerability. Maybe a tragedy has just befallen you. Your beliefs have been rattled, and you are seeking something new, a kind of salvation to help with the pain.

"Or you may be the child of a cult member, raised in a vacuum to believe nothing else. All the people you know are members. Even if you want to leave a cult, the obstacles are virtually insurmountable."

Sarah paused for a sip of water then went on. "Let's concentrate on these children, raised in a cult to do the bidding of the Great One and his minions. There are, I suppose, cults that are as innocent as flower children. These are not the ones I am discussing here today. I am talking about cults as platforms for the misuse of human beings. In these cults, children are regularly and systematically abused."

Laura was aware of chairs squeaking and whispers in the audience but her attention was riveted on the speaker. She felt revulsion at what she was hearing but was compelled to stay and listen.

"While it is popular to believe these abusive cults are satanic, I am sorry to tell you that is not always the case. There are cults that can call themselves Christian which practice systematic torture techniques on their little ones. Children may be imprisoned in the dark, or buried away. Their pets may be harmed. They are kept from anyone they love. Inevitably sex is a control mechanism. At best, nudity, at worst, pedophilia, rape, sodomy all performed for the personal pleasure and aggrandizement of the leadership. Or maybe for a reason even more diabolical. One that is a profit-making venture."

Laura heard grunts of derision, some of it angry. A few attendees rose noisily and marched out. But she, and most others that she could see when she looked around, remained fascinated. She felt she was learning what had happened to Colleen and David.

"We've come to the hardest part to accept unless or until you have seen it for yourself. In the case of at least one cult I have observed, the leaders can create, yes *create*, Multiple Personality Disorder in the very young."

This time, even Laura drew in her breath. The *creation* of multiples? Was Sarah crazy? Was it really possible that David's church had actually forced him to burst into shards like a broken mirror? *Why?*

"Think *Manchurian Candidate*, if you will, fiction not so far from fact. Children can be programmed through torture and abuse, which leads to dissociation, in order to do cult bidding. The individual does not know he or she is acting on its behalf; that knowledge is locked away into the deepest recesses of the system of personalities. As a child grows into manhood, he may steal on behalf of the cult, procure drugs on behalf of the cult, commit bodily harm to protect the cult, and worse, procure children to perpetuate the cult. A woman may actually present her baby to the cult. They become willing participants in sadistic activity, the same types of activities that shattered them to begin with. This is the way they were raised; this is the way they believe things should be.

"These are the most emotionally damaged people on earth. Creations of madness. Our job as counselors is to help them surface above their pasts, and to survive well enough to live in the light." She looked down for a moment then, in a softer voice, said, "And in my experience, with limitations on time and money, we fail far more often than we succeed."

She looked up again and asked her audience if they had any questions or comments. She was asked about her own cases, and provided a written list of sources for anyone who wished to take one. One delicate little man nervously asked, "I'm confused. If these Multiples are created by evil, what are they doing at counseling?"

"A very good question," Sarah said, reassuring him. "A Multiple rarely comes in with that diagnosis unless he has been transferred from a facility with a psychiatrist. He or she may have been imprisoned first for any kind of crime, or been picked up in a dissociative state by the cops. And, of course, in any one system there may well be personalities trying to break cult control, to be free of their backgrounds."

Most questioners were polite and intrigued with what they heard. But one man was openly antagonistic, saying, "You've made serious accusations here. And proven nothing."

Sarah smiled sadly at him. "We practice a science where there is often no proof but our own experience and the experience of others. I base my beliefs on what I have read and what I have seen, not on what I can take to the authorities tied up with a neat bow."

"Some here don't even believe MPD exists, and now you tell us Multiples not only exist but are created like Frankenstein monsters," he continued, indignant.

"Yes, exactly. And like the Frankenstein monster, they are not responsible for their own creation. I do not believe that MPD is some dirty little trick of nature on a hapless few. It is always caused by childhood trauma. The trauma itself may not be expressly perpetrated in order to create multiplicity. But leaders of certain cults know it can be, and use it."

"So you are calling religious leaders boogey men?" the man fought on.

"Only those few who deserve the title."

"I don't know, lady. Maybe you're the one who deserves the title." The man stomped from the room, clearly offended by her answers.

Sarah smiled at the people still remaining in the room who were unnerved by such emotion. "I think that's enough for now. Thank you for coming. I'll be around the rest of the day if any of you has more to discuss."

She came over to Laura to place her notes into her

briefcase. "Still want to be seen with me?" she murmured.

"More than ever."

CHAPTER SIXTEEN

Laura and Sarah each chose salad and iced tea in the convention hall cafeteria, then took a table for two next to a glass wall overlooking a small courtyard. A late variety of rhododendron was still blooming along with myrtle and a yellow ground cover Laura couldn't name. The site was a warm counterpoint to the utilitarian din of the cafeteria, conversations buzzing and plates clattering. The salads were described as a medley of fresh field greens, but were a disappointing choice.

"I guess field greens could include nettles and thistles so we should consider ourselves lucky." Laura raked through the greenery looking for anything tasty.

"At least they were really expensive," Sarah added. "So tell me, how are you doing with Tom McClaren?"

"Well, he is certainly trying to run a model department. Works well with state boards and funding officials."

"You don't like him either, huh?"

Laura laughed. "I can see that you are an intuitive counselor."

"Not really. Nobody likes him. Or so Lovella tells me. I thought it was just me until she spilled the beans."

"Running an orderly department is a higher priority for him than digging into issues that might prove controversial."

"Like MPD?"

"Exactly. Again with that intuitive genius." She pointed at Sarah with her fork.

"Right. He would prefer to deny the diagnosis even exists."

"But why? Why is he so hostile to it?"

"He's old school, Laura. In Community Mental Health, most nutcrackers come from a time when everything was called mental illness. If it looks like schizophrenia, it must be schizophrenia."

"You mean medicate and move on."

"Precisely. They're of the firm opinion that we're making this shit up. Or being hoodwinked by the clients. Or at least fanning the flames of mass hysteria."

"But everything I'm reading now is about post traumatic stress disorder. Surely MPD qualifies."

"So I believe. And you see more of it in Community Mental Health because you work with the most dysfunctional population."

Laura added more salt, pepper, and dressing to the salad in hopes of creating some actual flavor. "I admit I was skeptical until I saw it for myself. Meeting Weasel can turn your head around pretty quick."

"Ah, yes, David." Sarah stood. "Excuse me for a moment. I'll be right back."

Laura nodded, uncomfortable with how much she could discuss with Sarah without the client's express permission. *But Sarah was his counselor, too, so it's all hunky-dory, right?*

A couple minutes later Sarah returned with two enormous chocolate chip cookies and handed one to Laura. "Can't talk about this without sustenance. Field greens be damned."

Laura took the cookie gratefully. "Sarah, you left marvelous notes on most clients. But almost nothing about David's multiplicity. Why?"

"You've already answered that question, Laura. The less I said, the longer I could counsel him. I didn't have a PhD like yours to protect myself."

"Protect yourself?"

"Absolutely. Be sure to keep up the testing, cultivate relationships with the doctors, go after grants. It gives you the power to stay employed."

"You mean Tom actually fired you?" Laura was appalled.

"Like a missile. Worked out okay, eventually. I'm happy in private practice. Can see who I want and say what I want. I'm counseling a lot of children again, and I like it. So I'm fine now."

Laura picked a chip off her cookie and let the chocolate melt in her mouth. Then she said, "The church that David and Colleen go to, it's a cult, isn't it?"

"Colleen?"

"Colleen Garrison. David's sister."

"Colleen is his *sister*? Holy shit. I didn't ... but of course," Sarah's eyebrows soared upward as her dark eyes snapped full open. "She's not bipolar at all is she? Son of a bitch!" She bit her cookie and crunched rapidly, like a beaver attacking a sapling, before saying, "*Were* in a cult, *are* in a cult. It's so hard to tell when the system itself isn't clear what's past and what's present."

"My sense of it is that Colleen is less fractionated. David's Forum is functioning even now that you are gone. He's fragile but fighting to keep his balance. I think I can treat him best by enlisting her help. He's probably more secure with her than with me." Laura shook her head. "I don't know. I hope I'm right. But I do know your effort with David was amazing. The Forum is a masterpiece."

"Oh, my dear, thank you for that. We so seldom know the results of what we start. But keep in mind the Forum is a work in progress. There are personalities in there that are still not represented."

"I just don't know how hard to keep pushing. The books don't tell me. They don't go far enough."

"If you want my opinion, he can't get better until he knows his past. And he can only know that when he's strong enough to survive it. If you can use Colleen to his benefit without hurting her, then I'd say go for it. She may be the key to overcoming the poor man's conditioning."

"Conditioning?"

Sarah stared. "I thought you understood. I believe David is one of the *created* multiples I described in my lecture. Terrible things have been done to him, to prime him for doing terrible things. He needs a great deal of help, I'm afraid, to make the trip back from the edge. If I'm right, and if the cult is still active, it won't be safe for him to even try. Or maybe for you either."

Sarah dug deep into her bag and came up with a dog eared business card. "Call me when you can. Please stay in touch. I must run now, and prepare for the panel discussion." She turned to go, swung back for the last piece of her cookie, plunked it into her mouth, waved at Laura and was gone.

Laura felt dazed, as if lifted and whirled by a tornado then spit back out on ground no longer familiar.

This isn't Kansas anymore, Toto.

CHAPTER SEVENTEEN

After the conference, Laura met Rob at Washington Park's Rose Garden. When she lived in Portland she often came to this lovely place if the weather or work day was particularly gray. The explosion of color always cheered her. Today she was so jazzed that she was hoping it would calm her down. While Rob and she stretched their legs after a day spent sitting, Laura bubbled over with what she had learned and how much she liked her predecessor. She finally wound down after jabbering like a valley girl.

"Well, Dudette, I take it you thought it was bitchin'," Rob said, smiling at her enthusiasm.

"Damn straight, Dude. But frightening, too. Like, oh my God, gag me with a spoon." She rolled her eyes, then went serious. "I've learned plenty of bad along with the good."

"Let's hear it."

Suddenly, she felt a stab of paranoia. She stopped and stared at him. "Are you really sure you want to know more about this? Not many would. It can sound pretty nutty. Not to mention terrifying."

"Laura, I'm a reporter. I ask questions. It's my nature." He kissed her forehead, gave her a hug. Other walkers were forced to circle around, so they soon walked on, holding hands.

"Well, since you asked," she said. "You've heard the phrase Post Traumatic Stress Disorder?"

He sobered before he spoke. "I know guys who came back from Nam and have been given that handle."

"Right. It's been around forever, but that's when we really recognized it. What I'm beginning to realize is that it's happening all around us all the time. Trauma not only from war, but from domestic abuse. Similar pain, anger and fear."

"Feelings of hopelessness," Rob added. "That you can't do anything but give in or give up?"

"Exactly. Today I learned there are SOBs knowingly creating trauma in other people in order to cause dissociation that they alone can control."

Rob looked stunned. "You mean to make people do whatever they want? I've heard about government experiments, but ..." He shook his head.

"Here's the thing that's really scaring me. I was naïve in my shiny corporate offices. The trenches where I am now are deeper than I thought. These are seriously volatile people, and if I'm wrong in what I do, well ... I don't want to create bigger problems for them than they already have."

"All I know is what Wade said about you. 'Gram is pretty smart most of the time.' You won't make many wrong moves."

They took a seat on a park bench and sat quietly watching an Anna's hummingbird put on an air show as it zipped from bloom to bloom. Laura leaned against Rob. She loved his tall, clean frame, and how the breeze ruffled his slightly-too-long hair, and the way he squinted when he asked her a question, cocking his head just slightly to a side.

But his tolerance of the things that mattered to her? Well, that was the stuff that took relationships from one level to the next. Did she dare enter that elevator? It could just as easily take her down as up. She sighed. "I'm sorry for babbling. It just felt good to be with a group of counselors who are experiencing the same stuff I am. And not having a boss around to disapprove of everything."

"So you really believe in this created personality stuff, huh?" When he said it, Laura heard what she thought was skepticism.

She pulled back. "In the possibility of it, yes I do. Don't you?"

"I believe that you know a lot more about it than I do. I'm just trying to catch up."

"Nice recovery." She stood so they could begin walking again.

"I'd like to do an article on it. You're in unknown territory for most of us, the whole area of trauma. Since Vietnam, trauma has been a hot button, but we don't understand it."

She thought about it carefully. How much could she tell him without revealing confidences? "I'll help you with background data if I can."

"Could I meet one of your clients? Talk to him? Or her?"

"Nothing doing, my friend. You'll have to write it without them." She pulled her hand from his to give

him a playful punch in the arm. Semi-playful.
"But what they know might help others. Or at least make people more aware of their plight." Big sincere eyes pleaded.
"Oh, can the man-helping-man crap, you manipulator. I'll give you background info, and that's all. Really, Rob, it has to do with my obligations to my profession, and that's important to me. Now, how did you do today with your research on the cult?"
"So I show you mine, but you don't show me yours?"
"You've seen plenty of mine."
"And I intend to see it again tonight. But first, let's eat. Jake's okay with you? All this walking made me ravenous. You buy."
Laura laughed. "Now you sound like the Mule."
At Jake's, Rob told her what he had found about the Seekers of the Absolute Pathway. He'd located an interview from a few years back, with a woman who had left the group. "She called it a fundamental militant organization. They celebrate the Absolute Pathway as a sort of utopia on earth, and their Prophet is the conduit. What he says goes. Everyone in the membership is expected to turn over all their worldly goods to the Prophet. So unless they have someone back home to take them in after making that blunder, it's hard to leave.
"The Prophet is a dude who calls himself Abishua, which means something about deliverance or salvation. And he has a son named Cadman who's his henchman. The rest of the article wasn't about the

Seekers in particular, but about how hard it is to leave any cult." He took a swig of Henry Weinhard's. "There's more to learn here. They're not just a bunch of harmless moonbeams communing in the desert. I'll keep digging."

"Good. As long as you keep my clients confidential."

"That won't be a problem. I don't know your clients."

"My lips are sealed."

"Not always they're not."

"Do you want this last shrimp?"

"Another sign of affection?"

"Absolutely."

That night they made slow, sweet love on the awful sleeper sofa. "This is the last time," she promised. "I abandon it forever tomorrow."

"None too soon."

For a long time they snuggled and listened to night sounds of the city. It was one of the things she missed about Portland.

"Tell me a story, Rob," she whispered lazily. She was spooned against him so she could feel his smooth hard body, from her shoulder blades to the backs of her knees. It was like wearing another skin, one that was warm and strong and protective. She'd never felt this close to anyone, not even her ex.

"The one about the handsome man and the princess who was helpless to resist his magnificence?" Rob's voice slurred, as if he were close to sleep.

"Tell me the one about Ace Reporter Rob Cooper

in Chicago."

"An old, boring story." Rob sounded more awake.

"Nothing about you bores me," Laura said. "I'd like to hear it."

"How come women can never take no for an answer?" He sounded exasperated and rolled over on his back, away from her.

Startled, Laura rolled, too, pushing against him again and stroking his chest. "I want to know what's going on in there." Her hand came to rest over his heart.

"Some wounds are too ugly to reveal, even to a nutcracker who can't leave well enough alone."

"Wounds are what I'm good at," she said, getting up on one elbow and looking him in the eyes.

Even in the dim light she saw something in his expression harden. "I'm not your patient, Laura. I don't want to be analyzed or assured I am a peach of a guy whatever my sins."

The counselor in Laura rebelled. "That's not what I want either. I just want to get to truly know you."

"You're making me feel like a specimen in a test tube. I want a lover who takes me for what I am. Who judges me by today, not by yesterday."

"But Rob, who you are *is* about who you were. I can tell you're hurting, and I want to help."

He sat up swiftly, bumping her out of the way. "Just stop it, Laura. Don't be so damn competent. Don't try to solve in seconds the problems I've lived with for years. Makes me feel trivial."

"What I do is not trivial." Laura was not only hurt.

Now she was angry.

"That's not what I said. Oh, the hell with it." He got up and padded into the bathroom.

Laura heard the shower, then Rob dressing and stuffing gear into his bag. She said not a word, but thought the sounds of being left are among the saddest in the world.

Before he went, Rob sat on the bed, and touched her hair. "I could love you so easily, but I need some space with this. I'm good at asking questions, but not answering them. Talking things out isn't right for me. I believe in guilt and paying consequences for your actions. You shouldn't forgive yourself for everything."

"Take all the space you need," she said, holding back tears that she didn't want him to see. "But I think you'll find it feels pretty empty out there."

The next morning, after a sleepless night, Laura noticed the echo was back in the condo. She cleared out the few items that were still in the bathroom and kitchen, carrying most of it to a dumpster behind the building.

Helen called to ask about the conference and to tell her she had rented bikes and taken Wade for a ride in the park on Saturday.

"He must have loved it." Laura was thankful that Helen and Eudora were taking care of Wade. Maybe a real mom could always rally to put her kid first, but right now Laura's head felt too fuzzy and her heart too bruised. She was glad the little boy wasn't here to see her this way.

"He was really good at it. He won't need training wheels for very long."

"Maybe I'll buy him a little dirt bike when I get home."

"How about we take him camping next weekend? Mule and Rob can come along to pitch the tents."

"I don't think so. Seems Rob just rode off into the Sunset." *How damn hard was that to say right out loud?*

"What? I thought you two were becoming an item." Helen sounded genuinely upset.

"Apparently I'm too much of a counselor, wanting to delve around in all his secrets."

"That son of a bitch," Helen started then seemed to curb her annoyance at Rob. "Course, you can be pushy, and he is spooky about his privacy, and I warned you about that."

"It's so nice to know my best friend is on my side."

"Well, of course I am. I'm sorry, Laura. I thought you two might just make it."

"No, my record of failure is intact."

They promised they'd have lunch one day in the coming week, then Laura went back to packing. When she finished, she slipped a note under Gunther's door, telling him he could have the remaining furniture if he wanted it or have Goodwill remove it. Then she left to catch her flight back to Rapid River.

Alone.

CHAPTER EIGHTEEN

The parking attendant walked the three-story lot four times a night. It was the only sizable parking garage in Rapid River, serving office buildings and retailers like Meier & Frank. At night the lot was used by the restaurant and bar crowd or sometimes the theatre. Most of these fun-seekers parked on the ground level.

Tonight the attendant, Head Case his friends called him, was in a crappy mood. The boss had received complaints from a customer who saw rats in the lot, and the old man chewed the crew's ass about trash. Each crew was to clean up before shift change, but Eddie and Hot Shot hadn't bothered again. *Fuckers.* Now he'd have to do it while Gus vegetated in the front booth. And it was dark. Rats could hide under Subway wrappers or in popcorn boxes, and those mothers were mean. He was scared shitless of them although he sure wouldn't tell Hot Shot that. Next thing you know he'd find one in his lunch box.

Head Case thought about that girl he'd heard other customers call Cathy. She'd trudged up the ramp a half hour ago, and he wondered why she always worked so late. *Sucking her boss's dick, probably.* He himself wouldn't mind if she wanted a taste of his burrito, too. Nice ass, bouncy tits. Must be some lucky bastard waiting for her to come home every night.

He was late for this round because he'd watched the end of the Mariners game on TV only to see them lose in the ninth. *Chumps.* Maybe the Griffey kid they got in the draft would really help one day.

Head Case woke Gus in the front booth to say he was going to check the lot. He took the regulation Mag-Lite and a heavy weight plastic trash bag onto the elevator, then rode it to the top. At least it was a nice night. He hated it too hot almost as much as too cold. He circled around the top floor picking up what junk he saw. Not much but newspapers. Few cars were left this late way up here so it didn't take much time.

He walked down the ramp to the second floor where he saw that girl Cathy's car was still here. At the same time he heard small skittering sounds. His brain juggled two thoughts: *Why isn't she gone by now? Are those rats making that noise?*

Carefully, he approached the car, nervous because the scratching was getting louder. He aimed the beam of the powerful Maglite right near his feet so he wouldn't step on one of the furry little fuckers. The light created a bright yellow orb on the floor, making everything around it that much darker, as if all of the overhead lights in the lot had gone out. When he first saw the woman's hand, fingernails scratching at the bottom of the car door, it was like it wasn't connected to anything else.

"Jesus, Sweet Son of God," Head Case yelped or

maybe prayed. He shined the light from the woman's hand up her arm to the body of Cathy lying on the concrete next to her car. Nothing moved but her fingers, and the only sound other than the scratching was a tight gurgle in her throat. He squinted to see something around her neck.

Head Case set the Maglite down on the floor aimed at the woman's neck. He got on his knees, trying to find the ends of the cord that was crushing her windpipe. "I'll get you, sweet thing, I'll get you. Just a second, just a second." His hands shook. He couldn't find the fucking knot. Tears blocked his vision.

Suddenly the light was gone, and he heard more skittering. *Shit, rats are at her already.* He cried, "Why's that beam dancing around up there? Who's got my light?" Next he felt a tremendous blow to the back of his own head. And another. And another.

He saw the Maglite hit the ground next to him, splattering his eyes with a dark liquid before it rolled away. He thought it was kind of a joke that, outside the bright yellow orb, all lights for him truly were going out.

***

The Rage waited until David's wife quit clawing and was still, then dragged her body into the car and threw the Maglite in, too. Strangulation of a strong young woman had taken longer than anticipated, and the car with its cargo still had to be scuttled over a remote cliff, off a logging trail not used anymore.

The Rage had been given Cathy, but would be

punished for killing the lot attendant. Do no more than necessary, the Prophet always lectured.
But who is determining what's necessary now?

CHAPTER NINETEEN

"That's bullshit," said the Mule.

"I don't know. She's got her head screwed on pretty straight," Helen countered. "If Laura says they're creating Multiples out in the desert, I wouldn't discount it."

Rob had told the Mule and Helen about Laura's conference. He listened to their banter in the room the *Review* used for editorial meetings. It was also the garbage dump judging by the remains of bagels and donuts on the credenza. The old oak conference table was stained and charred with decades of coffee cup rings and cigarette burns.

From where he sat, Rob squinted at the front pages from past newspapers, framed and mounted on the walls. They were so crooked they seemed to skip gaily across the plaster. He got up to straighten them while the Mule and Helen bickered.

Joining in again, he turned to look at the photographer. "In Nam, I remember reports about mind control experiments. And you've heard about Project MK-ULTRA. I always figured you for one of the guinea pigs."

"Fuck you." Mule added a finger gesture for emphasis.

Helen recalled, "Oh, yeah. Lots of public outrage

in, what, the early 70s? The CIA used drugs and manipulation to alter brain functions ... got people to do anything they wanted."

"That's bullshit, too," said Mule, as stubborn as his namesake.

"Maybe, maybe not," Rob said, adjusting the framed story about a flood on Rapid River. "The Director destroyed lots of the files. Either way, it's not such a giant leap to think that mind control and dissociation are pretty similar. If Uncle Sam can do it, then Absolutists might have figured it out, too."

He sat back down, took a sip from a cold cup of coffee, made a face, and looked at the framed pages to be sure they were now straight. "The thing is there's a story here. Maybe a series. At least a follow up on that woman's interview I read in Portland. I'd like to talk with the Absolutist leader and some of the current members. If there's shit going on, maybe we can unearth it."

"Will I have to learn secret handshakes and mumbo jumbo?" The Mule rocked back on his chair and stretched, the poster child for skepticism. He wiped sprinkles from a donut off his shirt. "Hey!" he said in sudden excitement, slamming the chair down on all four of its legs. "Maybe I can take pictures of a helpless virgin tied to an altar. I've never seen a real virgin, you know."

Helen scowled, but otherwise ignored him and concentrated on Rob. "The group won't cooperate, you know. I tried to talk them into a piece years back."

"Too bad Laura won't share the names of her

clients."

"I have an idea. Maybe I can give them a little push in the right direction," Helen said, a smile wiping the scowl from her face. "I'll do an op-ed piece on what really goes on in the cult in the desert. It'll get the public looking their way. That'll piss them off. They'll contact us, and bingo, we'll get an invite to do a real story."

"You're a devious woman."

"That's why I'm such a fabulous editor," she said, then grew serious again. "Don't want to piss Laura off, though. I'll let her know what we're doing, tell her that we'll only call her a reliable source. We won't use anything from her that we couldn't confirm elsewhere."

"She's pissed enough as it is already," Rob nodded, feeling a stab of remorse at how he had left things between them. He wished he could rewrite the whole lousy scene.

"Not at me. I wasn't a jerk. You were the jerk," Helen said, pointing at him. "I told her you weren't. And you made a liar out of me."

"Me? Why am I the jerk?"

"Because you're my employee, and she's my friend. That makes you easier to push around. You make up with her, or I'll have you writing obits until the day you're featured in one."

"There must be union rules against this kind of abuse."

"Before you file your law suit, have you written the follow-up on that parking attendant?"

Rob opened a pocket-sized notebook and consulted it. "Gathering info, but there's not much to add yet. The attendant – everybody called him Head Case – was bludgeoned to death with the ubiquitous blunt instrument. Sheriff Elwood told me today that the guy manning the toll booth has admitted he slept part of the night. So a car could have gotten past him. And monthly parkers don't have to go through that booth at all. Hell, the killer might not have even come by car. The sheriff's office is checking the whereabouts of everyone with a monthly pass, but that will take ages and probably prove next to nada."

Mule pretended to hold a phone to his ear. "Why yes, Officer, I *did* park in the lot last night and murder the attendant. Funny you should ask."

Rob continued. "Elwood said there was a bag of trash next to the attendant's body. According to the lot manager, he was expected to pick up garbage on his rounds. And his flashlight was missing. Other than that, they haven't found a thing. Nothing to identify the killer or a vehicle if he had one."

"Does Rita think the missing flashlight was the blunt instrument?" Helen was on a first name basis with the county sheriff.

"It's her guess at this point. Lab reports may tell more. But if it was, that would indicate the murder was not planned. That the killer had some other reason to be there than to take out the lot attendant."

"Write up what you've got," Helen said, getting up and heading toward the door. "And Mule, get some photos of the guy from the toll booth." She walked out of the room. The door slammed behind her, making the framed stories jump around on the walls once more. Rob watched but gave up on them. "Come on, Mule, let's go to work."

"Just one little 'I told you so,' dude," the Mule said as he followed Rob out. "I told you if she's Helen's best friend, that Laura would be hell to get along with, too. But nobody ever listens to me."

***

Laura was energized following the conference and tried not to think too much about Rob. *Yeah, right. Good luck with that.*

Eudora told her that she and Wade had done beautifully over the weekend together. On Sunday, he'd chattered all about his bike ride with Helen the day before, and how he was going to be a bike racer when he grew up. "So much for being a cowboy," Eudora told Laura. The older woman had helped Wade make a pizza, then they had watched *Short Circuit* on the VCR.

Wade was in bed by the time Laura got home. She hauled her suitcase upstairs, then quietly opened his door to check on him. He was still barely awake, so she sat on the side of his bed, leaned over and gave him a kiss. He smelled of shampoo, toothpaste and clean sheets.

"I'm glad you're back, Gram." Wade rolled onto his back and smiled up at her.

"Me, too, sweetheart." She noticed on his bulletin

board a new drawing of Trooper Snoop holding a stick figure animal with four legs and whiskers. *I'm not thinking about Rob now, not at all.* "Is that Spock with Trooper Snoop?" she asked, tickled that Wade would draw his kitty in the arms of his favorite cartoon character.

"Yes. Spock didn't like him much." Wade rubbed his eyes.

"Wade, Trooper Snoop is a cartoon, and Spock is real. They'd like each other if they could really meet." *Nope. No Rob here. Not thinking.*

"They did. And he didn't."

"What?"

Wade sighed. "They *did* meet, and Spock *didn't* like him."

"You mean Trooper Snoop is a real person, too? Not just a cartoon?"

"Uh-huh."

"And he really came to your day care?"

"Yeeessss," he said. She recognized herself in the tone of exasperation he used.

A costumed guest, a real policeman, maybe a parent? Laura considered that for a moment. She was still new to this parent thing. Other mommies and daddies probably did all sort sorts of things for the school. Read stories and hosted field trips and made cupcakes. Probably she should be volunteering, too. She determined to ask Miss Judi what she could do.

But ... but why would Wade think the cat didn't like the trooper? Hopefully, Spock didn't chose a policeman or parent to bite. Maybe she'd ask Eudora for advice tomorrow. No, probably not. She received too much advice from that quarter as it was.

"I'm sleepy, Gram." Wade snuggled up against her and she stayed until he drifted off to sleep. She kissed his forehead then went to her own room, unpacked and went to bed.

"No Rob here either," she muttered. Even that awful sleeper sofa felt better than this.

CHAPTER TWENTY

The next morning, Laura saw a large bowl of what looked like colorfully wrapped candy on the reception desk.

"A whole bowl of sex," the receptionist chuckled, tipping the dish for Laura to get a better look. "Free condoms in every color of the rainbow. They're for clients, but I'm sure nobody would tell if you grabbed a handful for yourself. Well, come to think of it, probably I'd tell."

With AIDS and hepatitis and every manner of STD on the rise, mental health departments around the country were beginning to offer free condoms, no questions asked. But Laura didn't think many of her clients would get close enough to the bowl to weather Lovella's wise cracks. So she took a selection and, putting them in a clean ashtray, set them on a shelf in her office.

Much to her surprise they were responsible for another breakthrough in her next session with Colleen. The girl came in, her milky skin clear and her black hair in a thick braid threaded through with flowers. She was taller than Laura had realized, because she stood straighter than on past visits. Colleen smiled at Laura as she took the client seat and arranged her long skirt to drape neatly over her lap.

"Colleen, are you still doing okay without the lithium?"

The girl nodded, smiling shyly. "I like it so much better this way."

"Great. You look wonderful." Laura stopped to make a note that she would share with the psychiatrist. And, of course, it was a success that she wouldn't let Tom overlook. *Just wait until I see the pompous -*

"You're smiling, Dr. Laura. Are you writing something funny about me?" Colleen looked worried.

"Oh no, Colleen. I'm just thinking about something fun I get to do later on. Now, what is important for us to talk about today?"

"Um, um, um." Colleen's eyes wandered around the room, flitting from place to place until she lit on the ashtray filled with condoms. She stopped and went on point like a champion field dog. "Are those what I think they are?"

"Yes, they are condoms. Safe sex is very important. You're welcome to take some with you."

Colleen stood and took two, but it wasn't Colleen who sat back down. "Jesus, sweet cheeks, what do you think goody two shoes would do with these? Blow them up like balloons?"

Colleen threw her shoulders back and pushed out her chest. "And what's with this fucking tent?" She lifted the long full skirt until the length of her legs was exposed to mid thighs.

Laura was startled, but not dumbfounded this time when another person appeared like magic. "Hello. I'm Colleen's counselor. What part of her is here now?"

The girl considered the condoms in her hand and flicked them away. "What real man wants to wear a candy wrapper? Hey! That's funny. Sounds like a stripper! And here she is now, Miss Candi Rapper!" She stood to do a quick grind to a hip hop beat, then stopped and stared imploringly at Laura. "So call me Candi, okay? That's bitchin'."

"All right. Why don't you tell me about yourself, Candi."

"Why, Dr. Laura, I'm daddy's little girl, don't you know? And whatever daddy wants, daddy gets."

A cold chill climbed Laura's spine. "Where is daddy?"

"Honey, all the boys are daddy. Daddy. Daddy." And suddenly, it was no longer Candi but another voice pleading, "Daddy, Daddy, no!" Colleen crumpled into the client chair.

"You're okay, you're okay. You're safe here," Laura soothed. "What was Daddy doing?" She thought this presence might be Dolores, the one who carried the pain. But maybe not. *Yet another fractured shard?*

The girl looked around the room, behind herself and past Laura. "Is anyone here? Are they listening?" Her whisper was nearly impossible for Laura to hear.

"No, we're alone." *But is another part of her system listening? A dangerous part?*

"I've never told before. Not anybody." The girl leaned forward, and shushed with a finger as a child would. "He put, he put that prod on me. The one for cows. Down there. He turned it on." She began to sob in great nose-running gulps.

This is a child. Very young ... terrified. Laura handed her a wad of Kleenex and asked, "Your father put a cattle prod on you?"

Tears and whimpers. Then the voice sounded even younger. "He burned me down there. I screamed and screamed. He said he'd put it inside if I didn't stay still and shut up."

Laura wanted nothing more than to put her arms around this damaged child, but knew it would be a mistake to touch a client in such crisis. Colleen might believe her counselor was just another authority figure wanting to take her, molest her. Laura kept her seat and waited.

"I didn't want it in me. I didn't. So I was still. I didn't make a sound. But he pushed into me anyway. Pushed and pushed. Not with the one for cows but with the one of his own. I didn't even cry until he was gone. I had to be so quiet."

"When did this happen?"

"When I was four."

Laura couldn't help but gasp.

"And five and six and ... then one of the boys said, 'Stop Father! I'm not a little girl, I'm not a girl!' But it didn't stop him. He just showed me what happens to little boys. Why did I make my father do it? Why am I so bad?"

Her client cried until there were no more tears. Laura could not stop her own from spilling over. They stayed together for a long, long time until the girl sniffed, wiped her eyes, and smoothed her skirt back to a modest length. Laura could tell that Colleen was back, remembering little of what happened.

"I was thinking about my father. I've been crying, haven't I?" Colleen said, taking another handful of Kleenex and offering some of them to Laura. "So have you."

"Colleen, do you know Dolores now?" Colleen had denied her existence in their last session.

"It's hazy. But, yes, I think I've met her. She was here, wasn't she? I don't know where she's gone now."

"She is an important part of you. When you're strong enough, she lets you know a little more about your past. It makes you feel sad. But it also helps you get well."

"So she's a good person?"

"I think she's a very good person."

"And she's in me?"

"She's there."

"She wants me to be happy?"

"Yes, she does, and so do I. I think we can work together until you both know each other better and take care of each other."

Colleen hiccupped and sniffed, blew her nose like a trumpet. "That's kind of nice. Having a friend for always."

Laura was pleased that Colleen was relaxing, but she couldn't let it go at that. She needed to find out if the girl was safe. "Colleen, where is your father now?" *Hopefully spread eagled where buzzards are eating his genitals.*

"He's with the Absolutists. He won't talk to me anymore." Colleen looked crestfallen once again.

"Because you left?"

"It's more than that. Allen – my husband – was one of them. And he got scared for Gillian, our daughter. We didn't want her hurt. I let Allen take Gillian far away so Daddy can't ever find her. He was very angry at me and tried to make me tell. But I don't know where they've gone either. Now Daddy says he's ashamed of me. That I'll suffer for my sins against him and the rest. He scares me, but I miss him, too. He's my father, Dr. Laura. I want him to love me. Everybody I know is in that group. They're the only people I have, now that Allen and Gillian are gone."

Laura felt irate over the agony some people cause, and the bravery others need because of it. This brutalized woman had relinquished her own daughter to save the child's life. Laura did not like using terms such as evil. Like most psychologists, she believed that people are mostly the products of things that happened in their own lives. But lately she'd read that some might be born prone to malignance and use it for pleasure and profit. Isn't that *evil*?

"Colleen, listen to me. I know he's your father. But you must keep away from him. Let Dolores help you. You are not to blame for anything that happened. But you must keep away."

"Forever, Dr. Laura?"

"Until you and Dolores are strong enough that he can't hurt you again. She is your ally, and I want you to learn how to communicate with her."

"Okay, but it sounds weird. How do I start?"

Laura shuffled through her desk and came up with a small notebook. "When you go home, I want you to use this. Write to her."

"What about?"

"Whatever you're thinking or doing. Let's see if she writes back. Next session, we can go over the notebook and what you've talked about. Dolores needs to tell you things she knows about your past before you can have a safer and happier life now."

"I'll try it, but I've never written my thoughts before."

"Lots of people find it very helpful." As Colleen stood to go, Laura added, "Just one more thing. Do you know Candi?"

"I don't think so. Is she me, too?"

"We'll talk more about her next time. But if you happen to meet her, tell her that real women *do* make their men wear condoms. Okay?"

CHAPTER TWENTY-ONE

**THE DESERT CULT:
GODLY CONDUCT OR DIRTY LITTLE SECRETS?
by Helen G. Waring
Opinion Editorial**

The first cult to practice in Oregon may well have been at the turn of the twentieth century in Corvallis. Leaders of the Church of the Bride of Christ rolled around naked with their parishioners, apparently hoping to receive divine communication and general euphoria. According to record, they frequently received babies as well.

Today, in 1989, between the Rajneesh, the Moonies and rumors of Satanic orgies, Oregon is the capital of cult mania. Why? A main reason is the large amount of open space we have in the state for small groups of people to do their own thing in secret. But is 'their own thing' within the acceptable norms of our society?

The Seekers of the Absolute Pathway has existed in the desert west of Rapid River for nearly twenty years. They keep to themselves in general, but from time to time rumors of child abuse, multiple wives, and lost souls have surfaced. The group has been named again recently to this writer, by a reliable source, as the possible perpetuator of ugly practices, some of them certainly illegal.

By definition, a cult is outside the mainstream of belief. It can be genuinely religious, downright eccentric, or ethically unacceptable. While religious freedom must be protected, so must the law. Deviant and destructive behavior should be exposed.

It is time for the Absolutists to address the community around them, share with us their values, and assuage our concerns. As President Reagan said to Mr. Gorbachev last summer, we say figuratively to the leaders of the Absolutists: *Tear down this wall*. Open your doors and allow the public to learn about that which you hold in veneration.

If there is nothing wrong, there is nothing to lose.

***

"Well, that kicks some serious ass," the Mule snorted, having finished Helen's op-ed piece. "Give 'em hell, babe." Then he and Helen scrutinized the rest of the day's issue while they continued their breakfast in bed.

***

At Laura's house, Eudora got first crack at the morning news. "Damn! Any day now, Helen will be tackling that big story on the Virgin Mary found in an oatmeal cookie."

Laura didn't find it at all funny. "Hope Tom never finds the reliable source or she's in trouble to the max."

***

Rob was in his office cubicle, laying out the workday. He wanted to track down the woman he had read about in Portland, the one who had left the Seekers of the Absolute Pathway. He hoped a current member of the cult would reach out. In the meantime, he'd like to interview anyone in town who might have information about the Seekers.

He knew the paper would get calls today, mostly crackpots but some for real. *In the case of a cult maybe they're all crackpots.* Finding an interview would be easier if Laura would cooperate by naming a source or two. Keeping his mind on work would be easier if he could keep his mind off her. *Maybe Helen is right. I was a jerk. Maybe ...*

"Call on line six, Rob," the office intercom blared.

"Cooper," he said, picking up the line.

"The milk carton kids," said a muffled voice.

"Who is this?"

"The milk carton kids. They're out there in the desert."

"Which ones?"

"All of them. They've got them all." The caller hung up. Rob noticed that line four was blinking.

"Cooper."

"I have a tip for you."

"Yes, sir."

"They're all out there in the desert tipping cows, get it?" Click.

"Gonna be a very long day," Rob muttered.

***

Cadman was the first of the Seekers to see the editorial. It worried him, but not as much as showing it to his father. Cadman was a formidable bully, easy to anger. But his father could intimidate him as if he were still a snot-nosed child. He held Abishua in total awe, but he knew the feeling was not returned. Sometimes he wondered if his father thought of him as anything at all other than an order taker. But if that was all he could get, it was what he'd accept.

He gingerly approached his father in the office. Cadman quietly placed the newspaper on the man's desk, folded to Helen's column.

"Why do I want this?" the Prophet said with a frown.

Cadman pointed at the editorial, and the Prophet began to read. When he finished, he sat back, drumming his fingers on the chair arms. "Helen Waring is an interloper. Why pick on me to peddle her papers? Why now?" Abishua stared at the article again. "And who is this *reliable source*?"

"Maybe one of the town members let something slip?" Cadman was eager to assign blame elsewhere.

"Or maybe it's that new psychologist raising questions about us. Are you letting her get out of control?"

"No, father! We've seen nothing to indicate she's any more aware of our true purpose than the last -"

"It matters little. We'll show the news people our ranch. Be neighborly. Get them to turn the spotlight back off."

"But what if the editor knows -"

"She knows nothing," Abishua snapped. He ran his hand through his silver hair. "We'll give them the tour to demonstrate how content our people are. When that's done, I think I might pay a little visit to the newest member of our Community Mental Health Department."

Cadman saw the ice form in his father's eyes as the Prophet began to plan. As soon as Abishua said, "You may leave now," Cadman hastened from the room, feeling he'd done well to point out the article. And he was formulating a plan of his own, one that was sure to please his father. Maybe even enough to allow him his choice of rewards.

It was time he got to spend a night with Holly again.

CHAPTER TWENTY-TWO

Rob was in the editorial room helping the Mule select photos for a story he had written about a Rapid River elementary school class. A teacher had taken her third graders to the local airport, a field that was commandeered in the forties as a bomber base. Rob learned that, after WWII, the government had sold it to the city for one dollar. That explained why such a small town airport, like others in the west, had such long runways.

Two commuter airlines used it for service to Portland, Seattle and Anchorage. The school kids had presented a teddy bear to a flight attendant to start it on a journey, hoping airline passengers would take it plane to plane and let them know of its whereabouts. The Mule captured delightful shots of children exploring a cockpit with a pilot, helping take tickets, and tugging along the luggage cart.

"The circulation department will jump for joy over these."

"Yeah, parents will buy papers to send to grannies everywhere."

"Maybe these three," Rob was saying as Helen burst into the room. Her exaggerated strut would do a beauty contestant proud.

"Guess who just called?" she gloated.

"Ed McMahon offering a million?"

"Sean Connery offering you his hand?"

"No, you buttheads. The Prophet Abishua of the Seekers of the Absolute Pathway, that's who. The op-ed piece worked! He just can't imagine who would have said such hostile things about his flock, and he would so like to clear their name, and would be nothing but grateful if I were to give him that opportunity. He invited the *Review* to pay a visit to learn more about his fine, upstanding organization."

Rob gave her a high-five. "Well done, boss. You knew they couldn't resist a chance to set the record straight."

"And they get that chance tomorrow at two. You guys have an appointment with the Prophet, to walk the grounds and better understand their mission."

"We'll be there."

The Mule looked concerned. "I wonder if they'll show on film. You know, like you can't see a vampire in a mirror."

Rob and Helen both stared at him for a moment. Helen said, "Mule, I seriously worry about you sometimes."

"What'd I say wrong?" he said, looking bewildered.

"I caught an interesting call, too, Helen," Rob said, "from a man who thinks his granddaughter was abused out there a few years ago. Says he's willing to talk without naming names. I'll see him tomorrow morning."

"Okay, but I'm not wild about more unnamed sources." She started to leave, then turned back. "If you boys need any more help with anything, you know who to call." Helen swaggered out of the room.

***

In Laura's dream, the annoying racket was a school bell announcing the end of a class. Then her brain revised it to the clang of a railroad crossing, signaling an oncoming train. Finally, she awakened enough to know it was the phone ringing on the nightstand. By the time she found the light switch, it stopped.

Why the hell do I need a light to answer the phone? She stared groggily at the clock. 12:38. *Am or pm? Monday or Thursday? Portland or Rapid River?* She drifted off to sleep again. Then she heard a sharp knock at the front door, and the door chimes began singing their little song franticly, as someone held down the button.

Laura grabbed her silky robe and the flashlight she kept under her bed. It was the closest thing to a weapon that she owned. She galloped down the stairs. The knocking intensified to vigorous pounding. She saw her mother emerge from her bedroom holding the base of a lamp.

"Don't open that door until you're sure who's there," Eudora, wrapped in an ancient chenille housecoat, whispered to Laura.

Laura whispered in reply, "Go back to your room.

Lock your door." *Why the hell are we whispering?* She turned on the outdoor lights and yelled, "Who's there?"

"Laura? Laura, it's Rob. Please open the door."

Rob?" *Rob?*

"I need to speak with you."

He's come back! Laura hurried to unlock the door with one hand as she tried to finger comb her tousled curls with the other. But her first sight of him told her it wasn't romance on his mind.

When the door opened, Rob saw the two women, wide eyed as startled raccoons, one brandishing a flashlight and the other a lamp. "Unless you intend to blind me with light beams, put down your weapons," he said, crossing the threshold and shutting the door.

"Why are you here?" Laura asked.

Eudora huffed, "A little late for courting, Mister."

But Rob was deadly serious as he took Laura by the shoulders. "Laura, I tried to call, but you didn't answer. I want you to get dressed and come with me."

"What's wrong? Rob, you're scaring me," she said, reaching up and putting her hands on top of his.

"The Mule called me. Something's happened to Helen. She's had an accident, and she's asking for him. And you."

"Is she at the hospital?"

"No, sweetheart. No time for questions. Get dressed. I'll take you to her." Laura was already heading for the loft.

"What can I do?" Eudora asked.

"Maybe a couple of blankets," he said, sending the old woman hustling off on her mission without asking another question. He waited alone in the foyer, trying to control his own fear for his boss, his friend, Helen.

***

Laura appeared in jeans and an oxford cloth shirt she was still buttoning as she raced down the stairs with her Nikes under an arm. Rob grabbed the blankets from Eudora, who got Laura's jacket while her daughter tied her shoes. Rob and Laura dashed out the door.

"Tell me," Laura said as she buckled her seatbelt, and Rob sped out of the drive.

"The Sheriff called her cabin looking for a relative, and Mule was there, waiting for her. Helen was at the board meeting tonight for ... oh hell, what does it matter? She had a car accident out of town, on the way home. We're going there now."

There was no traffic at all on the early morning streets. Rob gunned the truck through the next light without stopping. Laura stared at him, but he wasn't making sense to her. "But why aren't we ... why isn't she at the emergency ward?"

He reached over and folded her left hand into his. She was clutching the seatbelt with her right. "Laura, she's pinned under the car."

"Oh my God," she moaned. Her hands jerked to her face, covering her mouth.

"The EMTs are afraid to move the car for fear of

jostling her." The Ford's tires squealed as Rob turned off the last city street and careened into the dark, racing down a county road toward the high country. Little was visible in the headlights but wisps of fog and the centerline ricocheting through dips and curves.

"But how will they get her out?"

"Laura, they're working on it," he said. "But she's pretty bad. She asked for the Mule and for you."

Laura felt the world screech to a stop. She couldn't think, she couldn't speak, she nearly couldn't breathe. *Helen.*

She tried to shut ugly images out of her brain as they approached a brilliant circle of emergency lights, next to the twisting road that led to Helen's mountain cabin. Once her eyes adjusted to the piercing brightness, she could pick out individual forms, emergency vehicles, and finally, Helen's SUV balanced precariously on its side. It was aiming steeply downward on a slope, away from the road where a cat's cradle of trees seemed to have broken its fall.

Near the front right fender, she saw a willowy form kneeling among a crowd of emergency workers. She recognized the Mule.

For Laura, time passed in a haze. Rob must have parked the car. She must have unbuckled the seatbelt, opened the door, run to the scene. But she remembered none of this. She was transported to her knees, huddling beside the Mule. He was holding Helen's hand and her head rested in his lap, but her body from the chest down disappeared under the two-ton vehicle.

An EMT whispered to Laura, "We've given her

morphine, so she's not in pain. But try not to move her." Laura reached out her hand to stroke her friend's forehead. She noticed deep red stains clotting in Helen's graying hair.

"Helen," she breathed. "Enough clowning around now. Time to wake up." She took a Kleenex from her purse and tried to daub at a cut on her friend's cheek. The skin felt so cold.

"Laura," Helen sighed without opening her eyes.

"I'm here. With Mule. And Rob. We're all here. We all love you."

Helen's body jerked, tensed, then visibly began to release its tension.

"Helen?" Laura whispered as tears soaked her cheeks and shirt. "Helen, don't ..."

"Tell Rob cult ... pals ..."

"Yes, we'll always be pals," Laura cried. "Friends forever." It's the oath they always used with each other.

That was all. The EMT checked Helen's heart and pulse and breath. He looked at the Mule and Laura, shaking his head. For a time, Helen's two closest companions leaned against each other and cried, until the emergency workers moved them out of the way.

***

Meanwhile, Rob was working, gathering all the information he could about the accident. The sheriff and her deputies all knew Mule and Rob from stories they worked in the past. Sheriff Rita Elwood told him what they thought had happened.

"Troopers found the car and called it in around 11:30. Hard to tell how long she's been here. Not much traffic this time of night." They walked over to the edge of the road, and she pointed out tracks that swerved all the way across the left lane. "Looks like she went off here, but we don't know why she lost control. An elk crossing in front of her, maybe."

"Find animal tracks? Or remains?"

"Not yet. Maybe at day break."

"Was she run off the road?" *Is this more than an accident?*

The Sheriff shrugged. "Maybe. I don't know much of anything yet, Rob. There are some road marks, but nothing definite. At least not tonight. Troopers will look for car parts in the area, and we'll search again tomorrow."

"She knew this road, Rita. Knew it well. She lived just up the way. You know that."

"Yeah, but there was a broken wine bottle on the front seat. Spilled all over the seat. And on her."

"Wine?" Rob frowned, then changed tack. "How was she thrown from the car? She always wore the seatbelt."

"We think she actually was able to get out of the vehicle. But she was on the downhill side. It must have been unstable. Somehow it rolled and caught her underneath. EMTs were afraid to move it until heavy equipment could get here to lift it off. She's been crushed, Rob."

That's when he, too, knew Helen had died. His breath caught. He couldn't speak, so he was glad when a deputy interrupted them. Rob recognized him as the one they called Big D, for his size and hometown – the Dallas in Oregon, not the one in Texas. Big D said, "They're gonna move the car now."

Rob turned and saw the Mule and Laura huddled together, watching the EMTs from a distance. The Bronco would be rolled away now, with no fear of hurting Helen any more. Rob got the blankets from the car, gave one to the Mule and wrapped Laura in the other. He spoke softly to them, then led them back to his truck. He had his arm around Laura, and the Mule followed along behind like an obedient hound, slouching more than usual. Rob asked the Sheriff if someone could drive the Mule's van back to the newspaper office, then he drove his two desolate friends back into town.

Helen was more than just his boss. She was the one reason the newspaper had been a safe refuge for Rob. She had not pushed him past his ability to deliver. Now it was time for him to forget his own sorrows and dig in as the first rate reporter he could be. He owed it to Helen.

In a voice so low he almost missed it, he heard the Mule vow, "If some son of a bitch is responsible for her death, that son of a bitch is going to pay."

Just as low Laura said, "And I want to help."

***

The Mule wanted time alone, so Rob dropped him at his apartment, telling him he'd come back after he took Laura home. She invited him in for a moment, saying that she had something to ask him.

Eudora had built a fire, and was waiting for them. She ushered them in, clucking and fussing like a hen. After receiving the news stoically, she brewed them each a cup of tea with honey, milk and a dash of whiskey. Rob declined, but she told him, "It's a sedative. So drink it, damn it all anyway." Then she left them to talk.

"It's late, I know. But I wanted to tell you what Helen said," Laura began. She felt curiously disconnected, as though she were floating. She knew it was a common effect of shock.

"Helen talked to you?" Rob asked. "I'm surprised she was able to say anything."

"She said, *tell Rob cult*." Laura separated the words and repeated them slowly. "That's the way Helen said them. Slow, but like they were connected."

He frowned. "Anything else?"

"She just said we were pals." More tears drifted down her cheeks.

"But no more about the cult? I wonder what she was thinking."

"Did she believe the Seekers did this to her? Did she maybe even recognize one of them? Oh, God, Rob. I'm the one that got her into this." Guilt settled on her, weighing even more than sorrow.

Rob put his arms around her and hugged her close. "Laura, we don't know anything. It was probably an accident. There may be more to see up there in the daylight. The Sheriff's good. If there's anything to find, Rita will find it. And the autopsy may show something."

"Autopsy?"

"Whenever there's a doubt about cause of death." After a pause, he asked, "Did you ever know Helen to drink and drive?"

Laura looked at him and saw that his eyes were far from dry. "Well, sure, when we were kids in college. But not since we got old enough to understand we're mortal. She wouldn't have driven if she was out of control. She'd have called the Mule ... or me if she couldn't reach him."

He hugged her again. "I'm so sorry, Laura. About Helen, of course. And about the way I acted in Portland."

"My fault, Rob. I pushed too hard. Not everyone wants to be dissected."

"This thing with Helen, if it turns out to be more than an accident, I *will* find out the truth."

"I have no doubt. Let me know what I can do to help."

"I will. And I think, maybe, we should all be a little careful for a while. Just in case."

"You think we're in danger?"

"If the Seekers had anything to do with this, anything at all, then they might have an eye on the Mule and me. Helen set an appointment for us to go meet with them tomorrow. And maybe they know about you, too, but I don't really see how. You were only called a reliable source."

"I don't care," she said. "If you need to name me, do it. I'm not afraid of them."

He touched her hair. "I knew you were smart and beautiful. Now I'll add brave to the list. And, Laura, there are things I want to tell you about my past. It's time to share. But not tonight. We're both exhausted."

As he stood to leave, she asked, "Did you mean what you called me earlier tonight?"

He looked perplexed. "What did I call you?"

"Sweetheart?" She had the grace to blush.

"I said that? Well, I never lie," he said just before he kissed her cheek. "Rest if you can. I need to swing by the Mule's place to check on him. He'll be lost without Helen. And it'll be a long day tomorrow for all of us."

After Rob left, Laura swallowed two aspirin and went to bed with her memories of Helen. Nothing had ever hurt her like this, not her divorce, not her father's death. Helen was her whole adult history. They had been 'friends forever' since college, knew each other's secrets and desires. The thought of all that life force crushed out beside the road was unbearable.

The sun was rising by the time she finally fell into a fitful sleep. It was late morning when she tried to open her eyes again. They were so swollen it was nearly impossible. Crying hadn't done her sinuses any favors either. When she finally peered out through narrow slits, Wade was peering in. He and Spock were right next to her.

"Dora said to be quiet and not give you any crap," he whispered.

"Wade, that's not nice," she croaked in a voice too low to be her own.

"It's what she said."

Laura groaned when she looked at the clock. "We're so late."

"Dora called your work and my school. Said we weren't coming. Before she said crap."

He tried to snuggle closer, but Spock positioned himself between them, raised a hind leg straight in the air, and begun cat ablutions.

"Did Miss Helen get deaded?"

"Yes, honey, she is dead." The lump in her throat was a boulder.

"Can I still get a bike?"

"Yes, of course. You and I will go riding together now." She rolled over on her side to face him.

"Will we miss her?" He was frowning as he wrestled with the concept of loss. Laura thought he'd had too much of that in his young life already.

"Yes, we will miss her."

"Did you love her?"

"I loved her very much." Laura could feel tears trickle from her eyes, burying themselves in her pillow.

"But she left you anyway?"

"She didn't mean to."

"But you're sad anyway."

"Yes."

"Then I'm mad at her."

"Don't be, Wade. She couldn't make me so sad

now if she hadn't made me happy so many, many times."

Laura realized that Wade was working his way through a bigger puzzle. "Mommy made me sad, too. Not just when she got deaded. Before that. She sometimes hit me. And made me stay in the closet when I was bad."

"I'm very, very sorry, Wade." She gathered him in to herself, hugging him tight. The cat gave ground, moving to the foot of the bed with a grumpy meow. "Those things will never happen to you again."

Did his mother hit him when she was drunk? Maybe she actually locked him away to protect him from her binges. How much more would he reveal?

Laura kissed the top of his head and said, "It's okay to have mixed feelings about Mommy. You can be sorry she had to go, *and* glad she is gone. Both things can be true." Laura told him he should never feel guilty about having lots of different feelings toward his past.

"If you help me get over losing Miss Helen, then I'll help you get over losing your Mommy."

"I love you, Gram."

Who was that woman who said she didn't know if she could love this child? Laura was suddenly absolutely positive that protecting him was her life mission.

"I love you, too, Wade."

CHAPTER TWENTY-THREE

The next morning was an ordeal. Rob had grabbed a couple hours sleep on the sofa at the Mule's apartment, then gone early to the *Rapid River Review*. He was aware that other staffers began to filter in, exchanging whispers regarding the boss and had she been drinking, and no, nobody had ever seen her out-of-control shitfaced but she did like wine, and what would happen to the Mule now? Helen was the heartbeat of the paper. It was hard to discern just what to do now that she was gone.

"You all know your jobs," Rob said, trying to restore order. "Now do them, just as if Helen were here. You don't want her pissed at you in the afterlife."

He asked a feature writer to handle Helen's obituary because he couldn't bear to do it himself. While he was talking to her about the assignment, he received a call from the publisher. John Landen owned the *Review* but rarely darkened its door since he retired a decade earlier. He asked Rob to share the role of editor with him until he could replace Helen. Rob agreed on two conditions: he wanted to continue on the cult story, and he wanted to investigate what really had happened to Helen. *It's really one condition if the two events are related.*

By ten a.m., he entered Liberty Park just down the

street from Laura's house. It was cool under the ancient Ponderosa pines. Their needles rustled in the wind, creating dappled patterns of sunlight on the pond and walkways. A man on the high side of fifty sat on a cast iron bench, watching a young girl feed squabbling mallards from a bag of torn bread. Two women further down the walk supervised their own youngsters, while casting baleful glances at the man.

Rob approached, then sat beside him on the bench. "Mr. Herkimer?"

The man continued to watch the child, apparently aware of the women's animosity. "A lone man can't be in a park anymore. If he is, he's a mugger, dope dealer or pedophile. Women are scared of us. They should be, I guess."

"You might get a friendly dog. It's okay to be in a park if you're walking a dog."

The man turned light blue eyes in Rob's direction and smiled briefly while they shook hands. "Thanks for the advice. I'm Ben Herkimer." He was the grandfather who had called the *Review* right after Helen's editorial ran. Rob had arranged to meet him here.

"Now we're agreed you won't print my name, right?"

"Not until you agree to let me."

The man nodded. He was dressed in a red and black flannel jacket that was nearly as old as he was. His small frame was slender, except for the beer belly that was imposing its own will, and his hairline had receded to the point of nearly disappearing altogether.

"How do we do this?" he asked Rob.

"You start talking when you're ready. Tell your story any way you want. I'll ask questions when I have any." Rob extracted a small notepad from his jacket pocket. He crossed one long leg over the other, ankle on knee, in order to form a sort of writing surface.

The man nodded again, then took out a pipe and lit it. Rob was glad the breeze was blowing away from him. Once the old bowl caught fire, and Herkimer had puffed it into life, he pointed with it and began to speak. "See that girl over there? The one feeding the ducks?"

Rob nodded, looking at the tow-headed child who was laughing as a squirrel dodged between the enraged mallards to snatch bits of the bread.

"That's my granddaughter. Annie. She's eight now. Loves to feed those damn birds. So when I come into town, I stop here just to let her do it. She's a nice kid, Annie. Maybe a little immature, but Mavis and me don't push her. Mavis, that's the Missus."

Ben looked at Rob. "Annie spent five years in that cult the paper wrote about."

"Seekers of the Absolute Pathway?"

"That's the one. They stole my daughter – Annie's mother – when she was no more than eighteen."

"They *stole* her? You mean like ... slavery?" Rob wondered if Herkimer was one of the crack pot callers after all.

"Might as well have been. Holly, that's my daughter, is the impressionable type. She met a couple of Seekers in town. They invited her to a service, and there seemed no harm in letting her go. She liked it and went again. They filled her head with notions that their leader was the one and only conduit to a better life on the other side, or a parallel life, or some damn thing. Never did get it straight." He stopped long enough to cast a knowing glance at Rob. "Finally, she met the big man in some kind of ceremony that was supposed to be an honor. He told her she was a chosen bride of the Absolute Power. Guess she never felt special before. Anyway, before long she refused to come home again. Wouldn't listen to Mavis and me. Said we polluted her thinking."

The sad little man stopped and puffed his pipe so long that Rob thought he might never continue. "What happened to her?" he prompted.

"Eventually, she got knocked up. Apparently the Prophet to the Absolute Pathway is really just a prick here on earth. Or that shoe fits one of the other Seekers. Holly wouldn't hear a word against them, what with being the chosen bride and all.

"But when it came time to have the baby, Holly wanted her ma, so she came home. Mavis and I took her in, got her to a doctor. She was underweight and underfed, but okay otherwise. The baby was a preemie, though. We huddled around that incubator for days as Annie teetered on the brink. No Seeker ever showed. Might have killed them if they did. Anyway, the baby was a fighter and she lived.

"Annie and Holly came home, and we got them both healthy. But not long after, a couple of the cult women showed up at our door. They wanted Holly back. We thought she'd given up on all that. But we were wrong. And back she went. Cleared out one night in secret, and took the baby with her. The law said there was no way we could stop her. Frankly, Mr. Cooper, I would have given up on our daughter right then and there. But Mavis had fallen for the baby. Guess I had, too.

"So we'd show up for visits when they let us. The whole group was hostile, but Holly was glad to see us, if only for the kid clothes and food we brought. Little Annie would light up when Granddaddy came along. This went on for four years, and then the cult asked us to stop coming. Seems they thought we were a disruption." He gave a bitter snort. "They thought *we* were the bad influence.

"It about killed us, not seeing that little girl. Mavis hounded me until I talked to a lawyer. Turns out grandparents have some rights, at least in Oregon. If you're denied access, you can see your grandchild as long as you can show that the parents don't act in the kid's best interest."

"Did you have that proof?" Rob asked.

"Didn't need it as it turned out. Armed with that nugget of information, I went out and confronted Abishua. He didn't want bad press or a law suit, and neither did I. So he agreed that Mavis and I could take the child for a day every other week."

Herkimer paused long enough to relight the pipe. Rob never did know anyone who could keep one of the damn things going.

"What he didn't reckon on was Mavis. She could

see that Annie was changing, losing the fire she had as a baby. She was worried the girl hadn't been getting proper care. So she made an appointment with a pediatrician friend, and we took Annie in on one of the days we had her. Neither of us was prepared for what that doctor found."

Herkimer faltered, clearly having difficulty controlling himself. "Mavis went into the examining room with Annie. She told me the child acted strange with the doc. A little too affectionate, rubbing against him during the exam, eager to remove her clothes. The doctor got suspicious and had a urine sample tested." His glanced at Rob with all the sorrow of the ages. "Annie had gonorrhea."

Rob felt a vile mix of shock and rage sear him like heartburn. "And she was what, just five?"

Herkimer nodded. "The doc feared she'd been taught how to act around men. We never took her back to those bastards. We threatened legal action. To shut us up, they gave Annie to us, along with a line about having no idea how such a thing could happen. Insinuated I had something to do with it. The doctor said he'd hush it up to protect Annie's privacy. Our daughter Holly chose to stay with the cult. We've raised Annie ever since."

"Is she okay now?" Rob asked, watching the child running along the river bank.

"Physically? Yeah, she's healed. Emotionally, I'm not so sure. But she doesn't have so many nightmares now, and she thinks she's safe with us."

"What do you mean, she *thinks* she is?"

"Well, that's one of the reasons Mavis and I are keeping our name out of this. Holly could take Annie from us anytime. She didn't give her the disease or they would have caught it when she was pregnant, so her claim would be valid. If we keep quiet, we keep Annie. Otherwise, she could be in jeopardy again."

He pinned Rob with an icy blue stare. "But, Mr. Cooper, I hope you find some way to skin those bastards for what they did to my grandbaby." Herkimer stifled a sob deep in his chest then stood slowly, stretched his back and walked away. "Come on, Annie, time to hit the road."

The girl ran after him, caught up and took her granddaddy's hand, waving and calling good-bye to the ducks first and then, much more shyly, to Rob.

Rob sat for a long time, listening to the river rapids, the birds, and the wind rustling through the trees. *Everything important is so fragile. When something is really vital to you, you have to cut through the fear of revealing your own flaws and self-doubts. You have to quit fucking around and make your move.*

He yearned to cross the park, walk up the street, and ring Laura's door bell. He would wrap his arms around her in hopes she'd return the gesture, and maybe just stay that way for days. But there was so much work to do for Helen's sake.

He returned to the paper to write an article, based on his meeting with Ben Herkimer. It was a heartrending piece, even without mentioning names. Rob knew it was seasoned by some of the grief that he was feeling for Helen. And for abused children everywhere.

Next he enlisted an intern and they both dug into research on cults. He wanted to be well prepared for his 2 o'clock meeting with the Prophet Abishua, and he still needed to call Sheriff Elwood to see if they had determined anything more at Helen's accident scene, today in the daylight.

Without the Mule he would have to ask that Neanderthal in their film lab to go along with him because photos were essential ... and that's when the Mule walked in. He looked like shit but, then, he was no beauty to begin with.

"What the hell are you doing here?" Rob asked. "You should -"

"You should shut the fuck up," the Mule growled. Then he shouted loud and clear across the small newsroom, "Everybody just stay out of my way. I know you're sorry and thanks for your thoughts. Just leave it at that."

He turned back to Rob. "I'm ready to meet the Seekers with you. Helen wouldn't want me to crap out, and she always gets her way."

***

Laura felt soft boiled and sliced open like an egg in an egg cup, unruly emotions tumbling out. Helen's death made her terrified for the safety of the other support walls in her life. Not long after telling Wade that she loved him, she padded downstairs and said the same to Eudora. Rob's timing with a quick call could not have caught her at a more receptive moment.

"Can I see you tonight?" he asked.

"Or sooner," she answered.

"I'm going out to see the Absolutists this afternoon, then I'll be over."

"Have you heard from the Mule?"

"He's here with me. I called the Sheriff to give her the phone number for Helen's brother. Mule says that's her closest kin. Elwood will contact him, I guess. Anyway, Mule wants to stay involved."

"Both of you remember that in all cults the followers believe their leader is some kind of messiah. They worship him and will protect him. They won't want you there. And the leader will appear normal, even cordial, but he's anything but. You guys be careful." *Fresh out of the egg and I'm clucking like a mother hen.*

***

The Seekers of the Absolute Pathway owned property where the high desert cuddled up to the Cascade foothills, sheltered from the highest winds and sprinkled with enough rain for crops to prosper. On the long drive out to the ranch in Rob's F-150, the two newsmen were silent. Rob wanted his friend to talk, but knew the Mule would reveal his thoughts only when he was good and ready.

Outside the town limits the musky scent of sage and juniper permeated the pickup. They drove an old asphalt road paved with patches through a bleak stretch of nothing much but yarro, bunch grass, and loco weed. Plants out here had to be tough enough to muscle up around lava rocks to bloom.

Finally, staring out his window away from Rob, the Mule said, "You know that wine they found in Helen's Bronco?"

"Uh-huh?"

"She wasn't drinking it."

Rob looked sideways at his friend. "You sure about that?"

"We were both cutting back on our chosen vices. She only drank when she was with me. And I only smoked one doobie a night with her."

"Couldn't she have fallen off the wagon just once?"

"Nope. I would, but you know ... knew Helen. She always did exactly what she said she would."

Rob nodded. "I didn't know she was cutting back, but even if she hadn't, she was no drunk driver."

"She might have had wine in the car bringing it home, but they won't find a drop in her system. Besides, it wasn't a brand she ever bought."

Rob mulled the whole thing over as they ascended, desert scrub giving way to mountain pine. There were certainly reasons anyone could have a new brand of wine in their vehicle. But Mule was right. If Helen said she wouldn't drink without him, then by God, she wouldn't. "So you're thinking it might have been a plant?"

"So I'm thinking it might have been a plant."

They rode in silence once more. When the photographer began to speak again, it was in a voice as barren as the landscape. "I'll never get over her, you know. In Nam, I learned that if you get to liking somebody, sure as shit you'll lose them. You're my only bud that made it back whole. Everyone else? Well, you know.

"So, I swore off getting close to anyone ever again. Didn't want to lose anybody else. Friend or lover. But Helen, she didn't play fair. She wasn't a looker, and she wasn't even always nice to me. I didn't see it coming, how hard I fell for her.

"Sometimes she'd get all pissy and kick me out, but Helen always took me back. She saved my sorry ass with that big ol' heart of hers. Stopped the drug nonsense, the most of it anyway. Healed a lot of mental breaks. Trusted that I could be something. She became a friend *and* a lover. How you going to resist something like that?"

He made a fist and slammed it down on the dashboard. "When her spirit drained away on that road last night, she took mine with it. The fucker who killed her, he signed his own death warrant."

His anger spooked Rob. The Mule was not the kind of guy to bluster. Once he got himself in gear, he was inclined to act. Rob said, "She gave me a safe haven, too. I owe her. But Mule, we don't know for sure these people are involved with her death."

"Maybe we don't have proof. But I can feel it. Cults are crazy shit, man, and it takes someone crazy to kill someone like Helen."

"We're just going there to learn today, Mule. You need to keep your cool, take your photos, and listen.

They're accused of abuse, and that's what we'll talk about. But if we discover a link to Helen, then I agree. They won't get away with it."

The Mule didn't speak. So Rob asked, "Agreed?"

Finally, he nodded. "Yeah, sure. I learned patience in Nam, too."

CHAPTER TWENTY-FOUR

Rob and Mule drove in grim silence. Few cars traveled these back roads, which primarily led to logging trails higher in the mountains. As if on cue, a logging truck far ahead of them slowed and pulled onto a gravel track, the same one that led to the Absolutist land. Rob and the Mule bounced along behind the monster, choked in its cloud of dust.

The truck was empty of logs, with its second trailer stacked on top of the first so it wouldn't swing and bounce on the roadway. Rob knew the driver would use a crane at the logging site to lower it back down, then both trailers would be filled with logs. When it left the site, it would be about sixty feet long with a gross weight of forty tons.

Rob was suddenly struck with an image of a truck like this barreling downhill at Helen, running her off the road late at night. *Jesus! Did something like that happen?* While he was scaring the crap out of himself with that grizzly vision, the logger thundered past the cult's buildings. Rob nearly missed his turn. He hit the brakes, swerved into a parking area, and his pickup rocked to a stop.

"Not nervous are you?" the Mule asked as they waited for the dust cloud to settle.

"Me? Hell, no," Rob answered as they got out.

Immediately, they heard gun fire. "Okay, *now* I'm nervous."

"Sounds pretty close," Mule said, grappling with his camera gear.

Rob listened intently. "A shooting range. Nearby."

The building in front of them had started life as a motor home, but a large porch and front entrance had been added. "Hard to make a silk purse out of a Holiday Rambler, but they've done it," Rob commented. The carpentry was both elegant and meticulous. He admired the unknown craftsman who built the addition onto the trailer.

Before they got to the front steps, a tall man came out and stood on the porch. He struck a stilted pose, back as straight as a military commander. He was hawk-nosed and dark complexioned either naturally or from working in the intense sun. His arms, akimbo, were roped with muscle. There was nothing welcoming about him. Rob disliked him from the get-go.

"Abishua?" Rob asked. *He's sure not the charmer that Laura told me to expect.*

The Seeker did not appear to notice the hand Rob extended. But a second man came out to the porch and moved to the front. "This is my son, Cadman. I am Abishua."

This one's a whole different horserace. His smile was genuinely welcoming as he shook hands with Rob then with the Mule. Rob guessed him to be at least fifty. His silver gray hair was full, and he exuded not only magnetism but vitality. His eyes were as caring as a veterinarian faced with injured animals. "I am very pleased to meet you, Mr. Cooper and Mr. Mueller."

He's done his homework, knows our names.

Another logging truck rumbled past, this one heading in the opposite direction, fully loaded. For a moment Rob couldn't hear above its throaty growl, and all four men squinted in the swirling dust.

When the truck was gone, Abishua addressed the logging business. "It's not our operation, but it's our road that gets them to their property. They pay a handsome toll. It's one of the many ways we support ourselves. But I am getting ahead of myself. I imagine I should begin with who we are versus who we are not. Come sit and we'll talk, then Cadman and I will give you a tour."

Rob and the Mule climbed the porch steps and sat on the handmade benches. Mule began unpacking camera equipment while Abishua seated himself on a glider. Cadman stood in an 'at ease' position, watching the Mule attach a lens to a camera body.

"Beautiful work," Rob said, running his hand along the polished grain of the bench's gracefully arched back.

"Carpentry is another way we provide for our group," Abishua said. "Quality workmanship is in short supply these days, but we have a very competent woodworker."

Rob thought he should give this guy the benefit of the doubt. Abishua seemed to be cooperative. "Why don't you begin by filling me in on the back story of your group. You know ... who, what, when and all that."

The Mule began to take photos of the ranch buildings. Cadman quickly moved to block the photographer's sight line.

"Cadman," Abishua said, and the man moved back to where he'd been. "Pardon my son's rudeness, Mr. Mueller, but he means well. You are welcome to photograph me or any other adult. However, we request that you do not photograph faces of any children you may see."

"Why's that?" Rob asked before the Mule could come up with a less civilized comment.

"It's hard for little ones to deal with the teasing or acrimony of outsiders if they are recognized in town. We prefer their images not be published."

The Mule aimed the motor drive at Cadman and clicked off half a dozen close-ups. "Fine by me. Adults only."

Cadman scowled, but Abishua thanked the Mule then turned back to Rob. "We settled on this land decades ago. As our group has expanded so has our property. We own 600 acres and receive all the tax considerations of any organized religion. This is a matter of public record.

"We began as a group of twelve. There are now forty of us here with a dozen or so living and working in Rapid River. I head our group, supported by a council of four elders, including Cadman. We call them Brothers." He stopped with a smile that looked almost shy. "I must admit to being proud of our growth."

"Since they are brothers, I take it no council

member is a woman?"

"They don't have the time. While we run the organization, they run the families. We work the ranch together, and we all seek the state of absolute grace. I am tasked with leading the way."

"Can you explain that to me?" Rob asked, trying to thwart his own opinion.

"My pleasure. We believe the Pathway is taking us not to some ethereal heaven of the type you might believe in, but to a genuine pure existence here on earth. There is no separation between church and state in our lives. Church *is* state."

"So you are anti-government?" Rob asked.

Cadman made a guttural noise similar to a growl, but Abishua merely leaned forward, elbows on his knees, hands together. "Only when the government is at odds with our Pathway. We comply when we can, but we are a militant ministry, protective of our state of grace."

"We heard gunfire when we arrived. Still hear it. Is that part of your militancy?"

Abishua laughed. It was rich and natural. "You are too literal, Mr. Cooper. We are militant about defending our beliefs, but the gun fire you are hearing is merely from our boys. Come. Let's begin our tour, and you'll see for yourselves." He rose and moved swiftly off the porch, causing the Mule to rush, fumbling with his equipment.

The four men began a circle around the outside of the compound, Rob and Abishua in the lead. To Rob, the grounds and the buildings appeared well-tended, surrounded by fields so lush they must be irrigated. They approached a shooting range where half a dozen young boys fired rifles while two teenagers supervised. As they walked, Abishua explained, "Each Seeker, or Absolutist if you prefer, is expected to contribute to the wellbeing of the entire fellowship. Here, our boys learn to shoot safely before they are ten. They provide meat for the colony. Birds, deer, elk, each in its proper season. They are capable of keeping cougar or bear away from our perimeter."

"Two-legged predators as well as four," Cadman muttered.

Rob frowned at him. This lout seemed intent on picking a fight. "So you've been hunting people?"

Abishua cut in. "Of course not. But we can protect our community."

Meanwhile, the Mule kept quiet and took photos, careful to keep behind the boys so their faces wouldn't show. And, Rob figured, so he wouldn't get picked off by a wild shot.

They continued walking the perimeter, touring grain fields, a dairy barn, beef cattle, a greenhouse, and a chicken yard. Everything on the campus appeared normal, at peace. The membership was hard at work wherever they looked. A large vegetable garden was tended by young girls who seemed to toil happily together.

"As you can see, there is nothing suspicious or violent going on here. They're all free to do their work in peace," Abishua said, then explained that their farm produce was sold through stores and farmers markets in Rapid River and beyond. They even had a vineyard. "Everything is organic, of course. It does no good to poison the body while you save the soul."

Rob asked a question that he knew would sound argumentative. He didn't care. "I've been told that a family has to turn over all its material possessions to join your group. True?"

The question didn't seem to faze Abishua. "Well, of course. It's part of the contribution of the individual to the wellbeing of the whole. We all choose to keep the Pathway clear by stripping ourselves of unhealthy influences and continuing our good work together. We share in all things."

While he listened, Rob observed that cult members wore simple utilitarian clothes made for working, not preening. Straw hats hid most faces, but nobody turned toward them anyway. Everyone ignored them completely while going on with their chores. "Why aren't any of them interested in us? I'd think you'd have few enough visitors out here that they'd be curious."

"They're not interested in you because you're a bad influence," Cadman answered.

Rob chuckled. "My parents thought so, too."

"Let me explain on behalf of my son. You represent the outside world, which they know to be wicked. Or at the very least you represent the kind of diversions that could lure them from the Pathway. They don't want to be infected with your practices and ideas."

"Guess they know you pretty well, Rob," the Mule muttered.

"I'm speaking categorically not specifically, of course," Abishua replied, smiling at the photographer who took that opportunity to snap the Prophet's picture.

The buildings were modified trailers and free standing structures that bore similarities to oversized log cabins. Abishua explained they consisted of married housing, dormitories for singles, a school, and a meeting hall.

Rob asked about the latter. "Is that where you hold your services?"

"Yes, although that's not what we call them. Our fellowships are presided over by me and the council of elders."

"But why at night?"

"How do you know that?" It was the first actual surprise that Abishua had shown. It stopped his spiel which had so far sounded as rehearsed as a Universal Studios tour to Rob.

"I've spoken with members in town," Rob answered, lying to protect Laura.

Abishua immediately regained his composure. "The town members are actually the reason why we meet in the evening. It is not an easy drive for morning meetings, but they can get here readily after work."

They stopped to watch a craftsman dado a groove in a drawer. Abishua introduced him as Nathan, their lead carpenter and woodworker. "I mentioned Nathan's ability to you before, back on the porch," he added.

"Your work is beautiful," Rob said. "I'm

impressed."

Nathan nodded his thanks, but then the click click click of Mule's motor drive appeared to enrage this mild-looking man. Like a mad dog he snarled. "Don't do that."

"Nathan," Cadman said sharply.

Nathan's stance changed immediately, and he smiled meekly. "I must continue with my work." He returned to his table saw.

"That was weird," Rob said as they continued with their tour.

"I should never have interrupted an artist at work," Abishua answered.

"Yeah, sure. Artistic temperament," the Mule muttered.

Rob wondered if the scar he'd seen on Nathan's cheek was from an accident with one of the power tools, or something worse. But he changed the subject as they passed the school. "Could we take a look inside?"

"We would prefer not, since it is in session. We don't want to disturb the education process, do we?"

As they walked back toward the office, Abishua said, "And now, I am sorry to say, I must leave you. The brothers are waiting for me. Cadman will show you out. Just one more thing." He looked directly into Rob's eyes. "I am sorry to hear about the loss of your editor. She was a woman of strong opinions, and I did not always agree, but such an accident is always cause for grief."

Rob felt like he'd been slapped. He saw the Mule

freeze. "It just happened last night, didn't make the morning paper. So how did you know about it?"

"You're not our first visitor today. Sheriff Elwood came by earlier."

Of course. "She thinks you were somehow involved?"

"Hardly. But your editor's tongue was sharp. We're not the only group to have felt its edge. I'm sure the Sheriff will speak with others before the event is ruled an accident."

Behind his father, Cadman directed a haughty smile at the Mule and added, "We'd certainly hate to think someone did it intentionally."

Rob took a tight grip of the Mule's shoulder, putting himself between the photographer and the Seeker.

"Thank you for coming, gentleman. Cadman, please show our guests out."

Rob called after him. "But what about the editorial? What *is* going on out here? You have been accused of undue influence on the young and confused. Possibly even abuse. One man has claimed a child received gonorrhea here."

Abishua stopped and turned back to them looking crestfallen. "I know the situation. The gentleman never had any proof that the child was infected here, or I would have dealt with it most severely. He could just as well have accused his own neighbors. Please do not repeat such statements."

"Shameful insolence," Cadman growled, clenching his fists.

"Stand easy, Cadman," Abishua ordered, then smiled at Rob. "The name Cadman means warrior. Perhaps I should have chosen a less aggressive name for my son. As you said, Mr. Cooper, yes we do take in the young and confused. The very people that your society has created then rejected. We give them hopes that you have dashed. These people are not browbeaten and brainwashed. I provide strict rules and doctrines of truth that take the burdens of strife off their shoulders.

"And now, gentleman, my time is rarely my own, but it has been a pleasure chatting with you. Cadman, please come as soon as you escort our guests out." Abishua turned and this time walked away.

Rob had to admit that the Prophet was impressive. He could see why people were drawn to him. Cadman walked with them to their pickup, and Rob made it clear he might call with follow-up questions.

When they got to their vehicle, an old woman was waiting for them with two narrow woven sacks. She spoke not a word, but bobbed a sort of a curtsy then left. Cadman handed the sacks through the passenger window to the Mule. "This is a blend of our own, our private label. You'll find it delicious. It's available in a few of the better stores in the state." He nodded and turned away.

"A going away gift? Probably bags of Gila monsters," Rob said to the Mule as he reversed the truck and pulled out onto the road. The Mule fumbled with the cloth tie on one of the sacks and pulled out a bottle of wine. He turned it to look at the label.

"Fuckers!" he yelped so loud that Rob winced. "It's *Seeker's Find*. The wine bottle in Helen's Bronco was *Seeker's Find*, too."

"No way," Rob answered. *Was Cadman taunting them? Or was it just a weird coincidence that ...*

"Go back. I'll make the bastard talk," Mule seethed.

"I don't think so," Rob said looking in the rear view mirror. "We've been noticed after all."

The work on the ranch had stopped, as the Seekers stared at them. The boys on the shooting range were poised with their guns lowered, but still in hand. No one smiled. No one moved. The atmosphere felt suddenly malignant, that electric tingle before a storm. The back of Rob's neck began to prickle. "We better get out of here. For now."

He drove away at a reasonable pace, but was unsettled by the logging truck that roared up behind them as they drove off the property. He put up with the tailgating part way back to Rapid River, but finally pulled onto the shoulder to let the goliath barrel past.

In the meantime, Mule had gone silent, staring off into a space all his own.

CHAPTER TWENTY-FIVE

Cadman was still grinning when he strode into the meeting hall where his father requested his presence. The hall was one large room with rows of chairs for the entire congregation. Now it was empty other than the three other council members and his father at the front of the room. They were seated at one side of a table on a raised platform. An empty chair had been placed on the opposite side as if ready for a court-martial.

Abishua watched his son enter, seeing the grin. *The boy is feeling proud of himself.* Pride was his son's flaw, encouraged by his father. Abishua taught him as a child that nothing in life mattered so much as his father's pride in him. Then, as the boy grew, Abishua used that need for approbation as a tool to keep Cadman in line. Now he caught his son by surprise when he stood, walked to him and slapped him hard across the face with his powerful open hand. "You have angered this council. And shamed me."

Cadman stumbled. His grin evaporated. He made no motion to retaliate, instead went down on his knees. His deeply tanned face burned red where his father's handprint began to show.

Abishua never experienced fear himself, but he'd certainly observed it. He saw it now in his son's eyes. He knew Cadman's body would be doing all those unpleasant things that went along with fear. His mouth would be getting dry, his stomach would start to churn, and weakening sphincters could force him to defecate right here in the meeting hall.

"But father ..." Cadman's posture lost its military stiffness. He crept forward reminding Abishua of a whipped dog.

"Silence. Sit and speak only when addressed." As his son climbed onto the chair that faced the table, the Prophet turned his focus to the other council members. Each of them looked nearly as startled as Cadman.

"My son has been very foolhardy. He is responsible for the death of the editor of the *Rapid River Review*."

"Surely not!" Joram exclaimed. Abishua wondered how the man dare question him. *Or is he merely surprised?* It was another of those emotions that Abishua never felt.

"But father, she was putting you in danger, exposing ... "

"I said silence." Abishua glared at his son then turned back to the council. "His ignorance has turned the light up not out. Now our actions will be even more scrutinized. The Sheriff will not let this die away. Neither will the newsmen. The ones who were just here, asking questions."

His council seemed deeply concerned by Cadman's action, but Abishua assumed they were privately tickled by anything that put a wedge between father and son. It might secure higher status for them. He turned to his son again. "What have you to say?"

"How ... how did you know?"

"Did you really think one of my creations would answer to you and keep it from me? Are you that much the fool?"

"I thought you would be pleased. I thought I was protecting the Pathway by removing the editor. I didn't realize my actions would put us under suspicion." Tears appeared in Cadman's eyes. "I see my error now, father. I apologize to you and the council."

"I can only hope you left no traces behind you at the *accident* scene. From now on, we all must be extra vigilant. No hint of the movies or drugs must leak. No one is to discuss any of our business outside of this room. Take no actions without consulting me first. Is that clear?"

Each member of the council said, "Yes, Prophet" as he stared them down one by one. Joram nodded most vigorously.

Abishua leveled his gaze on Cadman. The man may be little more than a thug, but he was ludicrously loyal. He was a value for that reason if no other. Abishua depended on none of the others like he did his son. The greatest retribution to Cadman would not be corporeal punishment. It would be loss of face within the cult. Humiliation.

"As your penance, you will no longer be allowed to call me father. You will address me as Prophet, as do the rest of the Seekers. And for now, you Joram, will sit at my right hand."

"Yes, Fa ... Prophet." The mortification that raced across his face was easy to read. And Cadman began to sob.

CHAPTER TWENTY-SIX

Laura wondered how Rob and the Mule were doing with the cult that afternoon, but mostly she grieved for Helen until her head throbbed and her nose hurt from blowing it. Like old friends everywhere, they'd shared stories and laughs nobody else understood. It was their own vocabulary, now a dead language, and Laura would never hear it again.

She might not have stirred for days, but she knew she was scaring Wade. So she decided to get out of the house and do something Helen would have enjoyed; she took him to purchase a bicycle at the new Walmart. Eudora joined them, winking at the greeter as they entered. She grabbed a cart and said to her daughter, "I want to buy something flashy for my date."

"Your date?" Laura asked, mystified.

"Harold from the Animal Shelter called."

"He did?"

"Well, you needn't act so surprised. I still have a womanly charm or two around here somewhere." She patted at her pockets.

Laura knew her mother was trying to cheer her up and loved her for it. "I'm just surprised he knew how to find you."

"He kept tabs on our phone number in the shelter's records. We're going to a get-together at the

Senior Center next Saturday."

Wade ignored their chatter, and tugged Laura toward the bikes while Eudora made a bee line to the women's clothing racks. He zeroed in on a selection of BMX models in a rainbow of brilliant colors. Wade sat on several, leaning forward to *Vroom! Vroom!* and scoffing at the idea of the training wheels. "I don't need them," he bragged. "Miss Helen said I'm awesome."

Helen. How I miss you. "You are awesome. But I want you to have them. Same with a helmet."

"You're a weenie, Gram."

"Did Miss Helen say that, too?" she asked, with an attempt at a smile.

"Yes. She was funny. I want her back."

"Me, too. Which bike do you think she'd choose?"

He pointed to the black one with red and orange thunderbolts. "She'd like that one. It looks like a motorcycle."

"Ba-ba-bad to the bone," Eudora rumbled, showing up just then with a red polyester blouse, slinking on a hanger. It had padded shoulders, a sweetheart neckline, and a sash to tie in a floppy artist's bow at the waist. "Your great grandma is pretty ba-ba-bad, too."

The shopping trip raised Laura's spirits, at least until she dragged the bike box into the house and set to work. She was still assembling the Huffy Thunder Road when Rob arrived that evening. Wade had long since given up on her and gone to bed.

Rob sat beside her on the floor of her living room, which was strewn with bike parts. He observed the operation in progress. "A wise man would not offer his input to his lady friend, is that correct?"

"A wise man would, indeed, keep a GD lid on his GD input." She'd already thrown two tantrums, knowing they were more about Helen than the Huffy instructions. "And he wouldn't mention that his lady friend's nose is as red as a Mr. Lincoln rose, or that her eyes match it."

"He thinks his lady friend is beautiful, even though she's had better days."

Once Laura finally wrestled the bike together, they ordered a victory pizza, and moved to the kitchen. Laura invited Eudora to join them. The old woman usually made herself scarce, but tonight, Laura figured they all needed company. Laura also thought, a bit late, to call the Mule and tell him to come over.

Rob hadn't eaten since the day before and he needed the fuel. The two women picked while he wolfed down several slices. By the time the Mule arrived, there was just enough left to feed another hungry newsman.

It was less than twenty-four hours since Helen died, but they had lots of information to share with each other. Rob started, telling them he had talked with the sheriff. "Elwood says that so far, there's nothing inconsistent with an accident. No scraped paint from a second vehicle, no cut break lines, nothing that dramatic. Now we wait for the autopsy to see if Helen had been drinking the wine."

"She hadn't," the Mule murmured through a mouthful of Italian sausage.

"There's no more they can do?" Eudora asked.

"They'll keep on it. She said they can't call it a murder, not yet. But a newspaper editor has a lot of potential enemies, so Elwood's making calls on obvious candidates."

"Like who?" Laura asked.

"Like the city council. That's where Helen was just before the crash. Several members had bones to pick with her through the years. She was always quick to point out their foibles."

"Waste of time. It's those bastard Seekers," the Mule mumbled, then seemed to remember that Eudora was sitting next to him. "Pardon my French, ma'am."

"Yes. Give it a fucking rest," Eudora answered, aiming a grin at the photographer.

Rob and the Mule told the two women about their trip to the cult, then Rob passed on the heartrending story of Ben and Mavis Herkimer's granddaughter, Annie. "Was that really only this morning? Seems like an endless day."

Laura, careful to avoid names, told them what her client Colleen had revealed about her abusive father. "It's another source that indicates the cult tolerates, even promotes, repulsive behavior. But she will never come forward. She doesn't even remember it herself half the time. She's way too traumatized to make a decent witness."

"Bottom line, we have nothing we can prove about the cult. Just hearsay of abusive practices and suspicions about Helen's death," Rob said.

They sat staring at the dirty plates and empty beer

cans. It was late, and they were too tired to make the next move. Finally, Eudora put her hands on the table, and pushed herself up. "My beauty sleep is very important to me," she said. She kissed her daughter, hugged Rob and then, before he could dodge her, gave the Mule a squeeze, too. "I ache for our loss, everyone. She was a great friend."

***

The next morning, the story of Helen's death was on the front page of the newspaper. Her obituary and Rob's interview with Ben Herkimer flanked the main article. Rapid River was a small enough community to be shocked by such a loss, and Laura found co-workers eager to discuss it. She let them chatter on, without adding to their conjecture.

"Do you suppose she was drinking?" Jenny wondered in the break room, where they were pouring their morning coffee.

"Or run off the road?" Diego joined it.

"There's something fishy," Lovella pronounced. "That woman was powerful. She had to have enemies."

"Her op-eds were not always well thought out," complained Tom. "Like that hooey about cults in the desert. Reliable source, indeed." He looked directly at Laura, even though she didn't think any of them knew that Helen was her friend.

The best bandage for Laura was to lose herself in her work, so she was glad to see David that morning.

"How have you been?" she asked.

"Okay, I guess. Working a lot. I'm kind of worried about Cathy. I don't know where she's gone."

"You and Cathy parted ways, David."

"I know. But I still keep tabs on her. She's not answering the phone. I've driven past her apartment a few times but haven't seen her car. Or any lights in her windows."

"Be careful that she doesn't think you're stalking her. You aren't, are you?"

"No, of course not. I just like knowing she's home safe."

"What about Weasel?" Laura realized the Defender was more bluster than bite, but she believed he might be the reason Cathy felt threatened by David.

"Fuck no. Why would I do that?" His body language telegraphed the switch from David to Weasel.

"I don't know, Weasel. You tell me. You're the one who scared her, aren't you?"

"Well, okay, maybe I yelled a little sometimes. But only when she got nasty to our boy. And I've never slapped her."

"You sure about that?"

"Nobody in the Forum ever laid a hand on her," he huffed in indignation.

"Weasel, she is important to David, so she is important to the Forum. Do you know where she is?"

"Would you believe me if I said no?"

Well, now there's a question. She'd believe Weasel, but not all parts of the David system. There could be activity that Weasel didn't know about. And maybe Nathan didn't know all about Weasel. Still, they were all one person. So would she believe? *Hmm.* "I believe that you, Weasel, don't know where she is."

"Nice save, doc. " He actually smiled at her. Or maybe it was more of a leer.

"Now may I speak with David again?"

He returned and continued, as if never interrupted by the Defender. "I'd try to reach her at the office, but she told me never to call her there."

"Have you called the police?"

"God, no. They scare the hell out of me. Maybe Nathan could do it, but I don't think his experience with them has been a whole lot better than mine."

"All right. I'll make some calls if you like. In the meantime, Cathy probably just took some time off, maybe a vacation or family visit. We can't do anything more for now, and it's too soon to worry. Okay?"

"You're the boss, Dr. Laura," he smiled weakly, but then sat back in a self-possessed posture. His smile turned to one of confidence. "You're only one of many, Dr. Covington. David has a lot of bosses."

"Who's speaking now?"

"It's Nathan. Thanks for the help with Cathy. When David's distracted, it's hard for him to perform his duties. The Seekers hold me responsible for that."

"You mean the carpentry, right?"

"Well ... yes. Of course that's what I mean."

"These Seekers. David's father is one, is that right?"

She was met with silence. She'd made a mistake to

ask a question like that so abruptly. Finally, David returned. "Nathan's gone. It's me again."

Laura was having a hard time concentrating. Her thoughts kept drifting to Helen. She decided to end the session early to avoid making other mistakes with this fragile client. "David, it's been a difficult day. I'll see if Cathy is still in town and let you know next time."

David looked troubled. "Are you okay, Dr. Laura? Have I made you sad?"

His concern nearly pushed her over the brink. *The counselor must not become the counseled.* "No, David. You've done nothing wrong. You don't need to worry about me."

***

David left the session, bouncing down the stairs and blowing a kiss to Lovella. But it was Nathan who left the building, and he was not sure everything was in order. He wondered if those newsmen who came to the compound had known who he was. Had Dr. Covington been indiscreet? It was just a feeling, but he thought he might have to speak with Cadman about her before too long.

***

"Why are you walking like that?" Rob asked Laura.

"Like what?"

"Well, with that little skip every so often."

"Oh. So I don't step on a crack."

"With your PhD and all, you still believe in that?"

"No. Yes. Whatever, Eudora's back is still fine, right?"

Willing to humor her, he began to watch his step, too. They were following Wade who pedaled his Thunder Road around the pond in the park. A breeze circled the ponderosas and fluttered the basswood and aspen leaves. It was a beautiful city park, with sidewalks intersecting lush green lawns like spokes in a wheel. Couples sprawled on blankets, families set up impromptu ball games, a small circle of women practiced Tai Chi. Joggers zipped past them, and they could hear the trills and whistles of the white-crowned sparrows above the squabble of Canada geese, wood ducks, and mallards around the pond.

"Okay, so here's what we think we know," Rob said. "First, you have two clients, brother and sister, both abused as children, probably in a cult."

"So it would seem."

Rob loved how she furrowed her brow in concentration, how she caught her lower lip in her teeth. "Second, one of those clients might be programmed by someone in the cult for some undisclosed reason."

"So it would seem."

"Third, the Herkimer's granddaughter, Annie, was abused while in this cult."

"So it would seem."

"Fourth, Helen died right after her op-ed piece threatened to shine a light on this cult."

"So it would seem."

"Stop saying 'so it would seem.'"

"I can't. It all sounds too bat shit crazy to be the truth." She looked up from the sidewalk and turned worried eyes on him.

"Bat shit crazy. That's another of those psychological terms?"

"Yes. It describes what cops would think if we told them this story."

"So we need more proof."

"More proof? How about *any* proof?" She ran her hands through her curly hair. Wade stopped pedaling and looked back at them. "You okay, Gram?"

"Absolutely. See if you can outrun any of those ducks." The child took off again and mallards scattered in noisy irritation.

Rob put his arm around her shoulders.

"There's more good news if you want to add a fifth item to your list," Laura said. "My client's ex-wife may be missing. I emphasize *may*." Without using names, Laura explained she had called the office where Cathy worked. The receptionist told her that Cathy was no longer there, so Laura then spoke with the HR guy. He was guarded at first, but based on Laura's job title, told her that Cathy had not shown up for the last couple weeks or answered his calls to her home. He had questioned her co-workers, and one told him she had recently left her husband and talked about leaving town. So he assumed that she had.

"It's most likely true, of course. She probably wouldn't tell an ex as strange as this one where she went," Laura said to Rob. "But I called the management company for the building where she lives, explained that she was not at work, and that people wondered if she had left town. The landlord said he'd check out the apartment."

"Find anything?"

"He hasn't called back yet. I asked him to, but if he finds anything wrong, he's more apt to call the police. And how was your day?"

"I talked to the woman who left the Absolutists several years ago. You know, the one I read about when we were in Portland. She wasn't eager to talk, but finally did."

Laura cocked her head and looked up at him. "What with you being such a smooth talker and all."

"There's that. In the years since the article appeared, she changed her name."

"Why?"

"It has to do with shame. She says a person is going through some weird personal shit to get involved with a cult to begin with. You're easy prey. I guess if you weren't, you probably wouldn't turn your back on everyone you know and throw all your possessions down a rat hole."

Laura laughed. "With insightful analysis like that, I may be out of a job in no time."

"Yes, I'd worry about that if I were you. Anyway, according to her, when you join, people on the outside think you've gone crazy. Then when you leave, people on the inside think you've gone back to the dark side. All in all, everyone thinks you're a fool."

"Did she say any more about cult activity?"

"She said the Prophet Abishua preaches that

outsiders infect the membership with unclean thoughts. So newcomers have to prove their allegiance."

"I can just imagine how," Laura said.

"Yep," Rob said, lowering his voice so Wade could not overhear. "Women who join have to stand before the congregation, divested of clothing, to be naked before the purity of the Pathway. Then they lay naked with the Prophet or the council member he chooses, and are taken as brides of the Pathway."

Laura shook her head. "How gullible people can be when they're desperate for something to believe in."

"This woman left the cult before they completely trusted her. She never saw anything illegal. But she knew there were ceremonies too secret for her to attend." He thought he'd come to an end, but then he remembered something else, something important. "Oh! And she heard rumors about drugs. Nothing specific. But it makes a lot of sense."

"Why's that?"

"Simple economics. Even with carpentry, farm produce and logging tolls, there can't be enough income to support a group that size. There's dozens of people out there plus another dozen in town. Got to be something else. At least it's a new avenue to investigate."

"Maybe we're on the verge of some actual proof of something. Enough to tell the cops, you think?" Laura asked, eagerly.

"Um, maybe not quite yet."

"Then how will you find out if the Seekers are

trafficking?"

"Well, I don't want to startle your sensibilities, but there's a chance the Mule didn't get his nickname just because he's stubborn or his name is Mueller. He might know a thing or two about drug runners."

Laura gasped in mock surprise.

"Come on," Rob laughed. "Let's go score some ice cream cones."

***

That night, Laura left Wade at home with Eudora, and she went home with Rob. The glass front of his A-frame faced Mt. Bachelor. "I've always thought it fitting for a loner like me. Not so much now though," he said, placing his hand on Laura's naked thigh. They were in his bed seeing just the faintest outline of the mountain in the dying light. At this time of year, there was some glow until after nine pm. They were experiencing a bit of afterglow themselves.

"I'm ready to tell you a story now," Rob said.

Laura rolled toward him. "It's not mandatory, Rob. Patience isn't one of my virtues, and you're right. You don't owe me explanations."

"If I want you to trust me, then I have to trust you. I owe it to myself to try. I'm just not very proud of this." To his relief and her credit, Laura shut up.

He told the story in a tightly controlled monotone. "I was just back from Vietnam, done with the army. Tired of writing military papers. Covert reports, bloody secrets. I ended up in Chicago in '69, after the Chicago Convention. Days of Rage. Chicago Seven. I worked the metro desk, along with the other rookies.

"We were all so hungry. We waged a war of our own, each trying to be first with the Big Story. I chose to make my mark on the crime beat. Like every other mutt in the pack, I struggled for months to establish a relationship with at least one police detective.

"You grovel and play bow, maybe make a badge look really good in one story, so he gives you a juicy tidbit for another. Over time, I got a reputation with the uniforms and dicks both for being dependable. Making sure their viewpoint was fairly stated. In those days, the Chicago police were under a lot of political fire, so a tame reporter was a valuable commodity. I never lied for them, but I always gave them the benefit of the doubt.

"Things went well for a long time. I'd done a couple favors for a homicide detective named Sam Pearson. He was a has-been, not the brightest bulb and needed a little good will. I did a feature on detectives with twenty years in the department, and talked pretty about him. It was a good story about a lot of men who believed in serving and protecting. Great public relations, so he owed me. Or so I thought.

"One night, a woman on the north shore was murdered. Nice looking woman, expensive neighborhood, as high society as Chicago gets. Grisly stuff with all the prurient details, the kind that's gold to a reporter. Her hands had been tied with her bathrobe sash and her nightie was pulled up then stuffed in her mouth. Left everything exposed. She wasn't raped, but penetrated with an instrument.

That's all we ever called it in the paper. Then she was knifed several times in the breasts, and the doer ejaculated on her there. The maid found her the next morning. Maybe she would have lived if a neighbor had heard anything, anything at all. Pearson called me and gave me the details, as long as I promised not to quote him. I had an exclusive. I was hot shit.

"The hubby was the prime suspect, as always. In this case, they were getting a divorce, and it was a nasty one. Lawyers were like piranhas. Neighbors didn't hear anything the night of the murder, but they'd heard an earful often enough before. She had finally locked the guy out, so she lived in this ritzy condo, and he was in a crappy little four-plus-one on the far north side.

"The night after the murder Pearson calls me again. Tells me the murder weapon was found in a dumpster just a couple blocks from the hubby's building. I break the story the next morning, and public opinion turns ugly.

"Hubby only had a divorce lawyer, right? Not a trial lawyer. He's too rich for a public defender and too poor for a good private mouthpiece, so he ends up with a lousy one. The trial was short, the guy was guilty, justice was done. I was there every step of the way, fanning the fires in the morning news. Detective Pearson was a hero. We high-fived after the verdict.

"It wasn't long before the husband hanged himself in the prison laundry by tying undershirts together. That would have been the perfect capper for my story, but about a week later, another prisoner confessed to the murder of the wife. Guy described the whole scene, even the nature of that rape instrument. It was a baton like a drum majorette would use. We'd never disclosed that, so the guy was telling the truth."

Rob rolled over to look directly at Laura. "And the final blow? He said he threw the knife in the alley behind her condo. Not in the dumpster up north. So. Was I set up? Did the cops find the knife then plant it near the husband's digs, just for an easy conviction? Did a bag lady pick it up in one neighborhood and have it stolen in another? Don't know, never will. But Detective Pearson stopped returning my calls.

"Fast forward to a couple weeks later, a girl comes up to me in a bar. Asks if my name is Cooper. I'm with the other reporters, liking this action, you know, playing a big man for being recognized.

"Then she says the dead woman was her mother. Raped with the baton the girl had used as a kid. She starts to yell at me, her face looked like that painting, the Scream. She said the real killer got away while Pearson and I accused her father. Turned public opinion on him. Hounded him. We were responsible for his suicide, too.

"She was hysterical, and some friends of hers finally dragged her away. I couldn't think of a goddamn thing to say to her. Neither could the other guys. They went back to drinking.

"I never could face them again. Or feel anything but duped. The thing is, the girl was right. I didn't ask the right questions of the right people. I'm responsible for that poor shattered girl, and that man dead before his time in a state prison.

"Bottom line, I wanted a big story, and I got it. But I didn't have the chops for it. I don't want that much power. The power to destroy a life by being so wrong.

"I left Chicago not long after that. I'm not cut out for the big city anymore. I'd rather write for a paper here, cover real estate scams or city council issues or llama ranchers. If I fuck up, nobody's likely to die. It's been a safe haven for years.

"But this thing with Helen and these poor kids? This time I want to be right. The bad guys won't get away this time."

CHAPTER TWENTY-SEVEN

They were all in the backyard. Annie Herkimer felt a light breeze. Her grandmother always said it showed up each evening to chase away the heat of the day. It was mostly quiet outside, other than the sound of the piña colada song on Grandpa's cassette player and her own splashing in the plastic pool. Annie was really too big for it now after that spurt of growth last winter, but it was still fun to roll around and slap the surface.

She was hungry and eager for the chicken on the grill to be ready. Grandma Mavis had set the patio table with paper plates and bowls of potato salad and mixed fruit. Grandpa Ben was peering into the barbecue, tongs in one hand and a large glass of lemonade in the other. "About time to flip you a bird, Mavis," he chuckled over the old joke as though it was the first time he ever told it.

Annie rolled on her back, face to the sky. She closed her eyes and smiled at the sun that warmed her cheeks as she floated, ears below the waterline. Later, she thought that's why she didn't hear the terrible sound of Grandpa's neck crack or the sizzle of his head as he fell onto the grill. She did hear Grandma scream. She surfaced in time to watch her grandmother strangled with her own apron strings.

Annie recognized the murderer. When Grandma

was finally quiet, she stood up in the pool and said, "You've come."

She stepped out, shivering in her bright print bathing suit, then knelt at the Rage's feet.

***

The next morning, Rob wrote his feature on the Absolutists, as well as a sidebar on the interview with the Portland woman who had left the cult. Then he met the Mule in the *Review's* editorial room, to go over photo choices for the lead article. Grief hadn't diminished Mule's talent. The photos were terrific.

"Helen's ghost is telling me to work faster, smarter, for Christ's sake," he groused. "I was kind of hoping her ghost might be easier to get along with than she was."

True to his word, he had taken no facial shots of children, but had several charming prints of the girls working in the garden. In one, a towhead was tickling another with a fresh pulled carrot. Their body English was of two happy little girls, one dodging the other. Rob decided on this photo as well as one of Abishua which had a moody aura caused by sun streaks the Mule had caught behind him while he smiled.

The Mule had also taken images of the buildings, and one of the log schoolhouse gave them both a chilling surprise. From one of the windows, a man in a blue uniform stared back at them.

"You know him?" Rob asked, squinting at the image. The man's face was deep in shadow.

"No … too grainy, but I'm pretty sure I know the uniform," the Mule answered, looking at the photo through a loupe.

"It is a city cop, right?"

"Yep."

"So a cop is a cult member?"

"Or someone pretending to be a cop."

"Curiouser and curiouser, Mule."

"Spookier and spookier, Cooper."

"We want to watch our backs, my friend."

Rob decided it was time to bring up drugs, a topic the two men no longer discussed. He had met Mule in Vietnam, when everybody experimented with everything. Rob dabbled, but the Mule was a heavy user. He'd been through years of suffering to throw that monkey. It was another reason Rob had come to Rapid River, to help his friend with the battle. Like Helen, he thought the Mule was worth the fight. Some of the language they'd used on each other during the withdrawal years was as graphic as anything they'd heard in Nam.

It was uncomfortable for either of them to recall those days now. As far as Rob knew, the Mule hadn't touched anything heavier than weed for years. But he might still know the culture, if that's what it could be called. And the players.

"Laura and I were talking about the cult last night," he said, sneaking up on the subject.

The Mule stared at another photo, one of Cadman. He said nothing.

"I told Laura there was more money keeping the

Absolutists going than they could make from selling gourds and building end tables. And I really don't believe that Abishua is in it just for the glory of the Pathway."

The Mule stacked all the photos except the selects and set them aside. "Are you building up to saying the Seekers are drug lords?"

The Mule could always surprise him. "It's possible. What do you think?"

"I think I need lunch. Come on."

They drove through a local dive called Burger-Teria, ordering two loads of salt and grease with large Cokes to go.

"This is the only kind of Coke I use anymore, Rob. You know that," Mule said as they sat in his van. The console between the front seats was littered with camera straps, lens caps, film packaging, and a fairly impressive selection of fast food wrappers. "But I know people who do things I no longer do. Friends, some of them. They talk in front of me, because they know there's no reason not to. I'm only telling you this because of Helen." He clenched his jaw as if willing tears away. When the moment passed, he stuffed in a huge bite of chili dog.

Rob watched chopped onion tumble down the Mule's scrawny chest. He said, "They wouldn't shut up a newspaper woman just to keep her from publicizing their group. Too little gain for taking that big a risk. There has to be more to it. They're doing something, and her spotlight scared them."

"My friend knows a guy who knows a guy who

tells him there's a lot of black tar for sale right now."

"Black tar?"

"Mexican heroin. It's cheaper than stuff that comes in from Asia through Hawaii. What it lacks in purity it makes up for in potency. The island boys and the Latinos are at each others' throats over the supply lines. Somebody will have to give way. Bunch of people gonna die either way." He finished the chili dog and attacked his fries.

"How does this involve Rapid River?"

"According to my guy, the Mexicans have a distribution syndicate pretty well set in the Southwest. It's easy to transport from there so it's become a choice route for the Northwest. An operation out in the desert near here buys from them and distributes around this region. My contact is pissed because this local supplier won't work with small timers like him. But they always have product for bigger dealers. At least that's what the street has to say."

"You think the local supplier could be the Seekers?"

"I think you can take that to the bank," the Mule said, finishing the last of his food then staring at Rob's. "You gonna eat those fries?"

Later in the day, after the newspaper was put to bed, Rob called Laura. He told her what the Mule had said. "Now I think it's time we see the Sheriff. She's going to question the abuse charges, but she has to listen about the drugs."

"We still have nothing but conjecture and circumstance."

"Yeah, but we need to do our good citizen thing. Besides, Elwood is nobody's fool. She'll gladly listen to two solid professionals such as ourselves."

"If she does, I'm worried about the caliber of law enforcement around here."

They made plans to go to the Sheriff's office the next afternoon then spend the evening with Wade. "Eudora has a date," Laura said.

"She does?"

"She met him at the anti-cruelty shelter."

"He must be a real animal."

"I'm sure she hopes so."

***

"She's going to laugh and call us names," Laura fretted. "She'd call the loony bin to pick us up if I didn't already work there. We need a peace offering." She had convinced Rob to take her to the bakery so she could purchase two dozen donuts for the Sheriff's department. "I've heard law enforcement types like these. With or without sprinkles?"

"Maybe *I'll* laugh and call you names," Rob said.

As they walked down the street a couple blocks to the Sheriff's office, Rob said softly, "Over there. To my right. That's Cadman with a carpenter named Nathan." He indicated the direction with a tilt of his head. The two men were unloading a table from a panel truck, but stopped to stare at the couple. Cadman nodded but the other one looked away.

"Why, that's Dav ..." Laura stopped herself.

Rob looked at her quizzically. "You know him?"

But Laura merely shrugged her shoulders, and they went on up the steps and into the Deschutes County Sheriff Office.

Laura was worried that Sheriff Rita Elwood might think she was revealing more client information than she should, so she had carefully prepared a preamble. "I am a PhD in psychology with years of clinical experience. I know the sanctity of a client's privacy, unless life is threatened. I have dozens of cases, and I will not tell you which of them provided me with information. That said, I am concerned about things I'm hearing about the Seekers of the Absolute Pathway." Following this set up, Laura carefully revealed what she could without stretching ethical lines tighter than a bow string. Rob added his own observations.

The offering of donuts did little to soften the blow. "So let me see if I have this straight," Sheriff Elwood said, after Rob and Laura told her their tale. They were stuffed into the Sheriff's cluttered office, trying not to knock over the piles of reports and wanted posters. Rob and Laura had paper cups of dreadful coffee, and the Sheriff slurped from a *Rapid River Rocks* mug. Laura noticed that she was pencil thin down to the waist but her hips blossomed out like a pear. The starchy brown pants of the uniform did her no favors, especially accompanied by the regulation leather belt with all the tools of her trade. At the moment, her attitude seemed as starchy as the pants.

The Sheriff began. "Two community mental health

counselors believe that one client is an evildoer created by a cult and that a second client has been raped by members of the same cult. But one of these counselors was fired and left the state, and the other admits her department administrator would not agree with this diagnosis whatsoever. In addition, this second counselor won't tell me the names of these clients so they can be interviewed."

"Yes, that's exactly right," Laura agreed, cringing at how the story sounded in the Sheriff's dry delivery.

"This counselor convinces her friends at the newspaper that these incidents should be investigated. But she won't tell them any names, either."

"Correct again." *Dying a thousand deaths, that's me.*

The Sheriff turned her icy stare on Rob. "So the newspaper editor and a big shot investigative reporter decide, based on no solid evidence whatsoever, to stir the pot by publishing an editorial that pokes the cult in the nose."

"Well, we *did* call it an opinion piece," Rob replied.

"Shortly thereafter, the editor dies in an accident that the reporter believes is foul play, also based on no evidence he knows of, except that the wine found in her SUV is the brand made by the cult, a brand that is purchasable, I might add, in more than one local store. In addition, he busies himself interviewing Ben Herkimer, a local citizen who may or may not speak with me now. And, icing on the cake, this crack investigator tells me he and his photographer sidekick saw a blue uniform out at the cult. Not *who*, mind you, not a name, just a scrap of cloth that could be a city cop."

Laura knew Rob must be squirming in his seat just like she had during her inquisition.

"Then based on hearsay from a source he won't reveal – and do give my regards to the Mule -- the reporter convinces himself and the counselor that this same cult is running drugs." The Sheriff leaned back in her desk chair and stared at one then the other. "Does that sum it up correctly?"

Laura felt like a child ready for the dunce cap, but Rob appeared moved to fight back. "Rita, I told you we had more concerns than proof. Laura has good ethical reason not to name a client. And I think there are enough circumstantial events relating to Helen's death to treat this seriously."

The Sheriff leaned forward like a cat ready to pounce. "Oh, I do treat it seriously, Rob. I liked your boss, and I resent any implication that I wouldn't be thorough investigating her death." She picked a file out of her in-box and flipped it open. "I'm going to tell you something from the autopsy I don't want to see in print, at least not yet. This is the one reason I don't boot the both of you out of here. Helen had no poison in her system, no brain aneurysm, no heart attack. No obvious wound other than those made by the vehicle. No *nothing* to say it wasn't just what it looked like ... a very unfortunate accident. But." The sheriff held up her index finger. "There's one little problem with something we *didn't* find. She had no alcohol in her system."

"Mule said she was cutting back," Rob said. "He

knew you wouldn't find any."

The Sheriff nodded. "He told me that, too. And it's an anomaly. An open bottle of wine was broken, and there wasn't enough spillage for it to have been full. But there was no cork in the car or anywhere at the site. Trust me, we looked everywhere. Maybe she was carrying around an open bottle of wine that she didn't drink. But I think it's more likely somebody wanted it to look like she was drinking, and put it there."

"But why?" Rob asked.

Laura gasped as an idea hit her. "Maybe to avoid an autopsy by making it look like a DUI." She gave the Sheriff a look of admiration. "It didn't work because you didn't buy it."

"Well, if it isn't Nancy Drew," the Sheriff said. "Somebody may have run Helen off the road. Driven straight at her, making her swerve into the trees. Then they rolled her car over on top of her, and planted the broken wine bottle. If that car was rolled, it would have taken more than one perp. Maybe more than two, depending on their size. Based on the position where the Bronco first landed, I'm having trouble believing it rolled on its own."

Laura remembered the last words Helen had said to her. "Just before she died, she tried to tell us. She said, *"Tell Rob, cult ..."*

"What else did she say?"

"Just *pals*. Which we were. She may have said more to Mule before I got there."

The Sheriff's phone rang, interrupting the conversation. While Rita listened to the caller, Laura silently seethed over what they'd been told. She was enraged that some son of a bitch had seen to it she would never hear Helen laugh, ever again.

When the Sheriff hung up the phone, her thin shoulders drooped. "That was Jerry Cassidy with the city cops. A neighbor just found the bodies of Mavis and Ben Herkimer."

"What?" Rob exclaimed, jumping to his feet.

"One strangled and the other apparently, ah, barbecued." The Sheriff visibly trembled. "Cooper, you're coming with me. I want to know everything Herkimer told you."

"What about the child, Annie?" He looked horrified.

"Cassidy said nothing about a child."

"Then we need to find her. Now. She's only eight." His distress made him short of breath. He turned to Laura. "Could you take my pickup to your house. I'll meet you there when I can."

Laura saw the guilt building in his face. She grabbed his shoulders. "Listen, you. Whatever happens, none of this is your fault. None of it. Ben Herkimer came to you with his story. He wanted you to know. To save other children."

But his tortured face told her he didn't buy a word she said.

CHAPTER TWENTY-EIGHT

By the time Laura drove Rob's truck down the alley to the parking area behind her house, she was in tears. On top of the strain of meeting with Sheriff Elwood, her concern for Rob, and the relentless grief over Helen, she simply could not drive a stick shift worth a damn. The lurching, squealing and grinding all across town might seem funny someday, but now it just fanned the flames of her misery. It didn't help when Wade burst out the back door yelling, "Mr. Rob! Oh, it's just you Gram."

She was granted no decompression time because the phone was ringing when she came through the back door into the kitchen, with Wade jabbering away about a game of *Go Fish* he'd played with Dora. The call was from the Mule.

"Laura? I'm out at Helen's cabin."

Laura knew that Helen had left her property to him. Rob had told her the Mule planned on moving in. "How's it going? Can I do anything?"

"Well, that's why I called. I have some things I think she'd want you to have, and some, ah, well ..."

"Would you like me to go through her personal items?" Laura asked. The Mule was grieving, too, and he could probably use her help.

"God, yes," he said, sounding relieved. "She

wanted me to live here. But she'd hate me pawing through her stuff."

"I'll come right out." She wasn't ready to face the job, but Helen would want her to be the one to do it.

"I'd be grateful. I probably won't be here when you arrive. Rob called about the murders so I need to pick up my equipment and get over to the Herkimers."

"That's okay, Mule. I have a key." *Best friends share things like house keys.*

"You keep anything you see that you would like, okay?"

"Thanks, Mule."

"And Laura?" She could hear the sorrow thicken his voice. "I owe you."

As soon as she got off the phone, Wade was pestering, "Gram? It's Saturday. What are we going to do today? Gram? Gram?"

I don't know about you, but I want to crawl under the covers with a mountain of snot rags. I'll just duct tape you to some table leg and go back to bed. But she said, "Let's go out to Miss Helen's cabin. We'll take along your bike so you can ride on her driveway." Helen's long curving drive was a hard packed dirt track, two ruts with a weedy strip down the middle. It was a safe place for Wade to ride on private property.

"Yay!" The child pranced around in a victory dance. When Eudora came into the kitchen and took a jacket from the pegs next to the back door, Laura asked her to join them. But the older woman declined. "I have to get ready for my date."

"Isn't that hours from now?"

"Field maneuvers have commenced. I'm marching over to Curl Up 'N Dye. I'm getting the works." Just two blocks from the house, Eudora had found an old fashioned beauty parlor with hair dressers not stylists, hair-dos not coifs. She would come home with a curly puff that could best be called a bubble, with flashy red nails to match her new red blouse, and with all the neighborhood gossip about people she'd never met.

Laura loaded Wade's new Thunder Road into the trunk of her Camry and as an afterthought, tossed in a couple empty cardboard boxes and a wrench, as well. It was not usually a long run out to the cabin. But Laura took a circuitous route to avoid passing the scene of the accident. When she finally got to the cabin, the Mule was gone. She set the bike out for Wade and watched him weave off down the drive, raising her voice louder and louder as he pedaled away from her.

"Do not get out of view of the front door, or else."

"Or else what?"

"The goddess of little bikes will remove it from your possession until you are thirty."

"Crap."

"What was that?"

"Nothing," he yelled back as he wobbled on his way.

She went into the cabin and stood for a moment looking around. Helen's collection of owl figurines, her rows of paperback mystery novels, her grandfather clock, a trumpet not used since her years in the college marching band. Everything seemed somehow diminished without its former owner, like a carousel with no riders.

Laura carried her empty cardboard boxes into the bedroom and placed them on the bed, sat for a moment rubbing her hand on the intricate stitching of the old quilt, and smiled at Helen's dresser. It was the only truly girly décor in the whole cabin. Every other piece of furniture was as unadorned as one of Helen's editorials. But this dresser was Country French, with scalloped moldings, bevel paneled drawers, antiqued milk paint, and carved wooden knobs. This was a dresser with secrets, an oasis of femininity that her employees wouldn't have associated with their tough, determined boss. On its top, she found a note from the Mule.

Laura: I put Helen's bike and skis in my van to bring to you. You're taller but not by much. You'll have to learn how to ski to keep up with Rob this winter. And I thought you'd like this scrapbook, too. Mule

"Keep up with Rob, huh?" she huffed, until she looked at the scrapbook, then all thoughts of Mule's words skittered away. It was a timeworn album that Helen had made in their college days.

Laura sat on the bed to open the cover. And there they both were, young and beautiful, full of joy and mischief. Two thorny roses, each ready to conquer the future. She shut the book, kissed its cover, and held it to her chest as she carried it out to the Camry. She would wait to look at it, sneak up on it a little at a time, so her heart wouldn't shatter with all the memories it contained.

While outside, she checked on Wade, then went back in. First, she packed two of Helen's suitcases with the few moneyed items in the wardrobe, including a beautiful wool Pendleton jacket, her jewelry box, family photos, and a collection of paperweights she gathered from her travels through the years. The Mule could go through these things when he felt ready, or just give them to Helen's brother. There was no hurry. Most clothing, including sweatshirts, jeans, socks and scarves, she put into the boxes that she would take to Goodwill. She hauled them out to the Camry.

Then she went back in to make a small collection of the toiletries and more intimate items to take home and toss away. When she opened the dresser drawers, she smiled at her friend's copy of Danielle Steele's *Star* tucked next to her hush-hush collection from Victoria's Secret. All the silky, strappy little numbers she discovered would stay Helen's secret ... Helen's and the Mule's.

When she was nearly finished, she went out and called Wade over to her car. "I think it's time for you to ride on your own two wheels." Working with the wrench she retrieved from the car trunk, she loosened the nut at the bike's back axle, removing the struts and training wheels.

Suddenly Wade was jumpy. "I'm scared, Gram."

"Of course you are. But after a time or two, you'll ride like the wind. Now, you start pedaling and I'll give you a push." She galloped down the drive, releasing the little bike long after Wade was under his own power. *Letting go of anything else today is too damn symbolic for words.* She cheered him on, then finally went back into the cabin and left her key on the kitchen counter. Her best friend didn't live there anymore.

Once the bike was loaded and Wade was back in his car seat, she gave him a *quena*, a Peruvian bamboo flute that had been Helen's. "Miss Helen wanted you to have it to play to Soccer the llama." After several miles of tuneless, breathy twittering from the back seat, she thought that had been a really dumb idea.

***

The Mule caught up with Rob at the Herkimer house. Rob explained that the bodies had been photographed and examined by crime scene investigators, then removed. Ben had been bludgeoned, falling forward onto a grill where he had burned until the tank ran out of propane. Either the blow or the fire could have actually killed him. Mavis had been strangled with her apron strings.

It was a morose group of investigators, without even the gallows humor that often lightened their oppressive task. Rob was aware that many of them had known Mavis and Ben, in this small town where strangers were the exception to the rule. They hoped to find the revealing footprint in the grass, or a complete set of villainous fingerprints, or maybe a tuft of hair wrenched free by Mavis. Rob, a war veteran and a veteran reporter, had found it nearly impossible to look at the macabre remains of a couple who only wanted a good life for their grandchild.

There was a sunny room in the little house, with all the trappings of a cherished little girl, from Cabbage Patch Kids and a Barbie Styling Head to Care Bears bedding as bright as a rainbow. But there was no sign of the child. The room without its occupant was nearly as frightening as the crime scene.

"She's only eight," Rob repeated to the Sheriff, looking around the room. "Her mother is named Holly. She was recruited by the Seekers just before she got pregnant by one of the men out there. From what Herkimer told me, I imagine she's still there."

"That's where we'll start looking for Annie," she answered.

As soon as Sheriff Elwood could leave the scene, she and two deputies headed out to the Seekers' ranch. Rob and Mule followed in the photographer's van. Rob noticed the bike and the skis in the back, but he was too focused on their mission to ask any questions.

"I got them killed," Rob said to Mule.

Mule looked sideways at his friend, and his reply was cold as ice. "The Herkimers knew the danger. They wanted to help, or he'd never have found you. You kept his name out of it, but someone recognized his story anyway. Hell, there's even a chance the cult isn't involved, that somebody completely unrelated did it. Whatever, you're a reporter. If I'm not wrong, that means you report. So shut the fuck up with all that self indulgent *I got them killed* crap. Bottom line, if we get Abishua through the Herkimers, it may be the only way to ever get revenge for Helen."

Rob had never heard Mule use so many words all at one time before. "Mule?"

"What?"

"I think maybe that bitchy part of Helen's ghost is rubbing off on you."

***

Sheriff Rita Elwood did not allow them to go with her into Abishua's office to speak with him. The newsmen sat outside on the beautifully made porch benches. Rob found the wait almost intolerable. "You got any Tums in the van?"

"Yeah. I'll take the other half of the bottle."

But then Rob saw Annie walking toward them, hand in hand with a young woman. He was thrilled to see her. "Annie?" he called softly.

The child stopped to look at him. The woman did, too. She looked so much like Annie that Rob knew she must be her mother, Holly. Both were ash blondes and fair as alabaster, but the child's blue eyes looked like windows to a dead zone. *My God, what those eyes have seen.*

"Annie. I met you in the park, remember?" Rob said. "I was with your grandfather. You were feeding the ducks."

"I remember," the little girl said with just the ghost of a smile. "Grandpa liked you."

Holly tried to lead the child past the newsmen into the office. But Annie pulled back.

"Come, Annie."

"No, Mama."

"Abishua called us, baby. We must hurry." She looked frightened.

"Grandpa said no. I'm never to go in there."

The office door swung open. Abishua and the Sheriff emerged.

"This is Annie. And her mother, Holly," Abishua indicated to the Sheriff. "Come inside."

The little girl quickly looked away, but continued to balk. "No."

The Sheriff smiled. She got on her knees in front of Annie. "Hi, Annie. Would you like a ride in a real patrol car? You can turn on the siren and flash the lights."

Annie raised her eyes from the ground and stared at the Sheriff. Then she stepped forward and whispered into her ear. The Sheriff looked at Rob.

"She'd like to leave, but with you Rob. Seems she trusts you."

"Is that wise, Sheriff?" Abishua cut in. "Surely she is safest here with her mother. And her community."

"We'll take Holly, too, Prophet," the Sheriff answered. "I think my department can keep them safe."

For the first time, Rob saw anger in the Prophet, in his clenched jaw and the narrowing of his eyes. In a flash, the wrath seemed to pass. He said, in a calm tone, "Very well. Holly, we will see you back here soon." He turned and went back into the office, closing the door tightly.

Holly shuddered. "He's angry. With us."

"I think he's angrier with me, hon," the Sheriff said. "My name is Rita. This is Rob and the Mule. Rob, you know someplace less intimidating than my office we can all go and talk? No uniforms? Maybe even the *Review*?"

Rob thought for a moment. "Better yet, Laura's place."

"Good call. She has to know more about this sort of interview than I do."

Rob felt the little girl's hand touch his own. He took hold and said to her, "I'll ride with you guys and maybe give that siren a try, too. Mule can follow in the van."

As they left the porch, Rob looked back directly into the cold eyes of Cadman. He'd been standing just out of view at the side of the porch. It was like a fist to the stomach when Rob realized Cadman must have heard where they were going. And that Rob had used Laura's name.

CHAPTER TWENTY-NINE

Eudora was getting ready for the date with Harold, so the kitchen was Laura's again. She ground more black pepper into her pot of vegetable beef soup. The room was redolent with the soup's rich aroma, plus that of the homemade loaves cooling on a rack.

Laura had begun to cook as soon as she and Wade got home from Helen's cabin. It soothed her nerves while waiting for news from Rob, almost as much as Spock did by making off with the *quena*. She was delighted with the little thief for putting an end to the irritating whistle.

Wade was on a stool at the kitchen counter building a Lego castle when Eudora wafted in on a cloud of Shalimar. She had chosen black knit slacks and patent leather flats with her shiny red blouse, along with a gold link necklace sparkling with artificial garnets. She struck a pose and vamped, "Eat your heart out, *Golden Girls*."

"You look lovely, Eudora," Laura said, meaning it.

"Not mutton dressed as lamb?" Eudora asked, revealing a pang of doubt.

"You still got it, so go ahead and decorate it," Laura smiled just as the doorbell rang.

"I'll get it!" Wade yelled.

"Wait," Laura instructed, as he pulled the door

wide open. "What have I told you about opening the door before you know who's there?" She frowned darts at him, then smiled at Harold. He was every bit as round as she remembered him, but in his dark suit, bright blue shirt and cobalt blue tie, he was easily the dressiest man in all of Rapid River.

"Hi, Harold, come on in. Wade, do you remember Mr. Harold from the animal shelter?"

Without warning, the child shrieked, "No! No! You can't have him back." He tore up the stairs calling, "Run, Spock! Run!"

"Oh, my goodness," Harold said, blushing from collar to bald spot.

"Wade! Harold, I apologize. I'm afraid he got the wrong idea altogether," Laura said, embarrassed for Harold and sorry for Wade's confusion.

Eudora appeared, saying "Don't worry, Harold, Laura will handle it."

"Oh, my goodness," Harold said again, but this time he was looking at Eudora. "I'll be the envy of the senior center for sure."

After the couple left, Laura called up the stairs. "Wade? Sweetie? Mr. Harold wasn't here to take Spock away."

After a lengthy pause, she heard a muffled, "No?"

"He was here to get Dora."

Another pause. "Will he bring her back?"

Laura stifled a laugh. "Yes, I'm sure he will. Spock and Dora both belong to you."

"We can come down?"

"The coast is clear. You have a Lego castle to

finish."

The bell rang again after she shut the door. "They must have forgotten something," she said, pulling it open.

But this time it was Rob. "Darling," he said sternly. "You know better than to open this door until you're sure who it is."

***

The whole bedraggled group poured into Laura's home: Holly, Annie, the Sheriff, Mule and Rob along with tension, confusion and fear. Laura felt it all as she sat everyone down around the kitchen table. The counselor in her was gratified that the cook in her had made an abundance of bread and soup.

"We'll eat," she said. "Then we'll talk." And sure enough, as the meal progressed the atmosphere began to discharge. The odd little flock even seemed to bond.

The ones who could, ate. Then Laura had Wade take Annie up to his room to play with his *Masters of the Universe* action figures. Holly managed a little of the soup, but she was still unsteady. Laura invaded her mother's stash and brewed chamomile tea to soothe the young woman's nerves. Then the adults gathered in the living room.

"Laura, I'd like your take on something," Sheriff Elwood began.

My take? Maybe she doesn't think I'm such a chucklehead after all.

The Sheriff was sitting on the ottoman, her elbows

perched on her knees. With her broad pear-shaped hips she reminded Laura of one of those toys you can't knock over no matter how hard you try. "On the ride here from the ranch, Annie told us she can't remember anything but playing in the pool and seeing her grandfather fall. Everything else is gone. What do you think about that memory loss?"

Laura thought for a moment. "Well, I don't have enough info, but if she were my client, I'd start with the assumption that the horror is too great for her to process now. The memories may come back, but may never. If the trauma goes untreated, it will manifest itself eventually in many different ways, none of them good. It's important for her deal with it soon. She'll need a lot of counseling to help with it."

"Right. For a start, we'll involve Children's Services first thing tomorrow. I know the woman who'll handle it. She's good. Annoyingly chipper, but good." Sheriff Elwood turned her attention to Holly. "But we need your input tonight."

Now Holly was the center of everyone's attention. Laura thought that she must be very pretty when the fragile skin under her eyes wasn't so dark. She kept her arms crossed over her breasts as though she needed a barrier. Laura worried whether she'd make it through interrogation. She knew first hand that the Sheriff could be tough.

Rita Elwood surprised her. The Sheriff used the warm homey atmosphere to her advantage. She tempered her voice so it felt more like conversation than interrogation. "Tell us what happened, Holly. I'll only stop you if I miss something."

In a voice that trembled like a wind chime, Holly began with Annie's phone call to the cult. "She called from my parents' house. I can't believe they're gone. I always loved them even when we didn't see eye to eye." Her tears began to flow.

The Sheriff asked, "How did she know how to reach you?"

"She must have looked for me in Mom's address book, the one she always kept next to the phone. Annie would know to do that. Mom had the office number for the Seekers."

Laura assessed Holly's tears as genuine grief for her parents. If she had been born in the cult, there'd be no outside affiliation, so the bonds to the Seekers would be virtually unbreakable. But Holly joined as a teen. If she was worried for her daughter - or if she believed the cult had killed her parents – she might come up with the courage to break away now.

Holly continued. "Cadman called me to the phone to talk to Annie. She was hysterical. I don't know if she saw the murders or the murderer. All I could understand was that Mom and Dad were dead. And she wanted me to come for her. Cadman said to tell her we'd be there. But she didn't wait. She left the house and ran along the road, coming to find me." She turned to Rob who was sitting next to her. Her daughter's trust in him must have rubbed off on her. "She was still in a wet bathing suit. She didn't even have shoes. Her feet were all cut up from running on gravel."

Laura imagined the ghastly scene. Had Annie

watched while her grandparents were slaughtered? How did she escape the murderer? Did she know who it was? Was she in danger for what she had seen? So many questions and all the answers were locked away in the little girl's head, where even Annie herself couldn't find them.

"When we saw her, she was almost all the way out of town. I'm glad she ran. I wouldn't want to see the house, the bodies." Holly gulped and sniffed.

The Sheriff asked, "What happened when you got her?"

"She hadn't seen me for a while, but she knew me. And I've seen her a lot. When I could get into town away from the others, I sometimes watched her play during school recesses. And I saw Dad with her feeding ducks in the park. She's beautiful, isn't she?" Holly blinked through tears and smiled at Rob.

"Yes, she is," Rob agreed, smiling back at her.

Laura was surprised by a jab of jealousy as irritating as heartburn.

Holly continued. "In the car, Brother Cadman demanded to know what had happened. He scared her. He always scares the children. If she did know, she doesn't remember now."

"Think hard about this, Holly." The Sheriff leaned toward the girl. "Did Cadman seem to know what happened to your parents before Annie called? Could he have ordered the murders done … or done them himself?"

Holly shook her head even before the Sheriff got the question out. "No, no. I heard him talking with the

Prophet before we got in the car to go get her. The murders took them by surprise."

The cult leader didn't know? Laura couldn't stop herself from asking, "Why do you think that?"

"The Prophet acted angry with Cadman, like maybe it was all his fault. But Cadman said something about rage out of his control."

"Rage? Out of control? What do you think that meant?" Sheriff Elwood took over the questioning again.

"I don't know. Maybe I heard wrong. I was scared and really only thinking about my daughter." She paused, then added, "But even if I heard wrong, I know it wasn't something that was supposed to happen."

"Why not?"

"A long time back, they said if I left the Pathway ever again, they would hurt my parents. That's why I stayed. As long as they were alive, Annie had a safe place to be, and Cadman had me. Without my parents to threaten, they don't have a hold on me. So I don't think they would have hurt them."

"You stayed to keep them from hurting your parents?" Laura cut in again. *Of course! That's why she didn't go back home.* The girl was not a silly fool after all ... she'd been living in fear for her family.

Holly nodded. "At first, I really believed in what the Seekers are trying to do. I still believe there has to be a better way out there somewhere. Don't you?" Holly asked, turning her baby blues to Rob.

"Uh, I guess, yeah, sure. We can hope so," Rob said.

Give me a break.

Holly turned her attention back to the Sheriff. "But then I was glad when Mom and Dad took Annie away. The Seekers told me they'd all be safe if I stayed. I guess I'm so used to doing what they say that it took me a while to realize today that I'm free."

"You think they'll try to find you?" asked the Sheriff.

"Oh, yes," she said.

Rob said, "They know where she is." He told them about Cadman overhearing them at the ranch.

Sheriff Elwood said, "I doubt the Prophet wants any more publicity. Maybe he won't pursue them."

Holly stared at the Sheriff as if she were impossibly naive. "He might not. But Cadman will. Annie and I have to get out of town. I have an aunt in California who might help us."

Elwood rose from the ottoman and stretched her back. "I know you're exhausted so just one more thing for now. Are you willing to testify against Abishua for threatening you? Or Cadman for, ah, whatever he's been doing to you?"

"No. Annie and I, we have to get away. Besides, who'd believe me over them?"

The Sheriff nodded, looking resigned, and glanced at Rob and the Mule. "I have no case against them then. Certainly not murder. Not yet." She looked back at Holly. "Wonder where I can hide you two safely for the night."

"The domestic violence shelter?" Laura suggested.

"It's full. One of my deputies tried to take someone there earlier today."

"They could stay here," Laura offered.

"Absolutely not," Rob said. "Too dangerous. For all of you."

"Rob's right, Laura. I guess the Rapid River Motel. It'll be easy for us to keep an eye on them there. A second floor room, no back way in. Well-lit parking lot. I'll station a car there for the night. They'll be okay."

Holly whispered something to Rob that Laura didn't hear. He looked grave, but they were interrupted by a childish argument from above.

"You're a smarty pants!"

"You're a dummy pants!"

"Wade?" Laura called up the stairs.

"Annie?" Holly called up the stairs.

The two kids flew down.

"She said Barbie was better than He-Man," Wade stuck out his lower lip at the absurdity of it all.

Annie, older and wiser, calmly said, "Things for Barbie always turn out okay."

It broke Laura's heart. She hoped things would turn out okay for Annie, too.

Everyone left, with Rob telling her that he'd be right back after he talked to the Mule. While Laura waited for him, Eudora came home. "Nice to get out of the house and kick up my heels," she said. "It gets pretty quiet around here."

Rob came back, and as soon as Eudora and Wade

both drifted off to bed, Laura turned on him. "You know Holly's been trained to act that way don't you? It's nothing personal about you."

"What? What are you talking about?"

"Holly coming on to you. It's how she's been trained to act around men."

"Coming on to me? What the hell are you talking about?"

Laura batted her eyes and parodied Holly's weak little voice. "Oh, you big, brave man. Thank you for saving me." Bat, bat. "And whispering sweet nothings in your ear before she left."

"Those weren't sweet nothings. She was saying she's scared of the Sheriff's deputies."

"What?"

"She's heard talk that one of them is a Pathway member."

"No shit! A city cop *and* a county deputy?" She shivered and felt petty for accusing Holly of flirting.

"Mule is going to watch the deputy who's assigned to the motel for the next four hours. Then I'll take over. Just to be sure Annie's safe."

"Oh, Rob. I'm sorry."

Rob grabbed her by the arms and pulled her in, with no resistance at all. "You know what I think?" he said, nuzzling her hair.

"What?" she pouted.

"You can really be a dummy pants."

***

It had been a long emotional day for them all. Tomorrow would be no better. Helen had specified no memorial service, and her body had been released to her brother in San Francisco. Rob told Laura that, left with no way to express their grief as a group, the newspaper staff planned ten minutes of silence in the morning. Laura, Eudora and Wade decided to observe the same ten minutes. Rob said he'd be at the paper, but the Mule would not. "He says that Helen hasn't given him ten minutes of silence since the second she died."

As Laura removed her makeup in the bathroom mirror, Rob showered. She called to him over the sound of the running water. "You realize you've saved that poor woman and her beautiful child, don't you?"

"How do you mean?"

"With the right counseling they both can recover. Find a new beginning. It'll be hard for Annie, but maybe the aunt can get her a good psychologist. One who specializes in children. I could help with that if she wants."

"I'll be sure Holly knows."

"You've done what the Herkimers were trying to do. You've saved that little girl. And think of all the other children you may have helped by getting the Herkimer's story out there."

The water stopped and a hand reached out for one of the thick plush towels on the nearest rack.

"You wouldn't be trying to counsel me, would you?" Rob asked, still in the shower stall.

"Not me. I just know you're thinking about Mr.

Herkimer and about that woman in Chicago. But reporting sometimes means hurting people."

"The Mule said something similar today. But not so nicely," Rob said. She could hear him toweling excess water from his hair.

"Reporting is like psychology that way. The truth isn't always the happiest thing to tell. Repercussions can hurt the bystanders." She replaced her day foundation with a fresh-scented night moisturizer. "And another thing, since I'm delivering a lecture: guilt is a useless emotion, Rob. One that is self-imposed. You are the only one that can let go of it. I think you're more than capable if you try."

He emerged from the shower, damp, warm, naked. His long hair was ruffled and wild as a mane. "Am I capable of fucking my counselor until her brainpan rattles? Or is that unethical?"

"Who the hell cares? Besides, I've already removed those dummy pants." She slipped off her robe and stepped nude into his arms, breathing deep of his scent to deposit it indelibly into her memory banks. She pushed against his erection and he cupped her buttocks in his hands.

CHAPTER THIRTY

Abishua was furious. That bastard newsman was the reason he lost control of Holly and Annie. The Sheriff nosed around because it was her job. But the newsman and the psychologist? They'd get their comeuppance. And soon. But first, Abishua needed to discover who actually had murdered the Herkimers.

Was Cadman responsible? It couldn't be, not after the fiasco with the editor. Surely he would never act without his father's permission again.

But who?

Abishua was feeling put upon, out of control, and furious about it. His Seekers kept away, like staying downwind of a wounded grizzly. At the moment he felt like sneering at the assholes. *Absolute Pathway? How fucking gullible can you get?* He needed them, of course, as a cover and as a breeding pool. But the Prophet wasn't in this to lead them to salvation. Far from it. He relished the wealth from drugs and kiddie porn.

And, yes, the power, too.

Abishua could abide the loss of Holly but, ah, the child. He'd been pleased to get Annie back. Her grandparents had interrupted his work when they took her away. The death of those interfering old fools was the only bright spot in his day.

Now Annie was gone again. He would have resumed her terror and pain, splintering her mind in stages as she grew. She had the imagination and life drive to be a superior creation, smart and calculating and cruel. She could have handled the toughest missions without him spoon feeding her every step of the way. She would have loved him, loved to serve him. And like all his creations, she would never accuse him of a damn thing. She'd have no memory of what she had done.

He had masterminded the whole thing. His personal little army of thieves, tormentors, murderers. It was the perfect set-up. He allowed himself a moment to gloat at his own genius. *No reason to pout, not really.* Annie was gone, but he'd just move on to another little project. It would help sooth his nerves. It always did.

Now let's see. Ah! The girl teasing another with the carrot, having fun when she should have been working. The one in the newspaper article for the world to see. How dare she! She hasn't been punished yet. Let's see, her name ... yes, Millie. One of my very own. We'll just see what we can do.

He found Millie once again working in the garden. The cloud of whispers and giggles that surrounded the flock of young girls dissipated immediately. They shrank from him as if his presence was a foul odor spreading across them.

"Millie, come."

Abishua knew that a normal child would have refused to approach such an irritated man. She might have even run. But Millie was a cult-raised child. She knew that submission was her only prayer.

"Kneel before me, girl. The rest of you gather." They dropped their pruning shears and hoes, then formed a semi-circle around their Prophet. Millie sank to her knees and bowed her head. Abishua waited until they were all still as stone. Squabbling crows and a logging truck rumbling in the distance suddenly sounded very loud.

Millie flinched when Abishua spoke. "Look up at me, girl. You have been shamed, and you have shamed us. You were photographed by the outsiders, shirking your duties. You have taken advantage of your sisters working here. And, worse, you have disobeyed our doctrines. Food is for the nourishment of us all, not for you to play."

Millie's tears began to flow. She couldn't know how her misery and humiliation appealed to him. She whimpered, "I am sorry, Prophet."

"I'm sure you are. But that is hardly enough punishment for the crime of disobedience."

"No, Prophet."

The circle of girls huddled closer together. Some took the hands of others. "You girls! Spread out and bring me another carrot. Whoever finds the biggest one will not be part of the punishment." They scattered into the garden. It wouldn't take them long.

"I said look up at me," Abishua snapped at the kneeling child who'd bowed once more. He grabbed her hair and pulled her head back. Millie's eyes shimmered with terror. He could see the delicate blue veins pulsing in her throat.

"For your sloth, you will work an extra shift, by

yourself each afternoon for a week. In the sun, no breaks. And because of you, each of these girls will work one extra shift as well. Now. What have you to say?"

Millie had heard apologies before, and knew the drill. "I apologize to each of my sisters, to you, Prophet Abishua, and to all of the Seekers for not contributing my fair share."

"Prophet Abishua?" said a trembling voice, distracting him. The tallest of the girls held out the carrot.

"Excellent, Elena. A nice big one. Give it to Millie. You will be excused from the extra work shift. The rest of you continue. Millie, follow me."

She trailed him to his quarters while he tried to decide what to do. Considering the options, he entered his private quarters followed by the dutiful little girl. He began loosening his belt as he closed the door.

Abishua sat on his bed and looked at Millie. "You know what to do."

She reached up to remove a band, shaking free her long silky hair. Next she pulled the loose frock over her head. Slowly, crying in shame, she removed her shoes, socks and underpants.

Abishua stared at the terrified child as her nakedness caused a blush to spread across her body. "Now send me Shana," he ordered. He watched as the child's demeanor changed to a far more accepting, even eager child. Millie was gone.

Shana smiled, rubbing her hand across her tiny budding breasts. "I am here, Prophet."

"Now, let's see, Shana. What shall we do with this carrot? I know!"

He didn't worry about her being overheard. She knew better than to cry out. *Besides, those idiots out there really believe that a session with me puts a child on the right Pathway for life.*

CHAPTER THIRTY-ONE

It had taken three full days, driving late Into the nights. Nathan spelled him with part of the driving, but at the moment, Weasel was in control. And he was worried. Just lately, he could feel himself losing control. The linkage was breaking up, getting less clear. Not everybody in the Forum was responding as quickly as he liked, and he was apprehensive for Rose and the Little Ones. He was their only real defender, and he was increasingly aware of an unknown presence, slithering up behind him in the dark. Something back in there was outraged.

It was night in the Arizona desert, as clear as he expected but much colder. He shivered in the lightweight black denim jacket. He knew he was miles from Piñon, and that was miles from anywhere else. He'd been here before and done this before. But it scared him every time, not that he'd ever tell Rose or the others. It scared him because David would be punished if he fucked up.

It would have been pitch black if it wasn't for the jillion stars in the desert sky. This was Indian country, Weasel had been told. The Navajo reservation. The rez. Not that he knew much about Navajos, but he wondered if they were sneaking up on him right now, moving as soundless as shifting sand. In movies, they were a sneaky bunch, changing shapes and becoming wolves. Of course, none of them could hold a candle to him. If he weren't also sneaky, they wouldn't call him Weasel.

He had parked the Chevy Blazer behind a pile of boulders while there was still a little twilight to see by, back when he left the road. He couldn't use headlights, of course, or he might be seen. It was a bumpy ride out into the middle of nowhere, miles off any road in any direction. But ahead of him, the desert floor was flat. Devil's claw and ragweed, candlewood and cactus, but pretty much free of rocks. He set out the road flares, not lighting them yet. That was for later.

When he'd finished the chore, he climbed up on the boulders. In the heat of the day, he wouldn't sit on these rocks because he was nervous about rattlers and gila monsters and tarantulas. Everything in the desert wanted to poison you, that's what Weasel figured. But now in the dark, it was too cold for all the poison boys. It was windy and he shivered again, but he couldn't sit in the Blazer with the heater running. He had to be able to hear the engines. Right now, all he could hear was the wind in the dry desert brush. Coyotes yipping off and on. And just once the flapping of an owl, followed by the shriek of something small dying in agony.

When he finally heard the engines, they sounded like an angry wasp approaching. It was the distinctive whine of the push-pull Cessna Skymaster twin. The night was so clear Weasel didn't have to shoot a warning flare upward. Instead, he just rushed to light the road flares he'd set out, zigzagging along a pathway that, when lit, became a landing strip. When he finished, the circling plane turned on its own lights and landed. It never came to a complete stop, but taxied to one end of the strip where an unseen crew pushed out a dozen tough, heavy bags while the plane turned. As the last bags hit the ground, the Cessna took off once again into the dark. The whole operation was complete in moments.

Even before the plane lifted off, Weasel had begun to snuff the flares by tipping them into the sand. He put their remains into the Blazer. It wouldn't be too many hours before the wind eradicated any other sign of the landing, not that anything was around to see the strip except the occasional sheep or wild burro.

He loaded the bags of black tar heroin into the back of the Blazer. He knew the plane had come from Mexico to make the delivery, and would return across the border. Piñon was about as far north as the Cessna could fly and make it back without stopping for fuel, skirting Winslow, the Phoenix area, heading southwest over Coronado National Forest into El Sásabel country.

When the hum of the plane had disappeared, the flares were dead, and the tar was loaded, Weasel sat in the Blazer, listening and looking. He heard and saw nothing new for ten minutes, then twenty. Finally he started the engine and began the long journey back toward Rapid River.

***

The first line of defense at the Mental Health Department was Lovella. Everyone who worked there knew that the quality of her service was dependent on how much she liked the caller. And Lovella liked David a lot. So that morning, she intercepted Laura in the hallway with the accuracy of a heat-seeking missile.

"I need to put a call through to you," the old warrior said, blocking the entrance to the ladies room.

"I'll just be a minute, Lovella," Laura said.

"No time for that. David's on the phone. He's panicky. He needs you now."

"But I -"

"Don't make me repeat myself." Lovella's wrinkles settled into an expression that could scare off evil spirits, then she trudged back down the stairs toward her desk.

Laura tried to sputter out a snappy retort, but could think of nothing. *If I don't go, I'll never get another message.* So with a shake of her head, and a very full bladder, she scurried back to her office. She got to her desk just as the call was ringing through. "David? It's me. Dr. Laura."

A frightened little voice answered her. "It's not David. It's Rose."

"Are you all right, Rose? Where are you?"

"I don't know where we are. The Little Ones are scared. I'm scared, too."

Laura's thoughts raced. How could she locate Rose/David? "Are you at a pay phone?"

"No. In a room. I've never been here before. Help

me, Dr. Laura."

The child might not be real, but the fear was. Laura wanted to rush, but needed to stay calm for Rose. "Of course I'll help you, Rose. Everything will be okay. Now, can you just describe the room for me?"

"The phone's on a table between two beds. I'm sitting on one of them. The bedspread is all soft and has lots of little bumps. There's a TV on the wall, and windows next to a door with a chain, and drinking cups with plastic on them, and I can't move the lamp. David's clothes are on the other bed in a suitcase. There's some heavy bags of something else in here, too. I tried to pick one up and I couldn't."

"Rose, it sounds like you're in a motel room. Is there a phone book there, maybe on a shelf under the table?"

There was a pause while Laura could hear Rose opening and closing a drawer.

"Here, I have it."

"Look at the front of it. What does it say?"

"It says *Presented by The Gideons*."

"That's very good, Rose, but it's the other book. Its cover is probably yellow."

"Oh." Rummaging sounds. "It says Redding."

Redding. California? "Rose, you are going to be fine. I can help you come home now. Especially if I could speak with David."

"Weasel took the phone away from him when David shattered the mirror and put him in a time out. He said I should talk to you instead."

What the hell is going on? "All right, Rose, can I

speak with Weasel?"

"Just a minute. I'll see."

Laura could hear the lower rumbling of a masculine voice. Her nerves wound tighter as she waited for the Defender. Finally he came to the phone. "Hey, doc, did you hear the one about the Multiple who went into a bar and said 'Do I come here often?' Ha!"

"Weasel. I don't feel like joking," Laura snapped.

"Well, shit, don't go all hard-ass on me, doc. I just wasted some of my best material on you."

"Weasel, what's happened to David?" She was so frustrated with him it was just as well he was in another state.

"He's okay. The pussy just cut himself when he broke the mirror. It hurt but I bandaged the wound. He's going to live. Don't be such a fusspot."

"Why did he break the mirror?"

It was a while before Weasel answered and when he did, he'd lost his good humor. "I can tell you some things, doc, because Nathan is asleep. So listen up. David saw the Rage when he looked into that mirror. I've tried to keep them apart, but sometimes I get so worn out, you know? He shattered it before I could stop him. He didn't break his hand, but I can't let him come to the phone. I don't want him to be this scared. It hurts us all when he gets a glimpse of what's creeping around inside. We could all shatter apart just like that mirror."

His voice broke and he sounded what? Exhausted? Defeated? Close to tears? "I don't know if I, if I can keep holding …"

The silence roared in her ears. "If you can keep holding what, Weasel? Are you there?" She wanted to be in the room with him, not hundreds of miles away and at a loss. She nearly pleaded, "Weasel, are you safe? What's going on? Where are you?"

And just like that, the smartass Weasel was back in control. "Hold it, doc. You forget how this works? You ask a question and give me time to answer it before you ask another one."

Laura took a deep breath. "Okay, start with the first one. Are you safe?"

"What the hell, I'll go for all three. Yeah, we're safe. Safe as we ever get. I've been driving for hours trying to get home from Arizona. I was dozing at the wheel, and Nathan was too beat to help, so he checked into this dump. They don't even have Magic Fingers on the beds, can you believe that? Anyway, I lost track of time, and David woke up. He didn't know where he was and went all scaredy cat. So he called you and panicked with the mirror. But I'm here now so we're all right."

"Why were you in Arizona?"

"I'm doing my job, doc. You like to see us work for a living, right? Good therapy and all."

Laura was confused. "I know Nathan helps David with his carpentry, but do you do that, too?"

"Shit, no. I have my own job. I don't want David anywhere around when I'm working."

"Why not? Are you doing something that puts David in danger?"

Weasel switched to a whisper, as though he didn't want to be overheard. "Just the opposite, doc. I'm trying to keep him out of danger. So I do what they tell him to do."

"You do what who tells him to do, Weasel?" Laura found herself whispering, too. And squirming in her seat.

"I pick up heroin in Arizona and bring it back to the Seekers."

Laura was stunned. "You're getting heroin for the Seekers of the Absolute Pathway?" Rob had told her about Mexican heroin, and now her own client could tie it to the cult. At least one part of her client. A part that only appeared now and then. *Shit. Like anyone but me would believe that.* "Does David know this?"

"Try to keep up, doc. David doesn't break laws. I do it for him. The brothers will punish him if I don't do it. Torture him. And you're the one who tells us we each have to keep the body safe."

That was true enough. She did tell them they were all responsible for its wellbeing. But she hadn't exactly had drug running in mind.

"I do the pickups so David doesn't know what's happening. If the cops ever stop us, he might look guilty as hell, but he could pass any lie detector test. Far as he's concerned, he really isn't doing it. Even if they still bust him, he can't lead them to the Seekers since he has no idea what's happening. They won't be touched. The Prophet set up the whole operation. Pretty damn smart, yes?"

"Yes, smart. But appalling to use a disturbed

human being in such a way."

Weasel snorted. "Sometimes I wonder if you're the sharpest pencil in the box, doc. They're not just using us for this stuff. They created us to do it."

Sarah Fletcher had told her it was true back at the conference. She'd said that some multiples were created. Laura heard the words then, but did not fully digest them. Not really. It was just too mind-boggling, too horrible a lesson to learn. She forced herself to face it head on now. *Abishua is creating people who will do anything he wants.*

She barely heard Weasel because he spoke so low. "I'm way out on a limb here, doc. He created us and can destroy us. Please, doc. Nobody can find out I told you."

"Weasel, that cult has no right to make you do this. We can go to the Sheriff -"

"You're our doc, doc. You can't tell." Weasel sounded on the brink of panic. "Something's happening in here, in the Forum. Something bad. I've said too much. Nathan may have awakened already."

Hearing his fear, she crossed her legs in one direction and then the other as she made a quick decision to shun Health Department codes. "Weasel, I will come get you."

"Yeah, right. A Valkyrie swooping in on her high horse." Weasel was full of bluster once more. "Fuck, no. I'll be back home by sundown. I have to be. They're waiting. But, hey, before I hang up on you, I'm sorry about your friend."

The hair on the back of her neck began to rise. "My friend?"

"That newspaper lady."

"How did you know about Helen?"

"The Sheriff's deputy told Nathan."

"How does he know Nathan?"

"Well, they're both Seekers, you know."

Jesus. Holly was right. A deputy was in the cult. Laura pressed Weasel about one more thing. "How did you know Helen was my friend?"

"Doc, you'd piss your pants if I told you everything they know about you and your newspaper friends." With that, he hung up.

Piss my pants. No fucking kidding. Laura scurried down the hall to complete the mission she'd started before Lovella had tracked her down.

She sat in the stall long after her bladder was relieved. But her brain was in turmoil. If the cult knew all about her and her newspaper friends, they must be watching her. *Wouldn't I notice them creeping up behind me?* Besides, how reliable a source was Weasel, a mentally ill guy who was not even real? David wouldn't be able to confirm any of this. So maybe they weren't really in danger. But then again, if the cult was behind Helen's death, they'd be capable of about anything. Her nerves prickled.

I'm a counselor. She wasn't a law enforcement officer, and didn't want to be. The closest she got to that was *Miami Vice* and, let's face it, she watched that mostly for the beefcake. She had no gun, no handcuffs, and no experience with manhandling bad guys. All she knew was how to help cure people.

She sighed. *At least I don't have to go get Weasel.* She'd rather not explain to Rob or Eudora or the feds that she was crossing state lines to pick up a drug runner. She needed to talk to Rob, though. They'd both seen Cadman and David the day they went into the Sheriff's office, although Rob only knew him as Nathan. Maybe it wasn't a coincidence that they were there right at that time.

First, I have to leave this ladies room. She went back to her office, which was only a little larger than the bathroom cubicle. She called Rob, but the phone rang and rang before the newspaper's switchboard operator picked up and said he was out on assignment.

"Why can't you ever find a reporter when you need one?" Laura muttered slamming down the receiver. "What the hell do I do now?"

She was gun shy about calling Sheriff Elwood with something else she couldn't prove. Hell, it was farfetched, but maybe the Sheriff was as involved as her deputy. Rob had seen a city cop in the cult photos Mule took, so Laura didn't want to call them, either. Besides, she kept coming back to the same old issue. As a counselor, she could reveal nothing about a client unless a life was in danger.

In fact, Weasel had said that if she told, she would put his life in danger. She now knew that the Absolutists were part of the industry that shoved narcotics into the veins, noses, and rectums of America. Was that enough for her to break her commitment to Weasel and get David in trouble, even though he knew nothing about the crime?

Besides, she still couldn't connect the dots between David and Helen. Maybe there was a link between another member of the cult, but not David. He was not Helen's murderer.

Was he?

Where had his wife Cathy really gone?

Maybe she should go to her boss, Tom. *Well, now there's a laugh.* He didn't believe in MPD at all, much less one personality keeping secrets from another.

When her thoughts were as tangled as a bowl of spaghetti, she had an idea that cheered her no end. Sarah Fletcher in Port Townsend, Washington, was the only person she could hash the whole thing over with and break no confidences.

She dove into her purse and unearthed a battered business card that was down there with some linty Tic Tacs, a bent paper clip, wadded Kleenex and other bottom feeders. Sarah not only answered the phone, she even sounded delighted to hear from Laura. "I've thought about you so often since the conference. Wished we could share another lunch. At least another one of those big cookies."

"You and me both," Laura was so relieved to hear Sarah's husky voice that she felt flushed with gratitude. "Do you have a minute to hear what's been going on?"

"Just let me get a cup of tea," Sarah said.

While she waited, Laura imagined the pudgy little woman's natural habitat. A light and airy office cluttered with heavy books and comfy seating in bright geometric prints. No family photos, not if she counseled people there, but something serene like a painting of the Washington rainforest or a pod of orcas ...

"Mmm, lemon ginger. Good for the digestion," Sarah said with a slurp. Laura could also hear the scrunch of a leather office chair. "Okay, shoot."

Laura gave Sarah an earful about Helen's death, the Herkimer murders and Weasel's drug running. Throughout Sarah made soothing little *oh, um, what* noises of interest and concern. Just sharing with her was a great comfort, that and the fact that she didn't accuse Laura of wigging out.

"Maybe I should have chosen mint medley tea to refresh my brain, dear. We need some serious think time."

Together, they hashed it over, kicking around Laura's concerns and next steps. They were both convinced she could not breech client confidentiality. That was a given. From there, they worked out several possible scenarios. Finally, they agreed on two action plans that Laura could put in play.

First, Laura would tell Rob about the heroin trafficking, making sure he understood that her source was a very disturbed man. The story supported the Mule's own claim that the cult might be involved. Rob was the investigative reporter, not Laura. He'd be better at it than she was. With these two leads, he would dig out more of the story. Besides, he was closer to law enforcement than she was. He'd known the Sheriff for a long time, and was in a better position to evaluate whether they could really count on Rita Elwood.

Second, Laura would press David to confront the truth that he was running drugs, under the cover of Weasel. She had to try to make him stop. If he would, then Laura's problem became moot. David would no longer be a criminal. She could live with herself for not naming him. And with the new self-knowledge he gained, she could help him see that he must stay away from the cult.

Sarah invited her to call anytime or come for a visit soon. "It's beautiful here. I see islands and mountains across the water. Very calming."

Laura was so relieved after their conversation, it felt like she had shared the tea and the view with Sarah. She calmly placed her second call to Rob. But there was still no answer.

CHAPTER THIRTY-TWO

Laura figured the end of the day had to go better than the beginning. *Nothing like a morning from hell to make an afternoon outing sound fun.*

It wasn't bowling this time, but an opportunity for the clients to socialize while sharing a meal. Rapid River Pizza Parlor let them come for a discounted price if they arrived after the lunch rush. Laura and Jenny loaded the van with Diaper Man, Woodrow, Vlad and four other clients to arrive at the little restaurant just after 2 o'clock.

Laura talked Colleen into joining them since she needed to socialize. The pizza parlor was near the library where she worked, so she could take a late lunch hour. Laura even cleared it with the girl's boss in advance.

"Nobody will want to sit with me," Colleen fretted.

"I promise you can sit with me," Laura answered. That sealed the deal.

Colleen was outside waiting for them when Jenny drove the van into the restaurant parking lot. In the gusty breeze, her freeform smock billowed around her tall slender form like laundry dancing on a line.

"You could have waited inside," Laura said to her as they unloaded.

"I didn't want to go in by myself." Self-assurance was always at a low ebb for Colleen, but at least today she looked happy, even managing a smile for Vlad. Or maybe at him.

A waitress led them through the restaurant to a large reserved table at the back. Jenny herded the group together, and Laura brought up the rear. Other late diners momentarily stopped eating or talking long enough to stare at them. They reminded Laura of ruminants interrupted while chewing their cuds. It irritated her, the normal judging the abnormal. *Of course, we are a pretty unusual group.* Laura glanced from Woodrow's aluminum hat to Vlad's white pancake foundation and black lipstick.

They each took their fill from the all-you-can-eat buffet. Colleen, who had claimed the chair directly across the table from Laura, stacked a plate with salad, then a second with chicken and potatoes, then another with pizza. Laura was amazed that such a willowy girl could eat so much. Finally she realized that Colleen and Dorothy and Candi Rapper were all eating. Along with heaven knows who else.

Everyone was having a messy, noisy good time until Colleen looked up from her plate and froze. Her jaw clamped tight on a bite of cinnamon roll, and her eyes were as wide as the full moon, staring at something just past Laura's head. Laura felt like Freddy Krueger must be right behind her.

But when she turned to look, it was a handsome man, tall and elegant. Laura felt instantly drawn toward him as if she were a divining rod. He was absolutely compelling, with silver gray hair and eyes such a light brown they could almost be called golden. Wolf eyes.

"Hello, Colleen," he said in a voice as smooth as velvet. He walked to the end of the table and stared down at her. "How nice to see you again." He might as well have slapped her. All the fun drained from Colleen's face, and she crumpled in on herself.

Laura was instantly on the alert. *Who is he? What does he want?*

The girl gagged down the bite of roll and mumbled, "I ... I have to go back to work now." She nearly knocked the chair over, scurrying away like a field mouse in terror of the hawk's shadow.

The stranger, beside Laura and close to her ear, said, "Goodness, she acts like I frightened her. Why do you suppose?"

She turned to frown at him. "Suppose you explain that to me."

He reached out a hand for her to shake. "Dr. Laura Covington, I presume. I am the Prophet Abishua. I am also Colleen's father."

A shockwave tore through her. She tried to be still as stone, hoping her face gave him no hint of how much he had distressed her. *The son of a bitch is Colleen's father. David's, too.* She'd known their abusive father was in the cult. But she hadn't known he was Abishua, the leader. How could anyone do what this monster had done to his own children?

She was in a restaurant with other diners. Her clients were all around, finishing their desserts. Jenny was even surreptitiously peeking at the handsome stranger. Yet Laura felt alone, endangered. Abishua not only brutalized her clients, but may have ordered Helen's death. She would never touch that extended hand.

"Yes. I have heard of you," she said.

Abishua dropped his hand then straightened the chair that Colleen vacated. He sat down across from Laura. His body moved with grace and ease. When he smiled it was positively breathtaking, as though goodness and strength radiated from within. *What charisma!* How hard to resist if she were a weaker woman. She felt awed by the mystery of such power.

New studies revealed psychopaths were biologically wired from birth to be without conscience. There was no known cure for such evil. As a counselor, maybe she should feel bad for him. But anger erupted in her system like lava, burning away any sympathy. He would not conquer her as he had so many others.

"And I have heard of you," Abishua said. "Colleen no longer visits our church, but you see another of our members. Nathan, our carpenter."

"I'm surprised he discusses it with you."

"Oh, my dear, we have no secrets at the Seekers of the Absolute Pathway. In fact, he mentioned this little event for your clients. He was too busy to join the festivities, of course. He must complete his chores for me before he can pass the time of day with you. I will always come first."

It was a blatant attempt to put her in her place. But two could play. "Is that why you're here? If I'm so unimportant, it's amazing you felt the need to waste your time on me."

"Oh, you're certainly not unimportant. In fact, I believe you have been quoted as a reliable source about my group. Although you have never met us."

"I can't imagine what you are talking about. As you said yourself, I have met at least two of your members." From the corner of her eye, she saw Diaper Man ogling the Prophet and pretending to fan his face, as though Laura had landed a major hunk. Jenny, with more of a question than a leer, was moving closer as she got the clients ready to leave. Laura raised a thumb, indicating to the caseworker that she was okay.

Abishua appeared to notice the exchange but ignored it. "I thought you might relish the opportunity to meet us all. At one of our fellowship meetings. We would certainly prefer you to your inquisitive newspaper friends."

She'd rather visit a vomitorium than the cult. Not only was this man hazardous waste, but she couldn't abide the thought of watching all those misguided wretches dancing to his tune. He would not get his rocks off by intimidating her. "I know all that I need to know about you, Abishua. It is enough for me."

"What could you possibly know about me?" he scoffed.

She let him have it. "I know you are a psychopath. You have no true friends. Anyone with genuine self-worth wouldn't choose to be near you. You are alone among those sad followers of yours. You have never felt real remorse or sorrow, but on the other hand, you will never experience true joy or love. You believe you are in control, but you don't understand the human animal well enough for that. You have so little comprehension of human emotion you don't even know that it will bring you down. And try as you might, you will never succeed in being one of us."

For a flash, she saw the monster within leer through his golden eyes. Then he recovered. "My goodness, such rhetoric." He looked around at her troubled little group. "I should prefer to associate with poor souls such as these?"

Condescending bastard. "I do not consider them to be poor souls. These are my clients and they deserve respect." She tried to remain her composure, but she knew her voice was rising along with her temperature.

Jenny approached, haltingly. "Laura? We should be leaving soon ... everything okay?"

"Yes, I'm fine," Laura said, standing and facing the Prophet. "I'm sorry we have no time to continue our chat. Of course, it would be unethical for me to say anything to you about Nathan anyway."

"Of course. But I am so pleased to have met you." Abishua stood, towering over her.

"Don't be too pleased. The Sheriff is sure to run you to ground, and I will certainly help if I can."

"Idle threats don't become you, my dear. There's nothing you can do, because there's nothing you can say. Those professional ethics you just mentioned."

She glared then turned to walk away, stiffening

her spine when she heard him say, "Nathan is right about one thing. You certainly are a beauty worth pursuing."

Was it a threat? Laura shuddered but never looked back.

As she helped Jenny buckle the clients into the van, she was sure the Prophet was watching. Her instinct was to run to Rob and tell him Abishua had frightened her. But as they drove back to Community Mental Health, she knew she wouldn't do such a thing. Rob might run him over with his pickup, then rock back and forth on the body. And Rob wasn't the one she wanted imprisoned for life. She decided to tell him little about the run in with the cult mastermind.

Laura was rarely foolish. She stayed away from dark alleys, haunted mansions, cheap motel showers, and all the other places fair maidens seemed compelled to go. But she hadn't been able to hold her tongue with Abishua. She would have to watch her back from now on.

***

Abishua intended to scare her, and he knew he'd succeeded. But her strength surprised him. She hid fear better than most. She was intelligent and resistant. It excited him.

How very intriguing she was in every way. She was stunning. Elegant, chestnut hair, creamy skin, full breasts, a beautiful face marred only by a frown. He wanted to run his hand high up between those long legs and probe the heat at her core. How he could humiliate her. And what a pleasure it would be when he brought her down.

***

Rob tried to reach Laura at the office only to be told by Lovella she was on one of those client outings. When he called her at home in the evening she seemed distant, or maybe just worn out from the strain of the day.

"At the restaurant where we took our clients? Abishua was there. So I've finally met him. What a charmer."

"Did he bother you?"

"Not really. Not as much as this part of the day," she said, changing the subject. Laura related her conversation with a client who confirmed the cult was part of a drug operation. But she still wasn't revealing any names. Of course, if the source was an imaginary character, what good would it do anyway?

The next morning, Rob sat in the Sheriff's office cramped beside the Mule, contemplating a very troubled Rita Elwood. Deputy Big D came in just long enough to drop off a pile of paperwork, and it felt like they were trying to wedge bodies into a phone booth. Rob recoiled, wondering if this was the deputy that Holly and Laura's client had mentioned. *Is he in the cult? Was he first on the scene after Helen crashed? Did he tip the car over on her?* Every instinct told Rob that he could at least trust Sheriff Elwood. *But.*

It was two days since Holly and Annie had left the Seekers. Rob knew they were with a representative from Children's Services, an indefatigable woman appropriately named Melody. She was arranging a handshake with a similar service in Chico, California. Holly's Aunt Lucille had agreed to take them in, at least until Holly got settled enough to know where she'd go next. The aunt's exact address was not being revealed.

"Not even your deputies know, right?" Rob asked.

"Even I don't know. Big D will take them to Medford, and the aunt will meet them there to drive them the rest of the way down to Chico."

Rob nodded. As county Sheriff, the investigation was up to Rita, with the small city cop shop pitching in. He knew that under her direction, they were doing all the proper things, canvassing door-to-door, following leads, indexing and cross-indexing information. But no arrests were on the horizon, and Rob knew the county commissioners were breathing down her neck.

Rita was currently untwisting a paper clip into as straight a wire as possible. She said, "The only helpful information from the crime lab is that the size and shape of the wounds in Ben Herkimer's head are a match to the head wounds on the parking lot attendant. Both were bludgeoned with the same device."

"I'll be damned," the Mule muttered.

"So one killer clubbed them both," Rob added. They'd never even considered it. "What possible connection could there be between an older couple like the Herkimers and a teenage homey like Head Case?"

"And if Holly is right, Abishua and Cadman were surprised about the Herkimers' murders. So that lets them off the hook." Elwood started in on a second paper clip. Rob and the Mule both watched distractedly.

"No buttons left at the scenes?" the Mule asked. "No hairs or threads or telltale fingerprints?"

"No matchbooks from a local dive, no business cards. None of those handy clues that TV shows are made of," Elwood replied.

"What about the drug angle?" Rob asked. He'd already told the Sheriff as much as he could of Weasel's story.

"Whenever drugs are involved, I have to alert the DEA. So I called. They told me that with a psychologist unwilling to name names, and street talk provided by a behind-the-scenes source," she paused to glare at the Mule, "and no proof of connection to the deaths around here, well, they'd rather I handle the whole thing. Insinuated that if I did my job better, they'd have something to work with."

"Asses tightly covered."

"Buns of steel." She sighed, dumping the tortured paper clips into the trash. "I wouldn't be talking to you two, but you're better than any investigators I got. Big D and Little D are good at the footwork, but not so much at the brainwork." Rob knew that Little D got his name because he was just barely big enough to be a deputy at all. He was currently manning the front desk and phone lines.

Big D tapped on the office door and said, "The

Children's Services woman is done now. I'm ready to take them to Medford."

Rob stood. "I think I'll just drive her down there myself, Big D. Save you the trip. Save the taxpayers some deputy dollars, too."

"Guess I'll go along for the ride," the Mule said.

The Sheriff looked at them both quizzically, and Big D began to protest, but she cut him off by telling him he was back on local patrol for the day. She needed all the help she could get.

The Mule and Rob headed out to the parking lot with Holly and Annie. Mother and daughter were pleased to have the newsmen as escorts. "We won't trust any deputy, since you don't know which one it is," Rob said to Holly. "We'll be careful that we're not followed. But Holly, common sense says the cult will give up on you now. They don't want to do anything too visible, not if they're into some of the other stuff we think they're doing." Rob hoped he was right as he helped her into the front seat of the van, next to the Mule. "I don't think you need to worry now."

"Okay, but you guys watch yourselves," Holly said. "Some of the Seekers have big shot jobs in town. They let Abishua know what's going on."

"Great," the Mule said, looking into the rearview mirror at Rob. "A cop, a deputy ... doctors, lawyers, Indian chiefs. Getting to be worse than the DMZ to live in Rapid River."

Rob sat in the back with Annie. He kept an eye on the road behind them, watching for a tail. But it was quiet as they travelled down Highway 62E toward

Medford, nearly two hundred miles away. It gave him plenty of time to worry about what might be waiting for them up ahead instead of behind.

All went according to plan. Aunt Lucille met them right on time in the Harry & David store parking lot. But just before the women drove away toward Chico, Holly dropped her last bomb. "So much has happened that I forgot to tell you one thing."

"Yes?" Rob asked, eager to be on his way.

"Annie said there were drawings of Trooper Snoop in Wade's room. She saw them when they were playing together."

"Yes?"

"The Seekers made up Trooper Snoop to scare the kids and keep them in line. A man pretends to be him sometimes. Somebody at Wade's day care is awfully close to that group."

Until that very second, Rob hadn't known you could literally feel like your blood ran cold. He leaped back into the van and told the Mule to get him to a pay phone. But he was too late. According to Lovella, Laura had already left her office to pick up Wade.

CHAPTER THIRTY-THREE

Laura had a late afternoon session with Carl, an obsessive-compulsive who could never remember whether he turned off his car ignition. She had suggested he keep a notebook so he could consult it instead of running out to the car repeatedly. Now he was compulsive about keeping perfect notes, writing them again and again. *That went well.*

When she arrived at Lil Pals, thoughts of Carl vanished. As usual, a boisterous circle of kids surrounded Miss Judy in their fenced side lawn, some on playground equipment and others waving projects they were eager to show to the parents picking them up.

Laura drove up to the front, looked around, then called from her car to the day care manager, "Hi, Judy. Where's Wade?"

"Wade?" Miss Judy looked around. "He was just here. On the swings. Maybe he ran over to Jumping Beans to meet you."

Laura swung the car around to the coffee stand's lot. She looked at the little tables where they often sat. No Wade. She got out and asked the baristas. No Wade. She jogged back to the day care. No Wade.

"He was right here with the other kids!" Miss Judy exclaimed.

"I need your phone." Laura hustled inside and called the police. *Answer, answer, please answer.* But when she did, the dispatcher said he was probably just walking home.

"No, he wouldn't do that. Not without me."

"You never know what kids get up to, do you? You just go on home, and remember, it won't do him a bit of good if you get hurt, so take your time and drive safely. I'll bet he's waiting on the doorstep. We'll send a patrol car right around."

Okay, this is how I walk to the car, and open its door, and put the key in the ignition, no, not that key, this key. I leave the lot like this, and look both ways, searching for him on the sidewalk, this side and that, all the way home. I don't panic. I don't. Wade. Wade.

He wasn't on the doorstep, but Eudora was. The old woman was holding their mail, trembling with fury, tears forging crooked paths through the wrinkles in her cheeks. "Look at this shit," she nearly screamed, thrusting pictures at Laura. "They were in our mail box."

There were two photographs. Both were images of little boys, one performing fellatio on an adult, the other being sodomized. Both photos were cropped so the man's face didn't show. The word STOP was hand scrawled across the top of each.

Laura had never seen anything so crude, so in violation of decency, so agonizing when your own boy was missing.

"Mama," she whimpered, using the word she hadn't said in years. "Wade is missing." Her vision narrowed to a tunnel, and she simply couldn't breathe.

A cop arrived at that moment, just in time to support her before she could fall. The muscular policewoman, whose name Laura never did get, lead the two terrified women inside then sat them down at the kitchen table. Eudora sobbed. Laura was struck virtually senseless, but she managed to get her lungs working again, forcing air through her system. *This is how I breathe.*

"Where might he go?" the officer asked, not unkindly but with firmness.

"Nowhere," Laura gasped. "He wouldn't go anywhere. Not without me, not without Eudora."

Her brain began to process the shock, and she knew. The photos were a threat. *They hadn't come for me ... they'd come for my son!*

"They took him! Not me! Him!"

Her shriek startled the cop. "Who, ma'am? Who took him?"

"That cult. Abishua. The Seekers out in the desert. They have him!"

"A desert cult? Why would they do that, ma'am?"

"There's no time for stupid questions. Get there. Find him." Laura realized she was shouting but couldn't stop herself.

What would he do to Wade? What would the sick bastard do?

The police woman spoke quickly into her radio. It burped and hissed as other cops and the dispatcher cut in and out. Finally, knowing Laura was close to hysteria, the policewoman explained they already had two cars out looking for a lone child, because he was so young. For an older child, she would have had to wait 24 hours before they assisted. And she had just sent another patrol car out to the Absolutist ranch.

"Do you have a picture of Wade, ma'am?"

Laura rose, so dizzy she nearly lost her balance, then tottered to the refrigerator. She pulled two photos from behind a starfish magnet.

"That's him with a llama. And this one on his bike."

"Did you recognize the children in the photos from your mail box?"

"No. Oh, God, those poor babies."

While Laura struggled to get control again, the policewoman asked, "Is that a picture of a policeman ...the drawing on the fridge?"

"Yes, that's Trooper Snoop," Eudora said, taking over for her daughter. "The kids at day care draw him, then hang pictures so he can keep an eye on them."

The policewoman made coffee, and gave each woman a cup. Laura and her mother held hands across the table. The cop told them they'd find their boy. Laura and Eudora told each other they'd find him. But Laura didn't believe it.

A heavy silence descended on this house that had grown so used to childish laughter. It was broken briefly when Rob called. "I tried you earlier. We're on our way back from Medford."

"Wade's missing. Come home."

Laura heard him gasp as though hit in the stomach. "I'm on my way."

The only other disruption was Spock slinking from room to room, meowing for his friend. The minutes ticked by.

***

Abishua was not at the ranch so no cop would find him there. No proof of involvement. Nothing at all. It made him smile to be so clever, as he looked down at the naked boy drowsing on a cot near a desk.

They were in the back office at Lil Pals, a place the children were taken for a time out when they misbehaved. Abishua had given Wade a triazolam hypnotic, enough to calm him, enough for Abishua to begin his work. He'd undressed Wade because, just like an adult, a child feels vulnerable and humiliated when naked.

At five, Wade was likely too old to become one of Abishua's more successful creations, as he liked to call them. *But can I terrify him, make him a sad little bundle for Laura to handle? Absolutely.* All it took was a child with no way out.

Abishua had ordered Trooper Snoop to begin the conditioning days ago when Wade brought his cat to school. Trooper Snoop reported that he'd told Wade he was very bad and took him to this room to be punished. He'd held up Spock by the scruff of his neck next to a cat pelt, and told Wade his pet would be skinned just like that.

Wade had pleaded for his friend's life. He'd be good, he'd be good, he'd do what he was told. So Trooper Snoop gave him one more chance. But if he told anybody what had happened, he would be skinned alive, too, along with his cat.

Of course, Wade had no idea what he had done that was bad. Abishua knew the boy would be in a state of fear, with no way out but to blame himself for whatever might happen. He would keep the secret to himself. Abishua had ordered this done to enough children to know exactly how it worked.

Now the Prophet would terrify the child again. He pulled a desk chair next to the cot, and patted Wade's cheek to rouse him from the hypnotic stupor. The child blinked and looked around. The room itself was enough the frighten him. He was in the punishment room.

"Where are my clothes?" Wade asked.

"I am the Prophet," Abishua declared in a deep, scary voice. Wade looked up at the big stranger. Abishua could see his confusion. "Trooper Snoop said you have been very bad. Again. I'm ashamed of you. Your Gram is ashamed of you. She's disgusted with you."

"No! I haven't! I haven't been bad. I haven't told."

Abishua patted his cheek, this time harder. "You will call me Prophet. Is that clear?"

"I don't know you. Gram says I can't talk to strangers."

Abishua slapped him hard enough to sting. "I am your Prophet. Now say it."

He watched the boy try not to cry. It tickled him to see the fire in the child. But he would bend.

He lowered his hand and pinched Wade's thigh.

"Answer me."

Wade, clumsy with the drug, tried to push his hand away. "Stop. You're hurting me."

"I'll stop when you call me Prophet." He added a vicious twist to the pinch.

Wade succumbed. "Pro ... Prophet."

"And you'll do what I say."

Wade nodded.

"Say it."

"Yes, Prophet." Now Wade cried.

Abishua released the boy's flesh. "Good. Stand up." He helped Wade stand, wobbly as the Prophet turned him to face the cot. Abishua sat right behind him, caging the child between his knees. From the desk behind him, he took an old fashioned metronome and placed it on the cot in front of Wade. He set it ticking at a quick pace.

"Listen to the ticking, Wade," he said, his mouth next to the boy's ear. "Tick, tick, tick. When you hear it sound just like that again, you will think of me. Tick, tick, tick. You will remember then to be a good boy for the Prophet."

Still trapping the boy with his knees, he picked up a bag from the desk. He opened it and pulled out a white bunny, placing it on the cot as well. Its feet were tied together. Abishua put a big kitchen knife on the cot.

"It's a pretty bunny, isn't it? Answer me."

"Y-ye-es, Prophet," whimpered Wade.

"All white and fluffy."

"Yes, Prophet."

"You can pet it if you want."

Wade reached out and touched the fur. "It feels soft. Hi, Bunny."

"Yes." Abishua picked up the knife and placed Wade's hand around its hilt. "Now I want you to kill the bunny."

"No! No! I won't." Wade tried to drop the knife, but Abishua squeezed it into his hand.

The metronome ticked. Abishua crooned into Wade's ear, "You will. You will because I command it." Tick, tick, tick. "You will or I will kill your Gram. Do it now, or she will die. It will be your fault. Nobody will ever want you again."

Abishua knew that if Wade were a little older he might figure a way out. But he was only a scared little boy, clouded with a hypnotic, one who had already lost a Mommy. After a few more protests, the child finally struck the rabbit with the knife. It shrieked so he struck it again. And again. Tick, tick, tick. He went on and on in a frenzy.

Abishua was sure in the passing of an instant another presence took shape within Wade and took hold of the knife. This presence accepted the Prophet as its master and liked the feel of warm blood on its hands. The only way the child could endure the horror was to fragment off a part of himself that had the power to withstand the abuse. There might be other splinters, too, but Abishua thought of them as trace elements. He only coveted the ones that could perpetrate and tolerate evil.

"You will tell no one about this, Wade," Abishua

continued softly in his ear. "You are a good boy now." Wade twisted around looking for comfort, and the Prophet held the sobbing child in his arms.

"You have saved your Gram by doing just what I say. How brave you are. What a good boy. When you awake at home, you won't remember much of this. But whenever you hear a tick, tick, tick just like this, on the phone or wherever you are, you will be ready to hear my words and do whatever I require. You can never tell your Gram because she will hate you if you do. I am the only person in the world who will ever love what you really are."

***

In the end, Wade was gone less than an hour. He appeared alone at the back door, entered the kitchen and staggered into Laura's arms. "Wade!" Laura and Eudora exclaimed together. The policewoman crossed herself, then contacted dispatch to call off the search.

"Don't be mad," was all that the child managed before he began to cry. Laura cuddled him close whispering how much they loved him, and that they weren't mad, and that everything would be okay. Eventually he said, "I woke up in the park." But he looked terrified when he glanced at the policewoman and would say no more.

Two more cops came in the back door, both looking jubilant at the boy's return. One of them asked to see Laura, so she gave Wade to Eudora to hold, then she went to the living room with the officer.

"I'm Jerry Cassidy," he said. He tried to dispel her fears, saying he doubted that the boy had been hurt, that the porn was somebody's idea of a sick joke. "The two events may not even be related," he said with an encouraging smile. "Just lousy timing."

Nonetheless they would take the offensive material and test for fingerprints. She should be assured they considered it a serious matter, even if the boy had been gone so little time there was no way anyone could have taken him to the desert cult and back. He'd just fallen asleep in the park. Kids. Still, did the boy have a particular doctor? If so, maybe Laura should contact him.

Laura nodded, then left a message on Dr. Latimer's emergency line. In Portland, she might have waited forever. But in the little town of Rapid River, the pediatrician came to her house immediately after his hospital rounds. He examined Wade, and told her the boy was definitely groggy, his pupils dilated. He certainly could have been drugged, but had not been harmed, at least not physically. There was no more than a fresh bruise on his thigh which certainly wasn't unusual for any active little boy. The doctor drew a blood sample for analysis, and suggested the importance of counseling to the counselor. But Laura was way ahead of him. Wade needed an expert with children now.

Eventually the police left, with *all's well that ends well* attitudes. But Laura knew that all was definitely not well. She didn't even think to thank the policewoman who had tried to be kind. She put Wade on the sofa, under a comforter, and Spock curled up with him, purring like a feline jackhammer. The boy fell instantly to sleep with Laura and Eudora both staring at him from the soft living room chairs.

"Well. We've certainly had nicer evenings," the old woman muttered before she, too, dozed off. Laura knew the shock had cost her mother dearly, and she loathed Abishua all the more. It was surely that bastard behind this, whether the cops believed it or not.

It had been an hour of pure hell. Something had changed inside of Laura, like tectonic plates shifting to create a harsh new landscape. After battling the emotional turmoil of Helen's death, David's confusion, Annie's plight, and now Wade's disappearance, she felt drained of sorrow and compassion.

She allowed a wildfire of fury to incinerate any inhibitions about doing whatever it took to protect her loved ones. She remembered Helen's last words. "Tell Rob cult ... pals." The newswoman had not just been telling Laura that they were friends. She'd been trying to warn Laura of cult involvement with Lil Pals.

I won't take more of this. I know how to stop it. It will take time, but this will end.

In that moment, Laura crossed from victim to aggressor. Her weapons would be everything she'd learned about the workings of the mind. She could fight dirty, too. No professional ethics would rein her in now. The stakes were just too high.

***

Rob arrived at eleven that evening.

"Is he ..."

"He's home. He's safe."

Rob's relief was clear. Tension drained from his face. But Laura saw it return as she told him the story. When he told her what Holly had said about Trooper Snoop, that the character was a construct of the cult, it simply strengthened her resolve.

"God only knows what's been going on. But from now on, I have to be smart, very smart," she said.

"I don't think that will be a problem, love. You *are* very smart."

"And I need your help."

"I don't think that will be a problem either."

"Will you stay tonight?"

"You couldn't get rid of me."

"I don't think we're in danger tonight, but I can use you if we are. I can use you anyway."

"I agree. The warning has been given. They'll watch to see what you'll do. You're not going to back off, are you?"

"Hell no."

"Nothing I can say would make you?"

"Hell no."

"That's what I figured."

"So first things first. I need a safe place to stash Wade and Eudora for a couple of days while I work things out," said the tougher, icier Laura.

"We weren't followed to Medford today, but the Mule and I may both be under surveillance by the cult here in town. Our places aren't safe enough for them."

"No. But nobody is watching Llama Lady."

Rob looked quizzical for a moment then grinned. "Of course!"

Laura called LL and explained that she was having some trouble with clients acting out. She wanted Wade and his great grandmother out of the house for a couple nights, and she couldn't think of a place Wade would be happier than the ranch. Would LL be willing to take in the littlest ranch hand and a feisty old lady who was one hell of a cook?

"No problem. I'll put 'em both to work. Besides, it gets lonely way out here."

"There could be some danger."

"Not on my watch," Llama Lady huffed. "We can see anyone coming a mile away. Besides, the llamas are damn good watch dogs. And I'm used to picking off rats with Old Thunder. We'll be safe."

"They'll be there in the morning, first thing. Rob will bring them."

Next she gently shook Eudora awake in her chair, and explained that she was sending her away. She cut off any possible argument from her mother by saying, "I'm entrusting Wade's welfare to you. He loves you and will listen to you. Nobody but you can do this for us."

Squaring her shoulders like a good soldier, Eudora agreed. She marched off to pack so she'd be ready to move out at first light.

Rob carried the sleeping boy up the stairs for Laura and put him to bed while Laura loaded a backpack with his favorite clothes. She put *Goodnight Moon* and his teddy bear in the pack the very last thing.

"You'll have to take the cat, too," she said to Rob.

"Glad he doesn't own a pony."

It was late when Laura finally came to her bedroom, stressed but resolved. Tears flowed down her face, but she never made a sound. Rob was waiting for her. He stood to disrobe her ever so slowly, until she was as naked as he was. Then he led her to the bed and told her to lie down on her stomach. He rubbed her neck and shoulders until her muscles could not help but release their tension. He worked his way down her back almost to her buttocks, slowly massaging with his strong hands. Then he moved to her feet, reflexing the arches and ankles, and worked steadily up her calves and thighs, back to her buttocks. She rolled to face him, threw her leg over him, felt his firmness, and murmured, "Please."

He entered slowly, expanding her gently to take in his size. Tonight, she knew this man was not just having sex. He was making love.

CHAPTER THIRTY-FOUR

The next morning, Laura left for work at the usual time. Rob watched the street for suspicious activity but saw only the usual dog walkers and mailman. He loaded Eudora, Wade and Spock into his pickup. Common sense told him anyone watching Laura would have left when she did, but he kept an eye out for followers as he drove toward the foothills. The further from town, the thinner the traffic. His F-150 was eventually alone on the road, other than a coyote that crossed far up ahead.

Wade was withdrawn, not willing to talk to Rob about the day before. He hadn't wanted Rob to put the cat carrier in the back of the truck, so Spock was in his case under Wade's feet. Together, they huddled between Rob and Eudora on the large bench seat.

Dora finally talked Wade into a game of counting cows on the way to the ranch. He beat her when a big herd was on his side. "No fair," she said, "there's nothing over here but unicorns." When Wade turned to look, Dora said, "Gotcha!" It was the closest Wade came to a smile since the day before.

LL met them in the driveway in front of her ranch house. After Rob introduced her to Eudora, the rancher sent Wade to go say hello to the llama he had named Soccer. "She's getting big now. You'll have to train her to walk on a lead while you're here."

"I can do that," Wade agreed as he hustled away toward the barn. Half way there he put on the brakes, turned and asked Dora in a frightened little voice to please come with him. She gave Rob the saddest of smiles, then took off at an awkward trot ignoring her tricky knee. "Bet I can outrun you, young man."

Rob's heart broke for this game old lady, the traumatized boy, and the psychologist who had committed to protecting them.

"Is Laura all right?" LL asked.

"Laura is ... Laura," Rob said. Then he told the rancher more about Wade's disappearance the day before. He confirmed that Laura was making plans to send him to safety. Eudora was to be his chaperone. Rob didn't even hint that Laura was protecting her mother, too. If Eudora caught wind of that, she would be as malleable as a sandstorm.

LL was happy to take in Eudora and Wade, but less thrilled about Spock. Looking down at the carrying case which was now complaining loudly, she said in a bemused voice, "Don't rightly know what to do with an indoor cat."

"Oh don't worry," Rob answered. "This one will set you straight in no time."

Rob was eager to be on his way back into town. He had things to do. Laura would handle the disappearance of Wade in her way, but Rob would in his. Someone would pay for scaring this family, a family he was beginning to think of as *his* family. He ignored speed limits getting back to the *Rapid River*

Review where he checked in with the cops. Then he tracked the Mule down in the editorial room.

"Can you believe it? Kiddy porn," Rob said. "No wonder the bastards have so many youngsters out there at the ranch."

"Probably porn is even more lucrative than the drug running," the Mule replied. "Stills and videos."

"Cops didn't find fingerprints on the photos, other than Laura's and Eudora's. So there's still no actual proof of a link to the Seekers."

"We're newsmen. Who needs proof?"

"And the woman at Lil Pals denies any knowledge of anything. She says he simply disappeared. Boo-hoo, mea culpa and all that shit. Goddamn liar."

"Well, you know, Rob, she may not know much of anything," the Mule said.

"She knows about Trooper Snoop, doesn't she?" Rob snapped back.

"Yeah, but I doubt Abishua and Cadman let women know much about what's going on. Maybe she just thinks it's an Officer Friendly kind of program, a good way to teach kids lessons."

"But what the fuck are the lessons?" The two friends mulled over their own thoughts for a time. Finally, Rob said, "They're too careful to leave us a tidy pile of evidence. We'll never be able to prove what we know. But the pricks have gone too far. It might be time to put a little Nam-type covert action to work."

"Not without me, you don't."

"And Laura doesn't need to know, right?" She had enough to handle without worrying about him.

"I like Laura, Rob. A lot. But you know this isn't about her for me. It's about Helen."

Rob wondered if their women were the best things about most men.

***

While Rob delivered Wade and Eudora to the Llama Lady, Laura spent her morning on the phone. She had Lovella cancel her appointments, and she shut her door. First, she called David to make an appointment for that afternoon. Then she called Sarah Fletcher to explain what had happened to Wade.

She started at the beginning, telling the counselor that Wade was already a survivor of a traumatic background when she met him. "I know almost nothing about his first five years. He was certainly passive when he first came to us. I read that as desperate to please, to keep Eudora and me on his side."

"Very likely."

'But maybe I was wrong. Maybe it was the submissiveness of an abused child. He's also capable of disappearing into a world of his own. Like he's working out issues he won't share with me."

"It's not your specialty, Laura. But it's one of mine. I see a lot of kids now."

"I know, and I need your help. Since he's been here, I've had him in day care. Now I'm sure it's a front for the cult."

"What? You mean the same one where David is involved?"

"That's the one. Then yesterday, he disappeared from Lil Pals." Her voice broke. "The bastards left kiddy porn in my mail box, and they kidnapped my boy."

"Dear God!"

"He was only gone an hour. The cops think he just wandered away. They aren't even going to involve Children's Services since the doctor found no wounds. But I know better. They had him for an hour, Sarah. What could they have done to him?"

"What does the boy say?"

"Only that he woke up on a bench in the park. And not another word. Sarah, you have to believe me. He wouldn't just run away."

"Of course I believe you, Laura. But why do you think Wade won't tell you about it?"

"Because he was told not to? They threatened him? Or Eudora and me? His cat? I just don't know, but if you talk to him, maybe you can find out."

"I'd certainly be willing to, but -"

"Could I send his great grandmother and him to stay in Port Townsend? I'll book them a hotel room. Nobody here will know where they've gone except the person who brings them to you. His name is Rob Cooper. When I can, I'll join them there."

"You'll leave Rapid River?"

"I have some things to do first. Then I'll have to."

There was a pause on the line before Sarah said, "Do you want to tell me what you're going to do?"

"No. You don't want to know." *This I do on my own.*

They made plans for Eudora and Wade. Sarah

would keep an eye on them until Laura could arrive.

Next, Laura called Rob to ask him if he could take her mother and child to Port Townsend. Her call caught him still in the editorial room at the *Review* with the Mule. After she explained what she wanted him to do, Rob flat out refused. "Nunh-unh. No way. I'm not leaving town with you here all on your own."

"But I need -"

"The Mule will do it. He can take them while I stay with you."

"I have to know they're protected by the only person I trust unconditionally," she said, thinking this kind of logic had worked on Eudora.

"You can trust the Mule, and you know that."

"Yes, but Wade doesn't know it. You're the one he trusts. For God sake, he was just terrified by some other man."

Rob had no answer for that. Laura knew she had him, because it was true. Wade did trust Rob.

"Shit, woman, you're too damn smart to fight with. You win. His safety is the most important thing. But I won't leave you more than two days."

"Thank you, my love. You are my Defender." She didn't think Weasel would mind if she used his title. "Wait 'til tomorrow to go. Give Wade a chance to enjoy LL's ranch. A day of calm will be good for him. And another night with you will be good for me." Next, Laura told him she didn't want to know how he would get to Port Townsend. "I think its safest if neither of us has all the information."

"Sounds a little paranoid, but I'm through arguing

with you, so I'll just agree right now."

They discussed options in general terms. Port Townsend was on the north coast of Washington's Olympic Peninsula, not quite 400 miles from Rapid River. Rob wouldn't use his truck, because he didn't want it to be recognized. If he chose to drive, he'd rent a car. Or he'd fly with Eudora and Wade out of Redmond, into Seattle and drive from there. He'd leave tomorrow from LL's ranch and call when they were safe in Port Townsend.

"I'll worry about you nonstop, you know that," he said.

"Don't. I have to tie up loose ends here at the department, then I'll be ready to leave myself. If I need any help, I'll call Mule."

"He's here with me now.' He put her on the speaker phone. She would spend that night with Rob at his place, and then stay there each night until he was back, or until she could head to Port Townsend herself. The Mule said he'd keep watch.

As Laura dismantled her carefully constructed new life, she realized she, Rob and Mule could all finally take action. They were done waiting for proof that would stand up in a court of law. It felt good to be on the attack.

***

After saying good-bye to Laura, Rob told the Mule they'd have to wait until he got back from Port Townsend before paying a visit to the cult. The Mule figured that was a good thing anyway. It would take a day or two, but he knew where to get a couple of weapons that couldn't be traced.

CHAPTER THIRTY-FIVE

Laura's plan was underway. She sat in her postage stamp of an office, reviewing her progress and gathering her strength.

Rob's taking Eudora and Wade to safety.
Sarah will help Wade with whatever trauma he's faced.
Colleen will be here later in the week.
David has an appointment with me today.

Laura intended to take control away from the Controller. She would make a weapon of David, a weapon to bring Abishua down.

She'd kill Abishua face to face, but the cult would never let her get that close. So she needed a guided missile to do the job. It would likely destroy David in the process, but that was a horror she was prepared to live with. She never would have believed she could intentionally damage a client. But that was before she had a son.

She tried to console herself that David was so far gone already that he would never be truly well. The rage Abishua had created in him was so deeply rooted, it had warped him forever. Weasel was a criminal, she was suspicious of Nathan, and she could no longer deny that some dark part of David's system had been instrumental in Helen's death. Maybe his missing wife as well. And the Herkimers. At best, he had years of prison ahead. At worst, he would continue to create misery for everyone around him. And for himself.

Laura also told herself that her plan would save other children, along with Wade. Get rid of Abishua, and no more kiddy porn, no more trauma, no more babies with STDs.

Make a weapon of David to turn the creation on the creator. Laura sighed. Deciding to do it didn't automatically mean she could. Failure was more likely than success. As far as she knew, it had never been tried before. There was no precedent in any of the books she'd read or lectures she'd heard. But then, who the hell would admit to something like this?

She planned to reach deep inside David, grab the rage and bring it to the light of day. She was banking on more of the system listening to her than to Abishua. She had to move at a pace no counselor should ever ask of a client. David would feel the massive pain of his own past long before he was ready for such a burden. If she pushed too fast, he could blow wide open. He could kill himself, her, anybody in an uncontrolled frenzy. But if she moved too slow, he might assimilate the changes, learn to accommodate them. She couldn't allow that if she was to succeed.

She decided on three days to expose his wounds and focus his rage. Then it was up to him. This was a dangerous game to play. If she didn't try, she might be a good counselor but a lousy human being.

It was the harshest lesson she'd ever learned.

***

"What's wrong, Dr. Laura? Why did you need to see me today?" David asked as he entered her office that afternoon. Anxiety clouded his normally mild expression.

"Come in David. Please sit down." Laura heard the new steel in her own voice.

"I don't have much time. Nathan and I are working on some furniture for the church, and he says I can't stay long."

"This is important, too, David. Nathan will wait. To move things along, may I speak with Weasel right away?"

"Eh, what's up, doc?" Weasel said, pretending to munch on a carrot.

"Hello, Weasel. We need to be serious today."

"Yeah, you're a little tight-assed if you don't mind my saying so."

Shit! He's so goddamn smart. "We've been working on difficult issues for a while, you and I, but this will be the hardest. It's time for David to confront his past."

Weasel frowned at Laura, looking as if his team had just lost the big game. At last he said, "Yeah. Things are changing now, aren't they, doc? Can't deny it."

"Yes, they are. Changes beyond the Forum's control."

Weasel seemed resigned to the truth of it. "We've done pretty well so far though, right, doc? It's been a hell of a ride."

"The Forum's been terrific, Weasel. But you know you can't hold it together forever. The best way for you to help David now is to tell him exactly what has happened to him. What is still happening. He's ready for the challenge."

This was it. The Defender was cunning. Would he believe her?

His iron resolve showed signs of weakening. "It's tearing the Forum apart, you know, trying to keep him from bursting into a million pieces. It's true. I could use a little help."

She nearly had him. "That's why you have to expose David to the truth. You've defended him for this very moment when he can take control. It's the only way he'll ever be free."

"So how do I do it?"

Success! Now to create her weapon, she needed to remove any gentle impulse within David's system. He must stay angry. "You stand aside while I talk to Rose. You can't interfere if you hear her cry while I speak with her, or come to her rescue. David needs to pick up the load that she is carrying. It's too much for a little girl."

"Take her job away?" Weasel asked, sounding incredulous.

"Yes. It's too much for her, Weasel. You know that. I want you to move over now. Please, may I speak with Rose?"

It was a breathless moment, waiting to see if Weasel would – or even could – comply. He looked at her with sorrow, then slowly closed his eyes. He gathered himself together, curling his feet around the front legs of the chair. His hands reached down and grabbed the sides of the seat and he leaned forward. It was as if a young girl materialized where Weasel had been.

Rose spoke. "Hello, Dr. Laura. Weasel told me you want to see me."

"Hello, Rose. I'm so very glad you're here." That much was true.

"Weasel says it's time to tell David what the men did to him when he was a boy." Rose began picking nervously at a thumbnail.

"Yes, Rose."

"But then I will have no purpose. No one will need me anymore. And I'll disappear."

"Oh, but you will be needed. You'll always be needed by the Little Ones. And loved by us. But it is for David's good. That's been your real job all along, Rose. Protecting David. He needs this from you. You and the Little Ones will let go and move to a safe bright place. Nobody will hurt you there. You will all be happy."

Rose's voice trembled. "I'm frightened, but I trust you."

Laura flinched, but could not allow herself to comfort this child part of the system. *Focus on Wade.* "Good. Tell me what you'll say to David."

"You already know a lot, Dr. Laura. You've guessed at it. The bad men tortured David when he was a small boy. A lot. His father let them beat him and stick their things in his bottom. He made David drive a stake through his puppy. They closed him into a box and told him they buried it underground. He finally burst apart just like they wanted. Like his father wanted. David wasn't whole anymore. The Little Ones were all born then. And I was there to take care of them."

Rose didn't cry. She didn't raise her voice. She stared at Laura and talked as though she were giving testament to a story old as time. "Sarah couldn't get everyone to join the Forum. Even we don't know who all's inside. I think some of them make David hurt people. Hurt them bad."

Rose suddenly gasped in fright. "Weasel's defying them right now, to help you. They want me to stop. They're meaner than he is, and there're more of them." She leaned further forward and whispered, "Nathan told you he's a White Hat, but he is one of them."

Laura was not surprised that Nathan was the system's spy. She knew someone must have been reporting on her.

"The Little Ones and I are what remain of David. Weasel calls us collateral damage. He says when the brothers break a body apart, some innocents escape the badness." Rose stiffened. "We have to hurry, Dr. Laura."

"All right. Tell everything to David, Rose. Do it now."

"I'll try. But Weasel might be overrun. And Nathan is angry."

David returned. He put his chin down on his chest and closed his eyes. Laura watched him carefully, as Rose was revealing his past to him.

At first David smiled. It would be hard not to smile

at Rose. Time passed. He began to moan. His face became a tragedy mask. Tears ran. Sorrow morphed to horror then to fury. David finally opened his eyes, threw back his head and bellowed, "I remember! They did that to me! My father, the rest of them. They did this."

"Yes, David," Laura said, staring rage in the face. *Don't lose him now, control it, keep him focused.* "Your father hurt you, made you hurt others. Your father. Abishua. The others were just doing what he told them to do. He's your enemy."

"Is he a maniac?"

"He is a cancer. Hear my words. Go home. Let yourself remember. Do not lose time. Do not go to your church tonight. More and more of the truth will return to you."

"Tell me now."

"No. You need to think about what has happened. Come back tomorrow. We'll learn how to handle the memories." Laura felt as desolate as David looked.

"I feel all raw, like rubbed with sandpaper inside."

"I know it hurts, David, but it will get better. I'll show you how. You'll be filled with new memories." Laura still wasn't done. "Now before you go, I need one last moment with Rose."

But it wasn't Rose who appeared. "You'll be in trouble for this, *Bitch*," Nathan hissed. "We'll all be in terrible trouble."

"It must be done, Nathan. Get me Rose. Now." Laura assumed the authority of a new commander taking dominion. At this moment, she was more powerful than Nathan. But that might not last.

"Oh, Dr. Laura, I did it. But David's so hurt."

"Thank you, Rose. You did it, and now he can get well. It's time to say good-byee, Rose. You've done your job beautifully and saved David's life. You are very brave. He could not have grown so big and strong if you hadn't taken such good care of him. But now he's powerful enough to accept the Little Ones' pain, so they can let go of it. They still need you to guide them, though, so you will always have a role. You are all free to move into the light, to happiness, with gratitude and love." She allowed her own tears at last.

The last word David said as he left her office wasn't David at all. It was Weasel whispering his own painful good-byee to Rose. He'd held off the others long enough. Rose and the Little Ones were free.

***

If David had called the crisis line that night, they would not have found Laura. She wasn't at home, but at Rob's house, and did not give them the number. She called in periodically just to check, but they had not heard from any of her clients. The session with David had totally exhausted her, and it would resume tomorrow. She was unsure how long she could control the rage she was freeing.

They were all subdued as she, Rob, and the Mule shared carry-out Chinese food around the coffee table in Rob's living room. She told them little of what she was trying to do. It sounded too fantastic. Besides, it would only worry Rob.

None of them spoke much. They were three resolute warriors, each contemplating the battles ahead. Rob would act for her, Mule for Helen, she for Wade. And all three would act for every child under threat from the cult.

CHAPTER THIRTY-SIX

After Laura left for work the next morning, Rob called Llama Lady and told her he would be by soon. First, Mule dropped him at the Redmond airport. Rob didn't tell his friend that he was not there for a flight. Instead, he rented a car. They had all agreed that nobody was to have the whole story, so nobody could easily lead anyone to Eudora and Wade.

Rob drove to a grocery store, bought a small cooler and filled it with provisions. Then he picked up Eudora and Wade. Rob planned to drive to Port Townsend, making as few stops in public as possible. Eudora offered to do some of the driving, but her technique on mountain curves scared Rob so badly, he made her pull over and wouldn't let her behind the wheel again.

After the mountains, their journey took them along the Columbia River where Eudora pointed out windsurfers, which wowed Wade. "I want to try that," he gasped, watching them race and weave. Rob was overjoyed to see the boy react with such pleasure. Maybe the kid was recovering.

"Someday you can try," Eudora said.

"When?" Wade demanded.

"When you're older than me."

"*That* old?"

North of Portland, they stopped at a small park near a brook for lunch. While Rob and Eudora set out their supplies on the battle scarred state-issue picnic table, Wade chased ground squirrels and used a stick to draw the outline of a fort in the fallen needles and leaves. Spock was not allowed out of his carrying case, and bitched throughout the picnic. Eudora made Wade's favorite peanut butter and banana sandwich, saying it had been Elvis's favorite but he liked bacon on it, too. Wade laughed when Dora sang about a hound dog and Rob played air guitar, dancing around and swinging his butt. After he ate his sandwich, Dora even let him have a handful of Jelly Bellies for the road. She said they were President Reagan's favorite candy, too.

In the afternoon, they drove through southern Washington, and on to the Olympic Peninsula toward the Strait of Juan De Fuca.

***

I wonder where they are? Laura couldn't help but think about her loved ones on a plane or a bus or in a car, somewhere out of her reach. It was terrifying not to know. Something could happen to all three. But still, it was the safest way.

It was Day Two of her own chilling mission. She felt drained from the day before, but needed to prepare herself for another day of battle. She gave herself a pep talk.

If a psychopath can create a multiple, then I can keep the personalities I need and neutralize those I don't. Sure I can. Rose had been dealt with. Now for Weasel and Nathan. Laura's goal for the day was to merge their strengths into David. Her weapon needed both their cunning and their anger.

David had obviously not slept any better than she had. "You told me not to lose time or see my church. I didn't want to go, but Nathan forced me. Without you, I can't back him down. He wanted to go there to talk with the brothers."

So Abishua now knew she was actively trying to break his hold on David. At least the psycho didn't know why she was cracking the system open. He would be too vain to believe she could turn his creation back on him. The fact that David was even here today proved that.

Nonetheless, the Prophet would be using Nathan to keep a close watch. So Nathan had to be neutralized.

"David, yesterday Rose told us what has been done to you by Abishua."

"Nathan says it isn't true."

"But you trusted Rose."

"I trust Nathan, too. He wouldn't betray me. Rose was just a little girl. Maybe she got things all wrong."

Betrayal is so hard to accept. "As the third member of the Forum, would Weasel have the final say?"

David thought about it. "Yes, I guess so. That makes sense."

"Then, Weasel, are you there?"

The Defender looked even more haggard than David. His brow furrowed as if his head ached. Was the skin under his eyes actually darker than David's? Were his eyes really more bloodshot?

"Weasel, I know you are tired. You won't have to hold on much longer. Could you confirm what Rose told David?"

There was silence in the office. Finally, David returned. "Weasel said Rose was right. But maybe Nathan just doesn't know the truth."

Laura realized he couldn't accept that he had been deceiving himself all this time. So she tried another approach. "David, you're right. Maybe he doesn't. So we will tell him. Weasel, I am speaking with you as well as David now. Are you listening?"

"I'm too close not to hear him, doc."

"I want Nathan to speak with me now, while you two both listen. Nathan?"

David's body switched again. Nathan was tense and backed away from her, pushing the chair to the wall, scraping its legs along the tile. He did not want to be there.

"Why are you making Weasel push me around? We all got along before you, and we will when you're gone. You're the only problem here. They need me more than they need you."

"Nathan, I understand you are angry with me. But I am trying to help you, too. I want to tell all three of you things you don't know. You've been keeping secrets from each other. Abishua separated you when you were little to keep you from being too strong for him to control. But you can break that control if you all listen to me. David, Nathan has been spying on you and telling your father all about you."

"Not true!" Nathan said in outrage.

"You have, Nathan. You just don't know it. Your father made you a snitch. He used you. He only needed you to control David. He doesn't love you, has never loved you."

The body lurched forward as if to attack Laura, but then slammed back into the chair. "Listen to her, Nathan," Weasel hissed. "I'm opening my memories to you. Listen and look. I was there when it happened."

Nathan lowered his head to his hands. He began to keen, every bit as bereft as mourners at a funeral. "He lied to me." It started low in misery, but swelled into fury. "My father lied to me!"

As Nathan mourned, Laura spoke to David. "Nathan did not willingly lie to you. He didn't know he was doing it. Accept him and forgive him. He is part of you. You are stronger together. He is charming and talented. He is the most comfortable of you all with the world around you. Allow him to become one with you. Do it now."

There was no flash of lightning or rumble of thunder. When the body lifted head from hands, it was David. But he had the easy smile, the attractive countenance of Nathan. The look he gave Laura was one of true delight. "Nathan is home. He is me!"

"How wonderful for you both. But you still feel anger at Abishua, right?"

"God yes. More than ever."

Yes! "Weasel, are you still there? I need to speak with just you now."

"At your service, doc. As always."

"It's time for David to know the truth about you, as well. Abishua created you to break the law so the cult wouldn't get caught committing crimes. David might have been convicted, but never Abishua."

"You sure this is the right thing to do, doc? To tell him he's a criminal?"

"You said you trust me. Tell him now, Weasel."

This time, David leaned back, eyes shut tight and head turned away. "Bullshit!" he suddenly burst out. "Is Arizona where I've been when I'm losing time?"

"Yes, at least part of the time. Weasel was born at the same time Abishua created the rage inside you. He's been defending you behind Nathan's back."

"Are you sending him away, like Rose?" He looked terrified.

"No, David. Weasel's job is not done. You need his strength. Weasel will become one with you just like Nathan did." She had come to like the Defender. He was the best of the system, the most complex of the personalities. She wished him a silent farewell.

"I am speaking to both of you now. Weasel, you have taken care of David for many years, been brave and kept him safe. You are clever, worldly, and strong. You are smart. All that you are should now become one with David."

Weasel expressed one final concern. "But all this rage in here, doc. If Abishua can't control it, who will?"

I will, Weasel, I will. "You will not have to worry about it anymore. Come together and be what you were meant to be. You are now one."

With no more ceremony than that, David and Laura were for the first time alone in the room. Weasel's presence was there in the way David gathered himself, squared his shoulders, clenched his jaw. His strength joined Nathan's anger. David no longer needed the defense of Multiple Personality Disorder. He was one outraged human being.

But the integration was as fragile as a new peace treaty between hostile nations. Laura had to keep it from breaking apart by giving the system a rest. Besides she was so tired, she was shaking as though her work had been physical. Her eyes watered. She breathed hard. "One more session, David. We will finish tomorrow."

"I need the time to get to know me now, doc." David spoke in Weasel's voice, strong and rich with a sense of adventure. The exhaustion was gone. He reeked of confidence. Laura smiled at this new man.

How sad he won't last for long. She wanted to beg his forgiveness. Instead, she walked him out of her office, down to the lobby, and shook his hand good-bye. She warned him once again to stay away from the Seekers.

After he left, she turned to look at a very excited Woodrow who was whispering to Diaper Man. Both were in the lobby, intermittently peeking out the blinds.

"What's going on with those two?" Laura asked Lovella.

"The aliens have landed." The receptionist cocked her head in the direction of the one in the aluminum cone hat.

"What's happening, Woodrow?" Laura asked.

"They're here!" He turned to her, round eyed with excitement.

"Are you happy about it ... or sad?" she was unable to tell.

"Well ... well ... I don't know."

"He's never been sure whether he's been keeping them away or directing them here," said Diaper Man. "But they're here now. And they're watching us."

If Diaper Man said it, could it be true? Laura took a peek out the blinds herself. They were being watched, all right. But not by aliens. By Cadman and two others. They watched as David crossed the street to his car and drove away. He did not so much as acknowledge them.

Cadman did not leave to follow. Instead, he continued the vigil on Community Mental Health. The cult's intimidation was visible. If Laura hadn't been in danger before, she was now. She took a deep breath and stood back from the window. It was time for her appointment with Diaper Man. She smiled at him and said, "Come on up, and let's get started. I have a favor to ask of you."

***

The Mule met Laura after work and stood guard at her house while she packed a couple of suitcases. He helped her load her car with her absolutely-must-haves. When they were done, he asked her if she'd like to get something to eat. She realized then she hadn't had anything since the Chinese food the night before.

"Have you seen anybody watching the house?" she asked him.

"The parked cars all look empty, and the only pedestrians have been children on skateboards. I'm just a photographer, not a trained bodyguard, but they didn't look too suspicious to me."

"Then a late night breakfast sounds great to me," she said, even managing a smile for this tall, gangly man. He followed her Camry in his van to Elmer's. They both ordered eggs, pancakes, bacon and potatoes.

"Comfort food," she said to him.

"You think they have enough of it to go around?"

While they waited, they stared vacantly at the large Norman Rockwell prints on the walls. "Life is not as simple as it is portrayed," the Mule observed.

"It surely isn't."

Two heavy platters of food arrived. Butter, syrup, salt and pepper were swapped between them. As they ate, the Mule began to speak about the two people they had in common.

"Helen and I used to come here after putting the paper to bed. She'd talk about how the copy might have been tweaked or the layout a little more appealing. That old saying about ink in her veins wasn't far from the truth."

Laura smiled. "I remember when she was at our college paper. An ass-kicking anti-war editorial she wrote was rejected, but somehow got into the paper anyway. She was bounced off the staff, but it got her an A in her journalism class that semester."

"She saved me from that war. I don't think I would

have made it back to my current normal self without her. Of course, I didn't have Nancy Reagan's *Just Say No* program back then to help."

"Yeah, like I'm sure that would have done the trick."

"Rob helped, too. He can tell you about it if he hasn't already."

"He doesn't talk much about the past."

"Well, it's not all been fun and games. He was orphaned as a young teenager. He's pretty sensitive about kids. Must have seen some stuff that made him figure he didn't want any of his own. That may be why this cult thing is bothering him so much. Along with your involvement in it. He had as hard a time in the war as anyone, and I know he's told you about Chicago. You're the first person to come along that he trusts in a long, long time." He looked up with a fork full of pancake. "Don't plan on pulling the rug out from under him, do you?"

"Are you asking me my intentions?"

"Yep."

"Well, I think they're honorable," she said with a chuckle. *How good laughing feels.* "We're a pretty matched set."

"Good. Then he's got you to live for. Like I have Helen to die for. If it comes to that."

"You see that it doesn't," she huffed, laughter gone in a flash. "No kidding, Mule. I know you two cowboys probably have something planned. I wouldn't expect you to just walk away, although I wish you would. Abishua is a psychopath. I have two clients that are his son and his daughter. He's brutalized both in ways you can't imagine. A lot of that cult may just be gullible souls, but you can count on it that Abishua has worked some black magic on his older son, Cadman, too. Watch out for him."

"You got that backwards, Laura. Cadman better watch out for me."

The Mule went back to his eggs and bacon. She still thought he was homely, ungainly, and certainly not a gourmet of culinary arts. But she suddenly knew exactly what Helen had seen in him.

CHAPTER THIRTY-SEVEN

Laura spent the night in Rob's A-frame. She tossed and turned through a few hours of troubled sleep, then watched the morning light reveal Mt. Bachelor. Rob was taking her family to safety. Reaching for the pillow he used, she clutched it to her chest, and buried her nose in its softness. It smelled of laundry soap, fabric softener, and yes, there it was. The faint salty, woodsy scent of his skin and hair.

Can he continue to love a woman who has become so ruthless? Or am I damaged goods, never trustworthy again?

The Mule had slept on the sofa downstairs. After they shared coffee and the two multi-grain muffins she'd bought at the restaurant the night before, he followed her to the public library. She left her Camry in a back corner of their parking lot, where a large stand of mature junipers screened it from easy view. Then she got in his van, and he dropped her off at work.

He leaned over to give her a kiss on the cheek. "You be careful, now. Nothing can happen to you, or my ass is grass."

Imagine coming to a mental health center as an oasis of safety. The thought almost made her smile as she climbed the stairs to her office. She hadn't seen the watchers out this early, but she had little doubt they would assemble before long. Scare tactics.

Will Abishua join them or just send his attack dogs? What will Tom think if he notices them gathering?

Lovella handed her a message slip. Sarah wanted her to call first thing.

"Did they get there all right?" Laura asked the minute Sarah said hello.

"Yes. They arrived last night, safe and sound. Rob tried to call but couldn't reach you, and they all bedded down here at my house. This morning, he checked them into a lovely B&B...it even has a view of the islands. The owners have a couple cats so they were willing to take Spock in, too. Eudora says she's tired, and Wade is subdued, but they seem to be holding up. But I need to warn you."

"Warn me of what?" *I really can't handle much more.*

"I talked with Wade a little. You're right about one thing. Trooper Snoop threatened him with hurting you and Spock. Wade isn't worried about me, so he told me that much. But he's not saying any more for now."

"What's happened to him, Sarah?"

"It'll take a long time to find the answer to that. But this is what I need to tell you. I'm pretty sure Trooper Snoop is more than a cartoon or some clown in a cop suit. He's a real cop. He did something to Wade, and he could do something to you."

So Trooper Snoop is the real thing. Probably the cop in Mule's photo of the cult's school house. "Great. I'm being watched by a cult whose membership includes at least one city cop, one county deputy, and maybe the whole National Guard for all I know."

"You need to get the hell out of Dodge right now."

"I'm nearly ready. Sarah, please don't tell Rob about the cop. I don't want him more worried for me than he already is. I'm scared enough for the both of us."

"I couldn't tell him if I wanted to. He's already on his way back to Rapid River."

***

It was the third day of Operation David. It would be her last. Laura felt like a heart-broken gladiator about to enter the Colosseum one last time. Mid-morning, Woodrow dashed in the front door to tell Lovella the aliens were back, and Lovella informed Laura.

"Street people usually know when something's going down," the receptionist scowled. "Assuming it isn't really aliens, I wonder what. Seems to me some people around here are keeping secrets from me. That won't do."

Laura locked her lips with an invisible key and walked away. *Can't tell you what's going on with your friend David. Hope you forgive me someday.*

Regardless of Tom's standing orders, Laura planned to hold today's session in the conference room. There just wasn't room for all three participants in her tiny office. She staged the room by shutting the vertical blinds to the street, blocking out the two "aliens" she now saw loitering on the other side. Not able to control her nerves while sitting in her office, she waited for her clients in the lobby.

"I'm going to see both Colleen and David together this morning," she told Lovella. "I asked Colleen to come early, but could you let me know when David arrives?"

"You matchmaking between the two?" Lovella asked.

"Hardly. They're sister and brother, you know." Neither Colleen or David considered it a secret so Laura wasn't worried about confidentiality.

"What? No shit."

"You mean I actually knew something you didn't?"

"Had to happen someday. But don't you know how to gossip, missy? You have something juicy like that, you don't keep it to yourself." Lovella gave her a ghost of a smile. Laura realized she would miss the old bulldog.

Colleen arrived, ending their conversation. She looked graceful in her long flowing dress, exuding an air of confidence that Laura hadn't seen before.

"We'll meet down here today," Laura said, and they went to the conference room.

"Wow," said Colleen, looking around in appreciation. "Totally rad. I must be movin' on up, you know, like the Jeffersons."

"We're meeting with your brother today so we needed more room than my office. There're things you two should share that can help you both. Is that okay with you?"

"Way cool," she said choosing a conference room

chair.

"You look very good, Colleen. More relaxed than usual."

"I feel it. The lithium is history, and I'm not all fuzzified anymore. I'm so excited to have met Dolores. We started writing each other notes, and sometimes now we even have long talks. It's scary sometimes, like after I saw my father at the pizza place. But I understand so much now."

"You won't go see your father again, right?"

"No. There's a fellowship meeting tomorrow night, but I don't intend to be there. It's not good for me. I know that now, thanks to you."

"Will Abishua run the meeting?"

"He always does."

So tomorrow night is the target. David has to be ready then.

Lovella ushered David in moments later. Sister and brother were pleased to see each other and hugged. "You two are big brother and little sister, huh? Nobody told me." Lovella shot a glance at Laura, then shut the conference room door, leaving the three alone.

"Is she mad?" David said, taking a seat next to Colleen.

"Not at you guys," Laura said.

David looked exhausted. Laura the Psychologist worried about him, but Laura the Warrior could not let up. She began the session.

"The three of us need to help each other understand a few things."

"Go for it," Colleen said, smiling at her counselor.

"I can't believe there's still more," David muttered.

"Each of you knows part of a story but not the whole. I know some but not all. This is our chance to share all of it."

"Feels sort of like *Truth or Consequences*," Colleen giggled. "I'm getting nervous." She began fiddling with a lock of hair.

"This isn't a game, and it won't be fun. It will make you both sad before it makes you feel better. But stick with it, and you *will* feel better. So let's get started."

She focused on David. "You were diagnosed with Multiple Personality Disorder. What you don't know is that Colleen is a Multiple, too. What we thought was bipolar disorder turned out to be wrong."

"Dr. Laura, is that true? Colleen, is it?" David said. "I thought you'd escaped all this." He looked both surprised and distressed.

But is he really? Laura must be alert to everything. *Is he even David? Is he still in control?*

Colleen sighed. "A lot of things are beginning to make sense to me that never have before. I understand so much, and it feels good, even if it's sad. I'm not so angry anymore. I know you never meant to hurt me." She reached for his hand.

"Hurt you?" David's surprise gave way to confusion. "I hurt you?"

Laura cut in. "Colleen, I would like to speak with Dolores. Dolores has carried the pain for Colleen, sort of like Rose did for you, David."

But Colleen resisted. "Please let me try, Dr. Laura. Dolores doesn't like to talk to anyone but me. We've had marathon conversations ever since my last session. I think I can tell David myself now."

She's beginning to heal just as I'm on the brink of abandoning her. The thought was deeply painful to Laura. She hoped the next counselor would finish the work she had started. "All right. David and Colleen, you both belong to the Seekers of the Absolute Pathway. Your father, Abishua, is a member. He is the leader."

"Yes," Colleen said.

David nodded. "Yes."

"Colleen, can you tell David what your father did to you?"

Sister turned to face brother. "Daddy hurt me for years, David. Others of the men, too. Like they did you, only I'm a girl. There was so much pain. And anger. But I thought Daddy loved me, that I was special. Until he moved on to some of the others. That's when he gave me to you, David. You did it to me, too."

"No," David moaned. He sounded feral and bereft, like an animal caught in a live trap.

Laura watched him closely. She could lose him if the truth was too much for the newly united system. He could shatter. His face began to tighten, his muscles clench.

"David!" Laura snapped. She was the force in the room. "Remember you have the strength of Weasel now. You can handle anything."

She nodded to Colleen who continued. "They made you do it. But you wanted to. You liked it. I was your first. You were just a boy. I taught you a lot and loved you." Colleen sighed. "You came to my room often. When you didn't, I thought I had made you mad, done something wrong. I didn't understand that it wasn't *really* you. Sometimes you were gentler than others."

David's face paled. He whispered, "I remember, Colleen. I remember now."

"Then I had your baby -"

"What?" he cried.

Laura fought to keep her jaw from dropping, but she wanted to shriek "What?" as well.

"I named her Millie, but I was never allowed to be with her. The older sisters raised her. I was still just a kid."

"Millie," David breathed. He turned empty eyes to Laura. "Nathan knows her. But not that she is his daughter. Our daughter. My daughter."

"Father made you stop coming to me after Millie was born. In time, I married Allen, and we saved my second little girl. But Daddy has sex with Millie now, trains her just like he trained us. The cult takes pictures of her to sell just like they did of us." Colleen stopped for a moment, as if gathering her thoughts. "I don't blame you, David. You're my brother, and it wasn't your fault. I love you."

"How could you still?" David asked as he began to tremble.

"You're all I have. I can't stay mad at you. But there is something else you need to know, something worse."

She had both David's and Laura's complete

attention.

There's more?

"You're still doing it to the children. It's a reward given to the rage inside you when you've done our father's bidding."

David pitched forward, resting his head on his arms on the conference room table. He sobbed. Laura was also stunned. David was abusing children? Was this finally the last of the surprises to bubble up to the surface?

Over her own tears, Laura said, "Thank you, Colleen. You've done very well. I am proud you had the courage to tell David what you know." The girl smiled at the praise. Laura continued, "Please go now, so I can help him understand. Just like Dolores has helped you."

Colleen kissed the top of David's head, whispered that she loved him, and left the room, quietly closing the door behind her.

David was still resting his head on his arms. Laura stared at him, feeling bereft for this likeable young man. But she steeled herself for what she must do next. She was about to brutalize him even further.

"David." Her voice was as cold as it had to be.

He continued to cry.

"David, sit up and stop crying. Now."

He seemed surprised by her tone but did straighten himself up. Without Rose or Weasel or Nathan, he had to face her on his own.

"I'm the only one left for guidance and support," she said. "You must depend on me alone now."

"I understand."

"Then hear my words. Your church did this to you. Your father tortured and raped you. He allowed other men to take you, too. They made you rape your sister. Abandon your child. Abishua created parts of you for his own use. Made you a criminal. In the name of the rage deep inside you, my friend Helen was murdered, an old couple, too, and no doubt your wife, Cathy. Your father made the rage in you do that."

Laura leaned forward across the table to get closer to David's face. "You're still following his orders. You're brutalizing children. Your father has done this to you. It's time to make him stop. You are no longer under his control. Punish him for what the Seekers have done to you. The rage is under your control now. Abishua created it for evil. Use it for good. Release your rage on Abishua."

The physical change in David was remarkable. His posture stiffened. He rolled his shoulders, looking bulked up and threatening. The teary film in his eyes gave way to a rock-steady glare. His lips drew back and his teeth clamped together. Weasel and Nathan were there fused with David, but more than that, Laura felt the blazing heat of a new presence.

She felt his rage.

For the first time, she was terrified of this man. Of what he might do to her, to himself, to others who got in his way as he stalked his father. She'd succeeded in constructing her weapon, but now could she control it?

She struggled to keep command in her voice with no show of fear. "You have work ahead of you tomorrow night. The fellowship meeting. Your father is sure to be there. Stay away from others until then. Use the time to plan your attack well."

David pushed back his chair and slipped away from the conference room in near total silence. He moved with the flowing grace and power of a predator on the hunt.

Laura exhaled. Her job was done. She sat for a time in the bright conference room and grieved for David. He was the product of human madness. He'd had no chance from the moment he was born.

CHAPTER THIRTY-EIGHT

Laura knew she must disappear before the cult found out that things had definitely changed. But when she went to her office to pack her briefcase, she seemed shackled to her tiny desk by despair.

This is what she had wanted, this job where her clients truly needed her. It wasn't them that made it impossible for her to stay, or forced her into using her skills in a way they were never meant to be used. It was the world that called itself sane. The scoffers like Tom, the villains like Abishua.

She flipped through her appointment calendar, looking at the names of the clients she would abandon forever. Some would easily transfer to the next counselor who filled this office. The regulars might miss her, but they had been through it all before. They'd be fine with a new person to share their woes.

But the others. The AIDS victims, battling depression along with their disease. The anorexics so underweight they hovered near death. The clients called Double Troubles, those with both mental illness and drug addiction. There was Juliet, pursuing a malicious stalker through the court system as long as Laura was in her corner. What will happen to her now? Or to Larry, paralyzed in a logging accident and toying with suicide. At least he knew her co-worker,

Diego...maybe the transfer would take.

And that was another thing. Piling her case load on top of the other counselors who already had frightful loads of their own. *I'm so sorry, my friends.* As she shut her appointment book on all these lives, she knew she would be missed.

And she was furious. *God damn Abishua to hell*. He had destroyed her new life.

But there was no time for this. Woodrow's aliens were outside now. She had released her weapon. Yet another new life waited for her. She needed to get to the child who this was all about. Her heart pounded as her adrenalin peaked. She felt danger all around now.

Move, move.

She called Diaper Man. "I'll meet you out back in fifteen minutes." During her session the day before, she had asked him for a ride today. "Woodrow's aliens are watching me."

"Oh what fun! Hide and seek. Can I wear a, well, you know?"

"Absolutely."

Next she stuffed as many of her notes as would fit into her briefcase, then grabbed her jacket. As she bent down for her purse in her bottom desk drawer, she was shocked by a knock on the office doorframe.

"Jesus!" she yelped, standing up so fast that she nearly lost her balance with light-headedness.

"Did I scare you, Laura?" Tom stood there. "You're so pale. A little jumpy, aren't you?"

"Yes, yes, I guess I am." *Like I need this now.*

"It might be due to poor decisions, you know."

She froze. *What does he mean? What does he know?* "What?"

"I'm told you saw two clients at the same time today. That can't possibly be wise."

"It is when they are family," she snapped, moving toward him. But he was in the doorway, blocking her exit.

"And you saw them in the conference room against my express -"

"Whatever, Tom. The conference room is all yours from now on." She shoved her way passed him and rushed for the stairs.

"Laura!" he called sharply. "What on earth is wrong with you?"

She didn't turn, didn't stop. Was he antagonizing her because he didn't believe in dissociation or because someone was pulling his strings? She didn't know. But she would not talk to him until after she was out of his reach. Who might he call to follow her?

Run.

Diaper Man was waiting for her in the alley behind the building, in an ancient Chevy Impala. No one would expect to find Laura in this hulk, but she ducked down nonetheless until they had thundered at least three blocks away. Diaper Man drove her to her car where it was parked in the library's lot.

Before she got out he said, "I have a present for you from Woodrow." He handed her a crumpled brown paper sack, one that a street denizen had probably used to hide a bottle of Thunderbird. "We both know something is wrong. Woodrow thinks it's aliens, but I know it's people. Either way, it isn't good."

Laura opened the bag and peeked inside. *Yikes!* A Saturday night special. What or who might Woodrow shoot at?

Diaper Man said, "Woodrow says it's a ray gun. But I thought you might rather have bullets than rays. I know it doesn't look like much, but I tested it so I know it works. And it's loaded."

Horrified, Laura closed the sack. She opened her quilted handbag, the oversized one she'd chosen for the trip, and gingerly placed the gun inside. She didn't want the thing. But even more than that, she didn't want to give it back to a nutjob like Woodrow. She'd find some place to dump it.

She broke a professional taboo by reaching over and hugging Diaper Man. "Thank him for me, and tell him I'll take out all the aliens I see. He'll be safe then. And thank you, too. I'm sorry I have to go. You all matter so much to me."

"I know. Just go, go. We all will miss you. Even Vlad, who is just a bit peculiar, don't you think?"

"You won't tell anybody, right?" she asked as she got out of his car.

"Now really. Need you ask?"

Laura knew these guys were as fond of gossip as Lovella was, so she didn't tell him where she was going. She wasn't too worried about them because who the hell would listen to a vampire, a UFO hunter, and a man wearing baby apparel?

Laura drove away with Wade's bike in the trunk, Helen's scrapbook on the seat, a Saturday night special in her purse, and a lump in her throat for all the sweet, troubled souls she left behind. No matter how frightened she was, she stayed strictly within the speed limit. The last thing she wanted now was to draw the attention of a city cop.

CHAPTER THIRTY-NINE

Laura drove north through the desert then west to the mountains. At the Columbia River, she turned east into Portland, then across the bridge into Washington on I-5. It was dark, and she was worn out after her long, disturbing day. In Kelso, she exited to a roadside diner. Huddling alone in a small wooden booth, Laura thought the place looked like something out of a Hopper painting, and she was playing the part of the lonely woman. She ordered coffee and a tuna sandwich, but found she couldn't eat.

The night-shift waitress was a tiny woman with muscular arms from years of dealing out platters of steak and eggs. Her name badge said *Who wants to know?* She looked critically at Laura's sandwich and asked, "You want something else?"

"Other than something to cheer me up, I can't imagine what it would be."

"If I had that, I'd keep it myself," said *Who wants to know?* dropping off the check and walking away.

Laura had worked up a first class sulk. She only ever wanted to assist people, had spent years acquiring the skills to do it. *And now I've created a monster who is planning a murder.* She was using David to her own ends, as much as his father had. She felt as guilty as Abishua should, but never would.

She opened her oversized handbag, then jumped as if a rat peered out. With so much to think about, she'd forgotten Woodrow's gun was in there. Now she gingerly shifted it aside to get to her wallet. As she went to the front counter to pay her bill, a man came in. She saw him only in passing, but had the impression of a big guy, beefy from sports or workouts. Her skin started prickling. Had she seen him before? When she looked again, his back was to her as he took a stool at the counter and pulled a menu out of the metal rack that also held mustard, ketchup and honey in a plastic bear.

There was a pay phone outside the diner. The night was cloudy but mild and the phone booth looked reasonably free of spider webs. She placed a collect call to Rob, keeping an eye on the man in the diner.

Rob had just arrived home from Port Townsend. "I could have come with you," he said to her, sounding frustrated. "God, I miss you."

"I had to get out. I was being watched. Mule helped me park where nobody saw my car. Diaper Man drove me to it and I got away."

There was a pause. "Who?" Rob finally asked.

"It's a long story. I'll tell you one day. In the meantime, if you see a guy wearing an aluminum cone hat, thank him for me."

"Can't wait for the details," he said. "I love you, Laura."

"I'm not what you think, Rob. I'm not even what *I* always thought. I want Abishua dead. I never believed I would say a thing like that."

"He hurt your child. Of course you want the bastard dead."

They talked about the near future. Rob would come to Port Townsend as soon as he could, and they'd make a plan. They both agreed it would involve each other. Rob said, "I have to stay here, at least until they get a new editor. Then I'll find you."

"I'll be waiting. But for now, you and the Mule be very cautious. There's a fellowship service at the cult tomorrow night. My client, the one you know as Nathan? He was severely beaten after one of their services. I think some of the Seekers did it. Stay away from him if you see him anywhere. He's a very angry guy."

"So am I. So is the Mule."

"I know. I was afraid I might be on their agenda for tomorrow's festivity so I had to clear out. But you guys might be, too. Be sure you stay where they can't locate you. Maybe at the *Review* office with other people. Be vigilant."

"Of course we will."

She hoped he was telling her the truth. After a few more very private words, she hung up and went to her car. As she pulled out of the lot, she saw the familiar-looking man leave the diner and head for a dull orange pickup truck.

***

While Rob was gone, the Mule had been busy. When they met at the *Review*, he opened the back of the van and Rob took a look inside.

"Helen's bike and skis are still in here," Rob said then looked at the Mule.

"Yeah, well, it's not like Laura's had a lot of time for sports. Look in the camera bag, asshole."

As Rob reached into the bag, the Mule said, "Glock 17s, both automatics. They're untraceable. It took a little conversation and a few bucks to a friend."

"I take it he's no supporter of the Brady Bill."

"Me either. Until after tonight."

"We need to play it cool, Mule."

"Of course we will," Mule said. Rob knew that was about as truthful as when he'd said the same words to Laura.

***

David rode on a tide of fury when he left Dr. Laura's office. He'd done everything his father had asked, only to be led astray. He'd never been loved, only used. They'd hurt him, lied to him. He was a monster.

It must end.

He would use the façade of Nathan to gain access to the brothers during the fellowship meeting. They knew him as a gentle carpenter. What could be more ironic? He would turn on them, using the oldest cleansing agent known to man.

Fire.

On any Seeker that got in the way.

On Abishua.

And finally on himself.

CHAPTER FORTY

A ceiling of fog snuffed out the stars, but the dashboard clock pinpointed it as just past midnight. Laura flipped on her turn indicator and negotiated the ramp to the rest area. Three long-haul trucks were parked in the remote lot, their drivers no doubt asleep in their cabs. The car lot was empty other than Laura's Camry. *Families don't travel much at night.*

Some of the lot's overhead lights worked, some didn't. "Vandals," Laura muttered as she saw the pop machine had also been obliterated by bird shot. It wasn't cold, but Laura shivered as she got out of the car, feeling exposed. She could hear nothing but passing traffic and the Camry's exhaust system clicking as it contracted. The dark walk from the lot to the ladies' room was just a few paces at a quick trot, then she shoved through the door. After checking every stall, even the one marked 'Out of Service,' Laura was sure the room was empty before turning off the light. In the dark, she slipped back outside, feeling her way around the side of the building then onto the grass. She wouldn't be seen seating at a picnic table under the pines, invisible in the night.

The orange pickup had pulled in slowly behind her, the driver apparently giving her time to collect her things, lock her car, enter the ladies' room, and go about her business. Somehow he'd found her in Rapid

River. Maybe he'd been following the Mule when she dropped her car at the library, then watched until she came for it. Maybe Tom the Asshole had called him. No matter...he was here now.

He might be wondering why she hadn't used the facilities at the diner. Maybe he was startled when he saw the light in the restroom go out, then scoffed at the Washington Department of Transportation for not changing bulbs before they blew. Mostly though, he'd be thinking she was trapped and all his.

He traveled the distance from the lot to the ladies' room in the swinging strides of an athletic man. After he pushed the door open he stood outside. Laura heard him slap the wall inside the door, feeling for the switch. When the lights blinked on, she saw the handgun he held down by his side.

"Come out, come out wherever you are," he crooned, advancing into the room. She saw him swing open the first cubicle door, then the next and the next.

"You called?" she said, sounding remarkably tranquil while her gut boiled in fear and anger. He spun around to face where she now stood framed in the open door, pointing Woodrow's gun at his heart. She knew enough about guns to have flicked off the safety. She was ready.

"What the hell. I saw you come in here," he said.

"It's a big damn puzzle for you to figure out. Drop your gun."

"You wouldn't..."

"At this range, I really couldn't miss."

He bent and dropped the gun to the floor. "I'm a

cop. I wanted to see if you were okay."

"I didn't recognize you at the diner in plain clothes. But then it clicked. You're one of the cops who came to my house when my boy was taken. Go sit on the floor, there, between those two sinks, you bastard."

"But Dr. Covington, I'm Jerry Cassidy from Rapid River. You're right, I'm a cop," he cajoled, moving toward her with a conciliatory grin. "We've been worried about you."

"Sit on the fucking floor, Jerry." He backed away then squatted down on the filthy dampness between the sinks.

She moved just inches to kick his gun into a bathroom stall, never taking her eyes off him. "What did you do to my boy?" She sounded like a rattler ready to strike and saw him give up the idea that he could deceive her.

An ugly smirk replaced his grin. "Trooper Snoop knows just how to keep little boys in line. Nosy newspaper hacks, too."

Laura smelled his nervous sweat. "You killed Helen?"

"It was a pleasure. Cadman and me? We even had help from your buddy David, you stupid bitch. Helen knew me, of course. Pleaded with me. 'Help me, Jerry.' But I told her I wasn't Jerry, I was Trooper Snoop. You should have seen the look on her ugly face." His lips curled back and specks of spittle appeared in the corners of his mouth. "And when I'm done with you, I'll find that boy of yours then give him something more to remember me by."

He was strong. He hoisted himself by grabbing the sinks and sprang forward at her. But Diaper Man had been right. The Saturday night special worked just fine. She shot the son of a bitch twice. Once for Wade and once for Helen. Then she shot him again. *That one was for me.* The echoes overlapped, careening off the porcelain and metal and tile.

There was little left for her to do. She placed her gun back in her handbag and looked out the bathroom door. No lights came on in the sleeping eighteen wheelers. No cars pulled off the highway. *Families don't travel much at night.*

Her mind bounced from thought to extraneous thought. *Goodness, look at that blood and those messy bits on the walls. It'll need a cleanup crew in here. Always wash your hands after using a restroom. Is that whimpering I hear really me?*

"Stop it!" she said aloud, and then she left. She must continue to Wade's hideaway.

CHAPTER FORTY-ONE

The next day passed painfully for David. His mind felt like an iceberg calving. Shards were collapsing. Ugly memories flashed through his mind. Dr. Laura was the only one he trusted now, and he had even hurt her, letting Cadman run that newswoman off the road. Helen lived through the crash, struggling out of the SUV. So they rolled it onto her, Cadman, the cop, and he, until it crushed her into the weeds and bracken of the forest floor. He owed Dr. Laura for that. Another reason to bring Abishua down.

In the early evening, as dark began to settle, David parked in front of the Absolutist office, pausing to look at the building with the beautiful porch he had built. The council always waited inside here while the congregation gathered in the meeting hall for evening fellowship.

He left his car and walked toward the equipment shed, but Cadman came out on the porch and stopped him. "You're early, Nathan. The fellowship begins at nine."

He knew how to look and sound exactly like Nathan, of course. Nathan would never lie to Cadman.

But David would. "I have work to do on the doors of that armoire. I should have finished by now, but there have been...complications."

"Yes. But you're done now with Dr. Covington and her nonsense. She's gone, leaving you just like the last one did."

"Yes. I thought she would go."

"And?"

"I serve only the Seekers of the Absolute Pathway."

"Good. Now do your work. Our father has arranged a reward for you after the fellowship meeting."

Our father. David cringed. Yes, Cadman must be his brother, a real brother. He went on to the equipment shed. In orderly sections, on shelves and pegboards, the tools that kept the Absolutist ranch up and running were arranged by task. Carpentry next to plumbing next to grounds maintenance. Every tool was tended and clean. Nathan was particular about that.

David walked the rows, considering each tool as a weapon. Claw hammers and nail guns and the propane weed burner. But things could be much simpler than that. Weasel knew all about flares.

And he was Weasel.

***

Rob had the Mule park the van in the shadowy depths of a turn-off, a couple miles from the ranch. He didn't want it recognized parked among the membership's vehicles. "This is probably the only place on the continent where a logging truck is less of a threat than an Econoline," he said to the Mule as he heard the next behemoth thundering toward them.

Rob stepped out into the road and began flagging it down. He stood his ground as its headlines picked him out. The truck shuddered and squealed to a stop. When its airbrakes at last expelled a dragon-sized puff, the Mule joined Rob, dragging along two large camera bags of equipment, plus a tripod.

"Takes damn fools or madmen to stand in front of a truck like this. You guys both or one of each?" The wizened driver squawked.

"I got fifty bucks for a ride to one of the ranches you pass on down the road a bit." Rob reached up to show the driver the bill.

"Well then, climb aboard."

They grappled with the camera equipment and did as they were told.

"It's the ranch owned by the Absolutists," Rob said as he settled between the driver and the Mule. "Appreciate the ride."

"Yeah, I know the place. They own the right of way."

"That's it."

"A little strange, ain't they? Some kind of commune, secret society, that kind of thing? If they worship the ladies, I'm in." The old man pointed a knotty finger upward, and Rob saw the ceiling of the cab was papered with Playmates and other bouncy babes.

***

Through the open door of the shed, David heard the membership gathering, cars and trucks arriving, greetings as town members joined the residents. Their conversations were muted. It was rarely boisterous at the ranch where one false step off the Pathway would plunge them into eternal nonbeing. There was still enough chatter to muffle David's footfalls as he left the shed carrying two cans of gasoline. If anyone saw him, they would think Nathan was finishing up another chore. David smiled bitterly, thinking they'd actually be right.

He disappeared with the gasoline cans into the darkness behind the office. No one could see him back there. After unscrewing the first gas cap, he dampened the foundation around the office, a rehabbed mobile home. There were no doors in the back, and the windows were closed, so David doubted the men inside would smell the unmistakable oily odor. After he had dribbled gas along the back and one end of the trailer, he circled to the other end with the second can. He finished by splashing the last of the fuel onto the porch.

He went back to the shed to bide his time. The council always waited until the hall was full of true believers before they went over together in a procession led by the Prophet Abishua. Just as the hall became calm and ready, that's when he would act.

He listened to the last cars trickling in with the town members. A logging truck rumbled up, stopped momentarily, then went on its way. Maybe it had been slowed by a car turning into the parking lot.

***

Rob and the Mule meant to crash the fellowship meeting. Whether the members were demented bastards capable of evil or merely lost sheep, Rob planned to confront them about the threats to Wade and Laura. He would determine whether they knew what their leader was really doing. "No more kids are going to be hurt out here," he said to the Mule.

"And I have a score to settle for Helen."

Rob was a reporter, not a gunman, but each camera bag concealed one of the automatics. He didn't want to use one, but he would if he had to. The logging truck dropped them near the front of the ranch, and they hung back until most of the congregation had entered the meeting hall. In the dark, Mule recognized Big D merely from his size, and pointed him out to Rob.

"And there's Nathan," Rob whispered as the carpenter left the equipment shed in the direction of the office.

***

By 8:45, David had heard no cars for several minutes. The hall was quiet, in anticipation of the evening. He'd seen that reporter in the crowd, but gave little thought to anything but the chore at hand. At nine, the fellowship meeting would begin. It was time.

He carried three bright orange plastic guns that looked like fat cartoon toys. The flares were formidable, 16,000 candle power of illumination meant to travel heavenward and burst into a bright frenzy, discernible from miles away. Instead, David shot the first flare directly at the foundation of the mobile home.

The gasoline whooshed into a wall of flames, startling him in its intensity and speed. He ran to the front porch, and entered the only door as two men staggered out, escaping the flames that were engulfing the building. Dave shot a second flare through the doorway, back toward the gas-soaked porch. Now the only exit was a barricade of fire.

Inside, there were still three other than himself. One was shrieking, a sleeve on fire. David thought it might be Cadman careening past him for the door, a human fireball bowling through the blaze. Another man crawled toward him, but went down. Too much smoke, too little oxygen for both lungs and flame.

The third man towered behind the main desk. He was a wraith shimmering through the heat waves, as he bellowed his own name. "I am the Prophet Abishua."

"I know who you are," David gasped, fighting for air. "Yours is a pathway to hell."

"You've listened to that ignorant nobody. You must obey your father."

It had always reined him in before. It was hard to resist now. But Dr. Laura was with him. "No. I trusted you, but you lied. She showed me the truth."

David called on his rage that he now controlled for his final act. He took the melting gun and shot the last flare into Abishua's heart. The flames incinerated them both as the mobile home with its beautiful front porch began to collapse on itself.

For the first time in his life, David felt no pain.

***

As the last of the membership went into the meeting hall, Rob and the Mule slipped in, staying to the back. They entered behind a pretty young woman in a long flowing dress, with flowers woven into her raven hair.

"Welcome back, Colleen," another murmured. There was a buzz among the women as they took quick peeks at her, whispered to each other, then hushed.

"Looks like an extra from Romeo and Juliet in that get up," the Mule whispered to Rob.

His voice caught the attention of a teenager who turned around and stared at them. Rob saw recognition dawn in his eyes at the same time he identified the kid as one from the shooting range. The boy's look was one of outrage. "It's them! The newsmen," he shrieked, repeating the call again and again. "The newsmen!"

The congregation looked around, a sea of surprised, confused faces staring at Rob and the Mule. Finally, the uncertain crowd organized. Several men moved toward their row, as if trying to box them in from both ends. The Mule and Rob turned back to back in order to face the rising tide in both directions.

Rob shouted, "We're just here to talk."

But suddenly a hot blast of smoke burst through the door. Towering flames and a shower of sparks outside lit the windows as bright as daylight. For a fraction of a second, everyone seemed paralyzed, as if frozen in a photo finish. Then panic galvanized them into motion. Fear, shouts, confusion, shoving. Everyone rushed the door, with the newsmen in the midst of the pack.

Before their eyes, the office building was swallowed by fire. A human in flames bolted past them, running to open ground, where it rolled over and over as it shrieked. Members of the congregation seemed at a loss. The Mule went after the flaming man while Rob tried to spur the crowd into action. "Get hoses and buckets," he yelled. "The fire department is too far away to do any good."

Two councilmen who escaped the flames staggered over and joined the crowd. But nobody else moved at all.

"Come on people, move your asses. Where's your fire equipment?" Rob ran among the crowd looking for someone to help. He stared from face to face, then finally recognized the look in their eyes. It was awe, spreading across the congregation. They were not frightened or angry or sorrowful. If anything, they looked transfixed as though their Abishua might be following the Path to a new level.

Then a young girl pulled away from a woman's hand.

"Millie, come back," the woman called.

But Millie walked to a broken splinter of wood

from the porch. It was burning on one end. It must have exploded away from the inferno, along with thousands of other flaming bits of debris. The child picked it up and heaved it with all her might toward the burning building.

Rob saw her look of triumph. This little girl was at last free of a savage existence. Her action broke the crowd's trance. The Seekers melted away into the darkness.

CHAPTER FORTY-TWO

When he saw the crowd dispersing, Rob grabbed one of the councilmen who escaped the blaze. The other had already vaporized. "You need to stay to wait for the Sheriff," he said. What's your name?"

"I'm Joram," the man managed in a hoarse gasp. Rob could tell he was suffering from smoke inhalation and helped him lie down on the grass. Rob opened his collar, telling him to be still and breathe as normally as possible. *Help will come soon enough to end the bastard's pain.*

Then Rob saw Deputy Big D heading toward his cruiser. "Wait up D. I'm not the only one who'll have questions for you."

"Go to hell, asshole," the Deputy snarled, then continued on to his car.

Rob gave it very little thought. He'd been ready to hit someone for days, and this seemed the perfect time, place and person. He said D's name once again, and when the man turned, Rob's hard uppercut caught him unawares. Big D caved like an imploding building.

By then, the Mule was back at Rob's side. They both stared down at the comatose deputy. Rob said, "He fell."

"Yeah, on his chin. I saw the whole thing."

Rob took the car keys that had dropped from the

deputy's hand, and threw them far into the night. "Seems he lost the keys in his fall."

"Guy that size shouldn't run in the dark. Dangerous."

"Were you able to help the fireball?"

"No. He died."

"Do you know who it was?"

"It was Cadman."

Rob looked at the Mule, and nodded. "Let's get to work."

They were, after all, newsmen. Rob began to take notes, and the Mule covered the holocaust in photos. The intense heat burned their faces as their backs shivered in the cool night air. It was not long before the shell of the mobile home and the porch collapsed completely. There would be no more escapes.

By the time they heard sirens from the fire vehicles and the Sheriff's department, the flames had died down. A huge pile of twisted metal, ash, and burnt offerings seethed and smoked. Rob and the Mule stayed out of the way because the area was a crime scene now. The Sheriff saw them, appeared surprised to find them there, then continued investigating as the fire department would allow.

A few members of the congregation began to reappear, offering the firemen cold beverages and clean towels. But many vehicles had been leaving the ranch, packed with possessions and loaded with people. Rob wrote down all of the license numbers he could get, in case the Sheriff would want them. Big D had long since come to, and was still meandering around with a flashlight looking for his keys.

By midnight, all Sheriff Elwood could tell the newsmen was that three bodies were found inside the building wreckage. According to Joram, one would be another councilman and one the Prophet Abishua. The third body had been removed, along with what appeared to be the remains of a flare gun melted to his hand. Nothing more could be done inside until the carcass of the building cooled.

If Sheriff Elwood was surprised to see so few mourners in what was left of a congregation, she didn't say anything about it to Rob. But he did see her approach Deputy Big D. She spoke to him, and he handed her something then turned away. From what Rob could piece together, he was no longer Deputy. He was just Big D now.

The officials didn't notice the fourth body immediately because it was so far outside the building. It was covered with burns, but just recognizable as Cadman. Oddly, he'd also been shot in the head with a nine-millimeter bullet.

Rob did not look at the Mule. But they turned away together and began the dark walk to the van still parked in the turn-off two miles away.

CHAPTER FORTY-THREE

RANCH FIRE KILLS FOUR, INCLUDING PRESUMED ARSONIST
By Rob Cooper
Review Staff Writer
    Four men died in a fire Tuesday night at the Rapid River ranch owned by the Seekers of the Absolute Pathway. The fire completely destroyed the office building of the organization. Remains of three adult males were found inside the wreckage, plus the body of one more outside.
    Identification of the bodies is underway. According to Deschutes County Sheriff Rita Elwood, one of the four dead is presumed to be the arsonist who set the fire with intent to kill himself along with the group leadership. Of the two additional bodies found inside the building, one is presumed to be the leader known as the Prophet Abishua and the other …

Rob knew this was not a crime with a clean conclusion, all the ends tied into neat little bows. In the days that followed the fire, he watched Sheriff Elwood do what she could, but she was down a deputy, and the rest of her team was overloaded. As a result, she counted on Rob and the Mule for investigative help, more than she might have otherwise.

The day after the fire, they were in her office. This time, donuts were shared by all three. "You can prove the fire was set with flares, right?" Rob asked, selecting an apple fritter, still warm and crunchy.

"Yep. Eye witnesses like, oh say, *you*, described the intensity of the flames. When we searched the area, we found an empty flare gun behind the building. Probably it was the one used to set the fire to begin with."

"Used by the carpenter Nathan?"

"That's what Joram says the cult called him. According to our records, he's David Hollingshead. He'd been known to the cops as a nutjob about town, not above bar fights or black outs. But nothing like arson before."

"He had easy access to flares?" the Mule asked.

"There was a stock of them in the equipment shed. Two kinds, actually. Bandoliers of aerial flares and a box of road flares. His fingerprints were on the gun we found outside and on the gas cans. He's for sure the arsonist."

And he was for sure Laura's client.

"The coroner said one of the corpses in the fire was shot with a flare in the chest. And another had traces of orange plastic on his remains."

"Abishua and Hollingshead?"

"That's the theory until the coroner confirms it. Looks like Hollingshead set out to kill the prophet before dying in the fire himself. I'm thinking the others were collateral damage." She sighed. "Kind of hard to tell whether the guy was a maniac or doing the community a good deed."

"Wonder where the Absolute Pathway is taking them now," the Mule mumbled.

The Sheriff stared at him for a while. "The big mystery is Abishua's son, Cadman. He got away from the burning office, rolling to douse the flames. He died of massive burns. Or maybe the nine millimeter bullet wound in his head. Where the hell do you suppose that came from? No gun was found. Well, other than a bunch of hunting rifles locked up in the equipment shed."

Rob rapid-fired all the options as he could think of. "Another Seeker taking advantage of an easy time to off him? A member tired of providing sexual favors? Maybe a drug runner? Lots of people out there, Rita. Lots of noise and confusion."

"Right," she said. "Or maybe it was somebody who thought Cadman killed a good friend, someone who exacted a little justice of his own." She stared from one to the next. "Oh well, I got enough other stuff to look into. No use digging into that unless someone drops a clue in my lap. You can't prosecute theories."

SHERIFF CONSIDERS POSSIBILITY OF ARSONIST'S CONNECTION TO OTHER LOCAL DEATHS
By Rob Cooper
Review Staff Writer

David Hollingshead, 24, alleged

arsonist who died in the fire last Tuesday night at the ranch owned by the Seekers of the Absolute Pathway, is under investigation for other unsolved crimes in and around Rapid River.

"He was a local man, a member of the community," said Deschutes County Sheriff Rita Elwood. "He has been a person of interest to law enforcement officials for some time."

The Sheriff is investigating possible connections to the death of Helen Waring, former editor of the Rapid River Review as well as…

Laura finally connected with Rob the afternoon following the fire. She reached him by phone just as he was coming into his office from the Sheriff's department.

"It's very beautiful here in Port Townsend," she said to Rob, looking for common ground to begin their conversation. "Wade walked down to the water with me to show me the ferry coming in from Whidbey Island. He wants to be a ferry boat captain."

"Is it a place you could live?"

"Yes, I think so."

"Is it a place I could live?"

"Yes, I know so. But I also know you have things to finish there. And a career of your own, of course." Did she dare hope he'd really move north with her?

"I've told the owner of the paper that he better get

a move on finding a new editor."

"He'll never be able to replace the old one." She may have Rob but she'd still lost Helen. And then there was David. Poor David.

Another day of mood swings. Laura knew she'd be emotional quicksilver for a very long time to come.

"No, nobody will really replace Helen. The sheriff believes that David Hollingshead, the arsonist, may also have had a hand in her death. She doesn't yet know he was your client at the Mental Health Department. But she will."

The pause was long and hollow on the long distance lines. "Yes, I suppose that is inevitable." Laura tried to muffle the sound of her tears, but failed.

"It's all right, love. I know you cared about him, as well as Helen."

"He had to go. I know that. But yes, I will miss things about him very much." *Good bye, Weasel. Good bye, Rose.*

"Elwood's trying to build a case that he was responsible for the Herkimers. It's a logical assumption. And she's interested in his missing wife. Not that there's any proof so far. She just says it's too many murders for a small town. This whole mess may be the end of her career if the commissioners turn against her." Now it was Rob's turn to pause. "You sent him there that night, didn't you? David. To the cult."

Laura sighed. "Do you really want to know? It might make you think a great deal less of me."

"I'll never think less of you. But I don't want you

wasting your life living in guilt like I've done. A terrific counselor's been helping me with that."

"Let's talk about this when you get here, not now, not on the phone. For now, can we just say I was fairly sure David had a score to settle that night? But I didn't know you and the Mule were going out there, too. I thought you were staying away."

"We really couldn't. Not if any more kids were being threatened. I thought I might put a stop to that. Turns out, David did."

```
RAPID RIVER COP MURDERED IN WASHINGTON REST
                    AREA
                By Rob Cooper
              Review Staff Writer
      A tourist found the body of Rapid
 River Police Officer Jerry Cassidy in
 the ladies' room of a Washington State
 rest area just north of Kelso. The
 body, in regular street clothes
 instead of uniform, was not identified
 until Wednesday morning. Why Cassidy
 was in the ladies room is under
 investigation, and his alleged
 association with the Seekers of the
 Absolute Pathway has added greatly to
 the questions surrounding his death …
```

The Mule and Rob were at the A&W, sitting in the van and chomping down Papa Burgers.

"Helen never wanted to come here."

"Laura either."

"Women," the Mule said. "And speaking of women, you suppose a female had anything to do with the death of Jerry Cassidy?"

"Well, a woman found the body."

"You know that's not what I'm asking about."

Rob chewed a piece of ice from his Coke cup. "Tell you what, Mule. You don't ask me questions about Laura's actions, and I won't ask you about yours."

"Fair enough. But just so you know? She's a mighty fine woman." He turned the ignition, and the old van shuddered into action. "And another thing? Helen's ghost seems a whole lot happier with me these days."

MYSTERIES STILL FOLLOW THE ABSOLUTE PATHWAY
By Rob Cooper
Editorial

"It's too many deaths for one small town," said Deschutes County Sheriff Rita Elwood. "Investigations are ongoing."

Are they all related to the Seekers of the Absolute Pathway? The Sheriff refused to speculate further, but certainly questions are unavoidable about these events:

The city police department is seeking information as to the whereabouts of Judith Loomis, former manager of the Lil Pals Day Care center. Loomis did not appear for work Tuesday morning and parents were unable to leave their children. The day care remains closed.

The body of Cathy Hollingshead, ex-wife of alleged arsonist David Hollingshead, has been discovered in automobile wreckage found in a chasm off a Cascade mountain logging road.

```
          The murder of the parking lot
     attendant Leon Jackson, known as Head
     Case by his acquaintances, remains
     unsolved ...
```

"I want my town back," the Sheriff mourned. "People happy, trusting each other again. There's been too much violence. It's like living in a big city, for Pete's sake. And there's still a bunch of stuff to work out." She leaned back and stretched. "The DEA is interested after all. And now that money is involved, the FBI is, too." She told Rob and the Mule that a small safe had been found in the remains of the Absolutist office, and a ledger in the safe indicated the cult had accounts totaling over two million dollars. But there was no record of where."

"No wonder the bureau is sniffing around," Rob said. "That much green sure isn't made by gardening."

The Sheriff agreed. "It has to have come from shit like drugs or porn. Interstate commerce of the lowest kind. From my point of view, I'm delighted to have them help clear up that distribution. But I'll be just as happy if they never find the money."

"Why's that?" he asked, surprised.

"My commissioners are sniffing around, hoping part of that meaty bone might belong to the county. They want me to stay close to the investigation. So my job is safe for now."

"Glad to hear it, Rita. You're too good an officer to have to put up with their crap."

"Hey, as they say at the movies, it's Chinatown. And it buys me time to do some real police work."

"Like Cathy Hollingshead?"

"Yep. Another murder. And guess what? She was bludgeoned with the same kind of weapon that took down Head Case and Ben Herkimer."

"The proverbial blunt instrument."

"In fact, a battered Maglite was found in her car. Based on fingerprints, it was the one Head Case was carrying, probably the night he died. No other prints, but maybe our boy David has several deaths to answer for."

RELIGIOUS GROUP DIMINISHES, BUT STRAGGLERS PLAN TO REBUILD
By Rob Cooper
Editorial

The ranch of the Seekers of the Absolute Pathway is a different place following the fire that killed two of their most influential members as well as the Prophet Abishua, leader of the group who was at one time convicted of sexual assault and paroled early from the Oregon State Penitentiary. The school is empty, and fields are unattended. Vegetables in the garden are rotting.

Both the FBI and the DEA keep a watchful eye on the handful of Seekers still at the ranch. The remaining diehards move slowly as if in a stupor, as opposed to the robust crowd that populated the ranch just days ago. None agreed to speak with this reporter, but one shouted. "We will rebuild. The Pathway is forever."

Nonetheless, an organization that was once strong and committed to the

```
single ideal of a Pathway to utopian
existence now seems scattered...
```

"Nobody in the cult is talking, huh?" Laura said on the phone.

"They look like a bunch of zombies, like they don't know what to do next." Rob explained.

"They probably don't. If it's like most cults, they were people truly looking for answers. Unfortunately, they got sucked in and ruled by fear. With Abishua's death, they're still looking for something to cling to."

"Here's hoping they go somewhere else to find it."

"How's the Mule?"

"Doing well. Says Helen lets him get some sleep now. That's another story to share with you when I get there. He asked if you would come back here now."

"Couldn't even if I wanted to. I talked to Tom McClaren, and he's plenty pissed I walked out. There's so much I can't tell him without revealing where I am."

"You still don't trust him?"

"Honestly, I'd guess he's just an administrator trying to run a department with as little trouble as possible. I'll never know his real motivation, but I'm staying away."

"Smart girl."

"I did call Lovella because I knew she'd be sad about David. She was glad to hear that the people he destroyed were the ones who destroyed him. Wish I could say good-bye to Jenny and Diego. They don't deserve to be left without answers. Maybe in time."

"The fewer who know where you are, the better."

"I'll get around to hiring a moving company to pack up our things eventually." The reality of all the long distance chores seemed overwhelming to her. She'd moved everything just months ago, and was not ready to do it again.

"I'll hire it done. Then Mule and I will rent a truck. No need to give your address to outsiders."

"Could you slap up a for sale sign on the house while you're at it?" She laughed, trying to sound positive about the obstacles ahead.

They said their good-byes, doing what Eudora would call their billing and cooing, then Laura hung up the phone.

She knew the deaths of Abishua, Cadman, another Seeker, and David were on her dance card, along with Trooper Snoop. But whenever she was cornered by remorse, she had a very simple cure.

She watched her son laughing at some damn thing his cat had done.

CHAPTER FORTY-FOUR

Ten Years Later

"I got a call referring a client with an MPD diagnosis," Laura said to her business partner, Sarah Fletcher. "I turned it down since MPD doesn't exist anymore."

They were in the Port Townsend offices of their company, New Horizons Therapy. It was their habit to touch base at the end of the day. Lately, they'd been planning Sarah's retirement. With the clients transitioning to Laura, she wasn't looking for anyone new.

"You mean now that it's Dissociative Identity Disorder." Sarah toasted Laura with her mug of chamomile. "Actually, it's a better name, I think. Recognizes that it isn't the number of personalities but the degree of dissociation that determines the severity of the disorder."

"Yeah. What you said." Laura smiled at her.

Laura scoffed at those who denied multiplicity whatever its name. Why do they think psychologists are lying or being suckered by clients all around the globe? Maybe they'd never experienced the kind of distress that she and Sarah had seen. She recalled one of her earliest thoughts when Tom McClaren had first cautioned her. *Just because you haven't seen it, doesn't mean it isn't real.* Now she added, *Or just because you didn't recognize it.* Other clients with Dissociative Identity Disorder had manifested through the years, but neither she nor Sarah had ever again seen such a fractured case as David Hollingshead.

Sarah asked Laura to join her practice not long after the younger psychologist arrived in Port Townsend. Laura had taken Sarah up on it. She had ample credentials so Washington State certification was no problem.

"I always told you that PhD was a magic carpet ride," Sarah had said.

Laura liked the antique Victorian town. But it wasn't the pristine environment or the partnership that made her stay. It was the counseling relationship between Wade and Sarah.

***

The first year was hellish as Sarah took on the locked room mystery that was Wade. It didn't require much time to get a quick peek inside that room, but actually cleaning it took months. Sarah began with the abandonment issues that Laura knew crippled the boy. Wade had no memory of his father. His mother might have loved him but if so, she couldn't see through her alcoholic haze long enough to realize how abusive she could be.

"*She locked me in.*"

"*Often?*"

"A lot."

"For long times?"

"I listened and listened but she wasn't there. I fell asleep in front of the door."

"Mommy should not have locked you in. But she was afraid something would happen to you so she tried to keep you safe. Gram says you can always leave your door open so you know you can always get out."

He'd suffered verbal assaults and spankings when he couldn't get a chore quite right.

"She called me bad and dummy."

"Do you believe that?"

"Mommy wouldn't lie."

"She might, Wade. Sometimes Mommies tell you things that aren't true. Other times they make mistakes. But your Gram is smart, and she's right most of the time. She knows you're not bad, and so do Rob, Dora and I. We all love you."

The result of his mother's problems was a wary little boy nearly desperate to please. Laura had seen it as passivity. Wade had seen it as a way to stay out of trouble. When his mother died, Wade would have done almost anything to oblige the next adult in his life.

"Gram leaves me sometimes."

"Isn't Dora or Rob there?"

"Yes, but Gram's not."

"And Spock is there?"

"BUT GRAM'S NOT!"

Sarah was pleased he could express anger. It was a sign he wasn't thwarting honest emotion, at least not with her. Sarah tried to help him understand that Gram sometimes did things or went places, that adults had work to do. But she'd always come back.

Of course, Helen's death hadn't helped. It reconfirmed to Wade that adults couldn't always be counted on to stick around. No matter what Sarah said, Wade stayed skeptical on this issue. And probably always would.

Lil Pals Day Care had been a devastating experience for him, and much harder to confront. Sarah counseled Laura, Eudora and Rob during this period to be prepared for his wild behavior swings. She was pulling a cork out of a bottle, and what bubbled out might be undue anger or extreme clinging or even violent acting out.

"We can handle it," Eudora said with a salute, and Sarah knew they could.

Getting to this kind of truth was difficult counseling, but Sarah was helped by knowing some of the facts about the day care. She was aware that Miss Judy had been a cult member and that Wade had been threatened. Sarah could only get at it through play therapy and, because he liked to do it, drawing exercises.

When Wade drew pictures of children with wings flying away or people diving, Sarah guessed he'd been told about a Pathway he had to stay on or else. Slowly, gently, Sarah convinced Wade that Miss Judy was simply wrong. She used an example from a story Laura told her.

"*Remember Gram telling you the llama didn't like to step over a hose?*"

"Yes."

"The llama thought it was a snake, remember?"

"But it wasn't."

"That's right. The hose looked like a snake, like something it wasn't. And it was safe to step over it, after all."

The time came when together they went out front and stood on the sidewalk. Sarah dragged a hose across, and she jumped over it. So did Wade. He laughed because it was fun. Then she jumped off the sidewalk onto the lawn. To her great joy, he followed. They high-fived. The symbolic pathway had been dealt with.

Trooper Snoop was as much an ogre in Wade's mind as he was in real life. In the early going, Wade persisted in drawing policemen with enormous hands, frowny faces, and people with eyes bigger than their heads. He only talked with Sarah about it after she and Gram and Dora and Rob all told him Trooper Snoop was gone forever. He couldn't hurt any of them. Finally, Wade began to believe it.

"He came to school sometimes. We drawed him a lot."

"What did you do with the drawings?"

"Put them up so he could see us."

"On the fridge?"

"And in my room. So he could see when we were bad."

Sarah slowly searched for clues in the locked room. Did the cult seek out which kids they could dominate, while providing normal day care to the others? Were they seeking imaginative children? Quiet, passive kids they could control? If so, Wade qualified.

Sarah could barely make it through Wade's story of the day he took Spock to school. Worse still was his time with the Prophet Abishua. It took months of play therapy, acting out the scene before he could reveal it in words.

"I waked up in the punishment room. They took my clothes."

"At Lil Pals?

"Yes."

"With other kids?"

"Just me. And the Prophet. And the bunny."

"A bunny! What did it look like?"

"It was white and soft. I petted it. It was nice."

"Bunnies are nice."

"The Prophet said kill it. He gave me a knife. I had to because I was bad. Kill it or he'd kill Gram. I stabbed and stabbed. The soft part got all red. The bunny got dead. The Prophet said I was a good boy."

"Wade, the Prophet will not hurt Gram. It will never, ever happen. You saved her. You did what you had to do. It's not your fault. You're not guilty or bad. It's okay to grieve for the bunny. You are not a bad boy."

"When I ran home, there were policemen with Gram. Trooper Snoop! So I couldn't tell her. Or Dora. I couldn't! You won't tell will you?"

Sarah believed she had gotten to Wade soon enough to help him make the long trip back from the edge. She spent months working out all the issues with the Prophet, made even more difficult by the aftereffects of some kind of hypnosis. Or drug. Wade was too young to tell her much about that.

She kept his confidences whenever she could. She shared more information than she might have with another parent, because Laura was her partner and capable of helping. But she downplayed what Wade had seen and how close Laura had come to losing him to the cult. Sarah suggested that Laura keep all the doors inside the house open, get rid of fluffy stuffed animals, and maybe not allow Wade in the kitchen while she was preparing roasts. She should not have any clocks that ticked loudly.

It was over now. Lil Pals was closed so children were not in danger, Miss Judy had disappeared, Trooper Snoop and the Prophet were dead. Slowly, Wade came to believe he was loved. In fact, he soon even had a daddy.

Once Rob left the *Rapid River Review* he moved to Washington and took a part time job at the biggest newspaper on the Olympic peninsula. It was only forty-five miles from Port Townsend. In his extra time, he began to work on a column he called *Cooper Goes Wild.* Each article was about fishing, camping, skiing or hiking in the Pacific Northwest. Eventually, it was syndicated throughout the area known as Cascadia, from southern Oregon through British Columbia.

He and Laura married on Wade's sixth birthday, and Rob adopted him, to the boy's delight. Finally, he knew Rob wasn't taking Gram away. And he took to calling them Mom and Dad.

The wedding was a small affair. Laura wasn't comfortable advertising her whereabouts, even though, according to the Mule, the cult was mostly gone. Wade was the ring bearer, the Mule was best man, and Sarah maid of honor. Eudora, Llama Lady and Diaper Man were the guests. Laura wanted Woodrow, too, but Diaper Man told her that he had disappeared, as street people often do. Maybe he was tearing about the universe in some intergalactic saucer of his own.

The Mule stayed in Rapid River, continuing to produce award-winning photography. Eventually, he made peace with Helen's ghost and began spending quite a lot more time with Sheriff Rita Elwood. The two of them flew up to see Rob and Laura now and then in the old Cessna that they bought together. On their most recent trip, they delivered the news that the State acquired the cult land for non-payment of taxes. There was talk that it would be turned into a park, a place where wildlife could return, and children were safe to play.

***

Now Sarah was retiring, and that's what they discussed as she drank her cup of tea in Laura's office. Laura was planning a retirement party, and they had sent out invitations, put announcements in the local paper and on their new website.

Wade, at fifteen, would be at the celebration. Sarah was no longer his counselor, but always available if he called, and sometimes she invited him to lunch just to catch up. She became another sure thing in his support system. He remained a contemplative, contained youngster, always standoffish around adults and nervous in crowds. He showed every indication that he was interested in psychology himself, and might consider it as a career, now that he no longer wanted to be a cowboy or a ferry boat captain.

The frightening past was no more than that...until the day on the waterfront at a nearby state park. Laura and Wade were walking the pebbly beach with his mutt, Tazzie. Spock was at home no doubt dozing on Eudora's lap, both of them purring in a comfortable old age.

As they ambled along together, Laura got that hard-to-explain but impossible-to-deny feeling that they were not alone. She turned and saw a woman in the distance walking behind them. When Laura looked again she saw that the woman was overtaking them. She felt a quiver of familiarity. Her attention was captured by the willowy figure, the flowing dress and long raven hair floating in the wind. The woman swung a flowered tote bag at her side.

"Hello, Dr. Laura. Remember me?" she hailed, when she got near. Laura and Wade stared, while Tazzie issued a low growl that would scare no one. Still, Laura was surprised. She'd never heard the mutt react to anyone in anything but a happy yap.

"Colleen? What a surprise!" Laura smiled broadly and waved. "What on earth are you doing here?"

"So you do remember. Since you left me, I thought you'd forget," Colleen answered.

"I would never forget you, Colleen." *How could she think that? Paranoia must still plague her.*

"This your boy? He's all grown up now."

Had she seen Wade before? "Um, yes. Wade, you can go on down the beach with Tazzie if you'd like. This lady and I need to talk about old times."

"No worries." Wade was always happy to avoid strangers, so he complied eagerly. It was Tazzie who had to be dragged away. They headed off together toward the shoreline, the mutt now back on a leash and Wade admonishing him to quit yapping.

"Colleen, I'm so glad to see you again. I've always been sorry I had to leave Rapid River without saying good bye. I bet your next counselor enjoyed working with you as much as I did."

"Oh, there was no next counselor." Colleen's face was unreadable.

"What? Why? Did you stop going to Community Mental Health?" Laura was amazed that someone so disturbed would make such a choice. *She's had no counseling for the past years? How is she keeping herself together?*

"That wasn't it. After you left, they wouldn't see me anymore. Can you imagine that? That was shit."

That son of a bitch Tom. He'd never believed Colleen was in such need of help. "How awful for you. It must have been a very hard time."

"Yeah, I was alone. Without you, without David. Only Dolores to talk to. And I couldn't always count on her to show up when I needed her." There was sorrow in her voice, but something else, too. Laura stared her in the eyes and tensed. She saw the anger as well as sadness. She'd seen it in David...and in their father.

"But finally I found a nice guy, so I didn't need you as much."

"I'm pleased to hear that. You deserve a good relationship." *Why is she here?*

"I'm still at the library you know. Saw the retirement party announcement on a website. Thought I'd come for a visit."

Laura looked around for anyone else on the beach.

"We're quite alone, Dr. Laura. Except for your boy. Shall I get him?"

"No...no. I don't think he should bother my clients."

"Bother? Well, maybe I'd bother him. I'm not at my best. Especially since that fucker Brad just dumped me. I've failed again. Now that he's gone, all the bad shit is roaring right back." Her voice was getting deeper and she talked faster, breathing heavily.

"How did you find me on the beach, Colleen?" Laura could see nothing to use as a weapon anywhere near her. No large rocks, no sticks. Every muscle tensed.

"I located your house then followed you here this morning."

"You've always been clever, Colleen." Laura turned just enough so the sun was not in her eyes. It was the best she could do.

She had a clear view as Colleen's face distorted with rage. "And you're the piece of shit who killed my brother." In one fluid, practiced motion, Colleen pulled a Maglite from her gaily colored tote and swung it at Laura's head.

Laura saw it coming and ducked, dodging the worst of the blow. But it still hammered the side of her skull, high above her left ear. She staggered, lost her balance, went down on her knees. Black wisps danced before her eyes as she fought to stay conscious.

"You," Colleen spit. "You made me remember it all. Then you left me. It wasn't David, you stupid bitch. He helped kill that friend of yours, but the rest of the murders were mine. My rage. Now I'm here for you."

Colleen towered over Laura and kicked her hard in the face, just below the cheekbone. Laura's head snapped back, and she fell onto the wet pebbles. Colleen dropped the flashlight, reached back into her bag.

Numbed by the blows to her head, Laura struggled to rise and failed, sinking back to the beach.

Colleen lifted a knife from the bag. The blade caught a kick of the sun. She held it so Laura could plainly see. Finally, Colleen smiled.

So this is how it ends. Abishua's revenge. Laura seemed to be looking at herself from far away. She turned for a final view of Wade, but what she saw terrified her back to lucidity. The swirls of mist parted. Her vision cleared. She saw Wade dashing toward her...yelling...a driftwood stick in his hand. Colleen would kill him...

"Run, Wade, run! Get help!"

Her shriek startled Colleen who paused to look up at the approaching boy. Laura could sense her concentration was broken for an instant. But it was long enough.

"Oh, you *are* clever, Colleen, just like Laura said," crooned a voice that was not Colleen.

What? Who is that voice? Laura fought to understand. Colleen had lost control long enough for another self to take over. Was it the one who carried the pain?

"Dolores?" Laura managed but was ignored.

"You are clever. But your rage and your pain have become too much for me to bear. I can't carry it any longer." With a profound exhalation of breath, Dolores plunged the knife deep into her own neck, severing the jugular vein.

Laura watched, stunned, as Colleen wobbled before her, knife in her own throat as blood drenched the dress billowing around her.

Colleen – or was it Dolores? – collapsed as Wade ran up the beach to Laura. He knelt, hugged his mother to himself and helped her rise.

***

The afternoon was a blur of police reports and medical attention. It wasn't until the next day in her office that all the pieces finally fit together for Laura. She was far too fragile from the head wounds both inside and out to see patients and had cancelled them all. She decided to go through the day's pile of letters and RSVPs for the retirement party.

It was there, buried midway in the stack. A letter to her from Dolores. Sent two days earlier from Rapid River, just arrived today.

Dear Dr. Laura,

As you know, I have always preferred writing to speaking. Unlike Colleen, I am not good with computers. So forgive me for not emailing or calling. I'm clearer in my head when I put my thoughts in a letter.

I have carried as much pain as long as I can. I have watched Colleen be overcome by her rage. Neither she nor I recognized it back when we were still meeting with you. But it was there all along, in her as well as in her brother. Abishua created it in both his children.

He was deeply upset when you exposed Colleen to her secret selves like Candi and me. She started to feel better about herself. You made her harder for him to control. So he won her back. He knew she loved her brother above all else. Abishua exposed her to her own rage by giving her a task she liked. He let her kill David's wife. Cathy had hurt David, and Colleen hated her for that. Besides, she was jealous.

Unfortunately, that parking lot attendant got in the way. 'Oh well,' she said to me. 'Too bad, so sad.' Anything gentle about Colleen slipped away.

Then the newspaper published that editorial about the Seekers and the article about the Herkimers. It didn't need their names for us to know who it was about. The publicity scared the cult. So Colleen killed that old couple, without asking Abishua. I can't even write what her rage did to Annie to keep her from speaking about that night.

Abishua was angry with Colleen for acting without his express okay. He gave her to her older brother Cadman again, and he was always so cruel. I carried that pain for her, too. I am so tired. And without hope.

When you spoke with David and Colleen together, she was pleased you helped him finally see how close they had been, that they had a baby together. But once he killed himself and their father, she was alone. She was there that night, watching the fire devour her family. She blamed you and turned against you. But you were gone.

With no counselor at Community Mental Health, her anger just festered. Finding a mate helped but he left her, too. When she found your invitation online, the Rage beckoned her again.

You tried to help us. Nobody else ever has. Everything that was good about Colleen thanks you for that. But I know what I have to do. I have just enough vigor left to kill her before she gets to you and your family. I will try. She's stronger than me, but I am smarter.

Is it homicide or suicide? I do not know. I leave it to you to decide.

Dolores, the one who carries the pain

***

Somewhere in Northern California, higher in the hills than the olive trees grow, Annie Herkimer lives a quiet life on her aunt's farm. For now. But in her, the rage stirs.

-- THE END --

AUTHOR'S ACKNOWLEDGMENT

The lifestyle and slang of the 1980s...the flora and fauna of Oregon...the overview of cults in general...the beliefs about psychopaths in specific. For these things, many fine resources exist, and I am indebted to dozens of librarians and websites for helping me find them.

For the way Multiple Personality Disorder – or Dissociative Identity Disorder as it is known today – was encountered by community mental health organizations in the 1980s, I am indebted to the courageous counselors who were there. I am also indebted to the clients who told their stories. May they, and those who follow in their footsteps, become who they were born to be.

For critiques that ranged from scrappy to joyful, I am indebted to my writers group, Heidi Hansen, Melee McGuire, Kimberly Minard, and Jill Sikes. Every writer should be so lucky as to have brave souls take them to task.

For seeing me through the birthing of this fractious baby, I am indebted to my dear friends Jan Shamberg, Mindy Mailman, and Renee Rosen.

For keeping my nose to the grindstone, my feet to the fire, and my writing on track, I am indebted to my sister Donna Whichello. This book would not exist without her passion for the subject and memory of the time.

ABOUT THE AUTHOR

Linda B. Myers won her first creative contest in the sixth grade. After a Chicago marketing career, she traded in snow boots for rain boots and moved to the Pacific Northwest with her Maltese, Dotty. You can visit with Linda at facebook.com/lindabmyers.author or email her at myerslindab@gmail.com.

CHECK OUT LINDA'S OTHER NOVELS

Fun House Chronicles

Bear in Mind

Hard to Bear

Bear at Sea

Bear Claus: A Novella

The Slightly Altered History of Cascadia

Secrets of the Big Island

Fog Coast Runaway

Please leave a review for *Creation of Madness* or Linda's other books on www.amazon.com.

Made in the
USA
Middletown, DE